THE BUS TO BEULAH

THE BUS TO BEULAH

A NOVEL

E.C. HANES

SPARKPRESS

Published by SparkPress, a BookSparks imprint,
A division of SparkPoint Studio, LLC
Phoenix, Arizona, USA, 85007
www.gosparkpress.com

Published 2022

Printed in the United States of America

Print ISBN: 978-1-68463-129-2
E-ISBN: 978-1-68463-130-8 (e-bk)
Library of Congress Control Number: 2021920009

Formatting by Katherine Lloyd, The DESK

Dedicated to

Lara Hanes Pierce and Philip Grenley Hanes,

my beloved children

"And Moses said unto the people,
remember this day,
in which ye came out of the land of Egypt,
out of the house of bondage;
for by strength of hand the LORD
brought you out from this place."
—Exodus 13:3

PROLOGUE

Maria figured they'd been driving for about forty-five minutes. She couldn't guess how far they'd gone since they appeared to be using narrow, bumpy back roads to avoid notice. She tried talking to the two men to convince them that what they were doing was wrong and dangerous, but neither would respond. They'd obviously been told to say nothing to the girls or even to each other. The only time either man spoke was when Paco needed to verify the directions. Jose was sitting in the back of the van with the two women.

Since the vehicle had apparently been used for some type of construction work, perhaps plumbing or electrical, there were shelves and bins along the far side opposite the sliding door. As a work van, it had never been fitted with seats in the back, so the seats put in for the girls and Jose were loose and ill-fitting.

Maria and Julietta sat on a narrow seat that looked like it had been taken from the back of an SUV. Jose sat in a low aluminum lawn chair. Maria guessed they were using the work van rather than the large white passenger van in order to be less memorable on the road. Julietta kept quiet, but occasionally she began to cry and tremble. Maria put her arm around the younger girl to steady her whenever she seemed to be breaking down. In truth, it steadied them both.

The road had become quite curvy, causing the seats in the back to sway and rock more than before. After a while, Julietta began again to tremble and then to gag. Maria hugged her tighter and asked, "You all right?" Julietta didn't say anything but leaned over like she was going to throw up.

"Stop the van!" Maria shouted. "Can't you see that she's going to be sick?"

Jose shouted, "Paco, pull over. The girl is going to puke, and if she puke, I puke." Paco slowed down and, seeing the turn off for a small dirt road on the right, pulled over. When the van stopped, Jose stood up and pulled the side door open. Paco looked over his shoulder and, as he started to open his own door, said, "Jose, you stay with the other one. I'll watch the sick one."

Before either man could react, Julietta jumped from the van and started to run. When Jose saw her running, he jumped from the van to catch her, but Maria tripped him, knocking him forward. As he fell, he hit his head on the side of the van's open door and dropped, dazed, to the ground. Paco leapt from the driver's seat and raced after Julietta while Jose struggled to his feet. Angry and bleeding, Jose lunged at Maria, hitting her in the face with his fist so hard that she fell back, her left eye closed and her nose bleeding into her mouth and down her neck.

Even though it was getting dark and she was having trouble focusing with one good eye, Maria could make out Julietta running wildly up the road with Paco in pursuit. The road was narrow with thick stands of pines on both sides. Through her good eye, Maria saw Julietta fall as she looked back over her shoulder. Paco was closing in on her.

Julietta managed to get to her feet, then, still looking back over her shoulder, darted across the road just as a pickup came through a wide curve up ahead. Julietta didn't see or hear the truck, even when the driver honked his horn and slammed on his brakes. The sounds and sight of the collision was something Maria would never forget. She turned her head and screamed, “Nooooo!” as she vomited out of the open door.

Jose was standing beside the van looking up the road when Maria vomited onto his pants. He jumped back too late, then, gagging himself, leapt forward and struck Maria again in the face until more blood, mixed with vomit, covered the floor of the van.

By this time, the driver of the pickup truck was out of his vehicle and kneeling in the road beside Julietta. Paco, assuming that Julietta was either dead or close to it, raced back to the van motioning for Jose to get back in. “Now!” he yelled. Jose pulled the side door closed as Paco leapt into the driver’s seat and in one motion started the van while accelerating into a U-turn, racing down the road in the opposite direction.

Sunday
September 22nd

DAY ONE

Sunday

10:00 a.m.

Maria Puente closed her eyes and turned her face toward the warm Mexican sun. She leaned back, stretched out her arms, and breathed in the dry, desert-scented air that blew down from the Sierra Madre mountains surrounding Monterrey.

After a brief pause she leaned forward, lowered her arms, and grasped the small, gold crucifix hanging from a chain around her neck. With her eyes now open, she turned and looked at her Aunt Marianna.

"Do I look okay? It's strange, but I'm excited and afraid at the same time. I hope Uncle Tomás and Aunt Sofia are pleased that they've asked me to come live with them, I don't want…"

Marianna raised her hand. "Maria, Tomás and Sofia are so excited you are coming that they have been working on your new room for a month now. Yes, my dearest, they are thrilled you are coming."

Maria smiled as tears formed at the corners of her eyes. "I know you're right, but still, you and Uncle Luis have been the only parents I've ever known. I know it was hard on you to add another mouth to the family after my mother died, but…"

Marianna again raised her hand. "Maria, you don't need to say anything. We were glad to bring you into our family. Your mother was very precious to me. We were the closest in age in our family and were not only sisters but best friends too. To not make you my daughter would have been unthinkable, but don't forget that your uncle Tomás has been a large part of your life as well. He has always been there for you just as he's been there for me and Luis. First, as your mother's and my big brother, but also as your uncle and provider. Luis and I couldn't have afforded to send you to the special schools in Monterrey without his help. Believe me when I say that he is excited to finally become an active part of your life. Do not worry. Your new job will be a challenge, but nothing you can't do. You're a strong young woman—ready for a new world."

"Yes, I know, but I don't want to let any of you down."

"Maria, you have never let us down—and you never will."

The AmTex bus that was to carry Maria north stood stark and motionless in front of the single-story white adobe building that housed the Monterrey, Mexico, headquarters of AmTex Transportation, Inc. Maria and her aunt stood close together on a brick patio under a tattered awning at the side of the building. In front of them, in the parking lot, were two to three dozen men milling about, speaking in low tones, each holding a small suitcase or backpack. Standing on the other side of the patio were the only other women who would make the trip, one young, about the same age as Maria, and the other older, perhaps Marianna's age.

Most of the men, both young and old, seemed hardened and world weary. It was clear this was not their first trip north across the border. They were part of the endless stream of seasonal agricultural workers who trekked north to do the backbreaking work in the fields of California, Texas, Florida, and in this instance, North Carolina.

Maria was going north on an H-1B visa, signifying that she was allowed to work in nonagricultural businesses with at least a three-year stay. The rest of the passengers had temporary agricultural visas, which meant that they were supposed to return to

Mexico after their jobs were completed, but many would not, thus blending silently into the burgeoning mass of illegal immigrants in the US.

Maria was thrilled with her new clothes, as close to what her aunt felt would be an American career look as she could find. Except for the nerves that kept her somewhat rigid, Maria looked as beautiful as always. Her dark hair flowed over her shoulders and down the back of her new blouse, and her face glowed with the natural beauty that for years had allowed her to make money as a model in Monterrey, but not as one of the wraith-like young girls featured on the covers of most high-fashion magazines. She was as tall as the others and had the beautiful skin and eyes of a model, but she was blessed with an athlete's body, strong and muscular.

Like all young women, Maria knew this day would come; that eventually she would fly from her comfortable nest of the last twenty-two years. This was not her first time away from home, but it would be the longest and farthest away. Five years before, she had moved to Monterrey for her last two years of high school and three years of college.

She had enrolled in one of the best schools in Mexico, the Universidad Regiomontana, a private school with one of the most respected technology curriculums in the country. Since the school was too far away for a daily commute, she had lived with her Uncle Luis's sister, Rosalie, during the school year.

While she always had the comfort of knowing that Marianna and Luis were nearby and that she could visit them on weekends, she took full advantage of her new surroundings and exposed herself to the exciting world of ideas that lay beyond Monterrey and Nuevo León. She had been a frightened young girl when she entered the school, but left a determined young woman armed with a cadre of new friends and the confidence to expand her world.

Marianna looked across the parking lot, "Maria, see that young man with the red hair standing beside the bus talking to those two men? Does he look familiar?"

Maria turned and looked over at the men standing beside the bus. After a pause, she said, "No. I don't recognize him. Do you?"

"Maybe. He isn't like most of the other men going on the bus. I mean, a light-skinned redheaded man isn't the typical Mexican on his way to work in America. And the man wearing the baseball cap? He, too, looks out of place..."

Maria looked again at the two men.

"Maybe the younger one, maybe he was with me in school, but not the older one. He is too old, but you're right, neither one looks like a farm worker."

A man came out of the building and yelled, "Everybody who's going on the bus to Beulah, please board now. If your luggage is too big for the overhead racks, please put it in the baggage compartments under the bus."

The men in the parking lot formed a line at the bus door, suitcases and knapsacks in hand. Those with large bags threw them in the baggage compartments under the bus, then got in line behind the others. The two women standing at the other end of the patio started walking toward the bus, so Maria, tearing up, turned and gave Marianna a long, desperate hug.

"I love you, Aunt Marianna," she said stepping back. "And I promise I'll call when I get to Uncle Tomás's, but let him know I'm on my way. I'll be fine, no need for you to hang around. The people at AmTex said the trip should take from thirty to forty hours depending on the wait time at the border, stops for gas and bathroom breaks, and any unforeseen problems. If that's true, we should arrive sometime late Monday afternoon or early evening. I'm guessing that a Sunday border crossing shouldn't take too long, but you never know.

"Please give Uncle Luis a hug for me, and call Rosalie and tell her that my adventure is starting."

Marianna, also in tears, said, "I'll call Tomás, hug Luis, call Rosalie—and pray that my dear Maria gets everything good that the world has to offer."

She touched Maria's damp cheek, then turned and walked away.

"Good-bye, Marianna. I love you. Dios bendiga."

Marianna turned and waved, but couldn't say a word, her throat being filled with quiet, small sobs.

Monday
September 23rd

DAY TWO

Monday

5:00 p.m.

The sound of the bus slowing down and the subsequent jolt caused by its running over some object in the road awakened Maria with a start. She looked out of the window and saw that the bus was pulling up to a pair of gas pumps at what appeared to be a small country gas station and convenience store. She looked at her watch, five o'clock, almost thirty-one hours since they left Monterrey.

The driver turned his head and said, "Last stop before Beulah. We're only gonna be here for a few minutes, so if anybody needs to stretch their legs, now's the time." He looked at the older woman who was seated on the aisle across from Maria, "Señora, if you and the señorita need to use the facilities, there is a restroom in the store." Over his shoulder he said to Maria, "Same goes for you, señorita."

It had been a long and largely uneventful journey so far. Maria had managed to sleep for a large part of the trip, waking every few hours or whenever the driver stopped for gas or a bathroom break. Since the bathroom on the bus was being used primarily by the men, and was, perhaps, of questionable cleanliness, the driver was good enough to stop and let the three women use the gas station facilities. The two other women had been silent and largely uncommunicative. The older one appeared to sleep for large parts of the trip while her thin, young companion seemed to have not slept at all. Whenever Maria tried to talk to either of them, the older one was the only one to answer, and then only in a terse, caustic voice. The younger woman seemed to want to speak, but whenever she tried, the older one would glance at her with a look that precluded any communication.

When the bus door opened, the older woman stood up and stepped into the aisle while motioning for the younger one to get up and step off the bus. After they had both gotten off, Maria stood up, stretched her back, and took the three steps down to the asphalt parking lot. As she started toward the small convenience store, Maria noticed that the older woman was talking to a man standing beside a white utility van parked in front of the store.

As she got closer, she heard them speaking in Spanish, even though they were definitely in North Carolina by this time. She couldn't hear what they were saying, but the woman was clearly trying to make a point to the young man, who seemed to be resisting. The younger woman stood by the front door some yards off and appeared to be waiting for her companion to finish her conversation. Maria smiled at the girl as she walked past and into the store.

The sparse, musty-smelling store was empty, its only employee outside filling the bus with gas. Maria paused to look for the restroom, spotting it in the back right corner of the cramped store. She walked around a shelf loaded with cans of motor oil and windshield-wiper fluid, past the cash register, and to a door marked with a stick figure of a woman. Spray-painted across the female figure was the word, "bitches."

While larger than the restroom on the bus, it was hardly cleaner, Maria smelled at once. There were two unflushed stalls and one grimy sink, none of which had been recently cleaned. She entered the second of the two stalls, the one next to the far wall. At least there was a full roll of toilet paper, plus a half-full box of seat covers on the wall.

She hung her purse over the toilet-paper holder since the

clothing hook on the back of the door was missing. Just as she had settled down, Maria heard a loud, angry conversation taking place in the store between the older and younger woman on the bus. Their conversation seemed to have morphed from a simple disagreement into what could become a brawl. As the voices grew louder and more violent, suddenly the restroom door slammed open and the two women crashed into the small space.

"Shut your fucking mouth," the older woman yelled. "You'll do what the hell you're told and stop whining about it!"

The young woman shrieked, "I was told that I was to be a cook at one of the labor camps, not one of your scummy whores. No way I'll do that!"

"Oh, really? Well, we'll see what your father has to say about that."

"He's not my father. He is just a mean drunk my mother married after my real father was killed, and besides, he's the one who told me I was to be a cook, not a whore."

The older woman laughed smugly at this. "He told you that to please your mother!"

The younger woman fell to the filthy concrete yelling as loud as she could, "I don't care, I'm not a whore like you. I—" Maria heard the slap as if it was against her own face.

"Shut your mouth and stop that foolish crying!"

The young girl paid no attention as she sat on the floor screaming and crying.

Maria was frozen on the seat. She slowed her breathing, and as quietly as she could, she raised her legs, hoping the women wouldn't know she was in the stall. As the young woman thrashed on the floor, the older one leaned against the first stall, causing Maria's purse to slip off the paper holder and onto the floor. As quietly as she could, Maria reached down and picked up the purse and held it in her lap. Still sitting with her legs raised, she hoped that she would go unnoticed. She closed her eyes and offered a small prayer, only to see the older woman peering at her through the crack in the stall door as she opened her eyes.

"You finished in there?"

Maria took a breath, "Almost."

"When you are, come on out. We need to talk." Maria put her feet down, pulled some paper off the roll, and then flushed the toilet.

"I'm through."

The young woman on the floor stopped crying after Maria spoke.

Maria opened the door and stepped out. The older woman didn't say anything at first, then said, "You didn't hear anything, right?"

Maria looked at the young woman sitting on the floor, her eyes red and a look of terror on her face, and said, "I heard two women arguing about something, but I couldn't say what."

The old woman smiled crookedly and said, "Very smart. Wait here with my young friend. I need to confer with someone." She turned and walked out of the restroom and into the store.

Maria looked at the young girl on the floor and held out her hand to help her up. "You need to get up and wash your face. You…" She couldn't go on because she had no idea what to say to someone so consumed with fear and dread. The young woman stood up, looked into the mirror and said, "I'm looking at a whore. What do you think? Is that a good-looking whore?" With this she broke into tears again, and all Maria could think to do was pat her on the shoulder and say, "It'll work out. You'll be okay. You'll think of something."

After ten minutes, the door to the restroom opened and the old woman came back in.

"It seems that the bus has gone on to Beulah. The young man

who I was talking to said that the bus couldn't wait any longer, so he sent it on."

Maria moved toward the door, but the older woman blocked her way.

"It can't leave without me," Maria told her. "I'm supposed to get to Beulah tonight and then be driven to Mussel Ford to my uncle's house. Please—get out of my way so I can stop the bus."

The old woman said, "I just told you, it's already gone. Luca Castro, the young man with the van, said that he'll take you to Beulah. Julietta and I were leaving the bus here anyway. We aren't going to Beulah."

Maria pushed the old woman out of the way and walked into the store. Luca Castro was standing at the door talking to Charlie Kiger, the proprietor of the reeking establishment.

"Mr. Castro, I was supposed to be on the bus. Why did you send it on?"

Luca looked at her and then at the older woman who had come out of the bathroom behind Maria.

"We—me and the lady—figured it would be best if you came with us."

Maria turned and looked at the older woman. She could see a small smirk spread across the wrinkled face. "Figured it best—why?"

The old woman said, "Well, maybe you didn't hear anything and maybe you did. We need to talk about that." With that, she turned and opened the door to the restroom, grabbed Julietta, and pulled her out into the store.

"Let's not stand here all night. We got places to go."

Maria, seeing that she had no chance of escape, walked to the door.

Luca waited for the old woman and Julietta, then opened the door and led the three of them to the van. He looked at Maria and said, "I took your bag off the bus. It's in the van."

Monday

6:30 p.m.

Downtown Beulah had more or less shut down, since Latham's Hardware and the Dollar General closed at six. The only businesses still open were Blackie Wilson's Country Store and Gas Station, Mozell's Diner, and the Motel 6 at the north end of Main Street.

Blackie's gas station had three pumps, one of which always seemed to be broken, an air compressor that cost fifty cents to activate, and a self-service car vacuum that charged a dollar for two minutes.

The country store part of the business clearly relished the "country" part of its name. The walls were covered with neon beer and soft-drink signs, twenty- year-old chewing tobacco ads, and a collection of stuffed deer heads, flying ducks, and jumping fish.

In between all this local decor was a seasonally adjusted selection of local produce, a basic inventory of canned goods and home necessities, local honey and molasses, plus assorted candies, cakes, and soft drinks. Also, a small take-out counter offered a daily selection of Southern foods; pork barbeque, fried chicken, country-fried steaks, and a mixture of over-cooked vegetables. Being always on the lookout for new sales opportunities, Blackie had begun offering Mexican dishes—tacos, burritos, and eggs smothered with what he called "pigante" sauce.

The only reason Blackie's was still open at this hour was that

Blackie Wilson had negotiated a deal with AmTex Transportation to supply cheap gas to their buses and vans, which could arrive at almost any hour.

AmTex and its affiliate, the North Carolina Farmers Collective, known by the initials NCFC, were owned and operated by Albert Waters, or, to be more precise, Albert Ruffin Waters, known to his close friends as Ruff Waters. As AmTex and his other businesses grew, and thus his visibility as well, Albert realized that he needed to soften the hard edges and sharp elbows for which he was known.

AmTex and NCFC needed the cooperation of the various governmental agencies responsible for the regulation of seasonal migrant labor; so Albert needed to develop a patina of respect. Not that he needed to trade in his JCPenney suit for a $500 custom Hickey Freeman, but he did need to clean up his language, learn everything he could about US immigration laws, and lose his dingy John Deere ball cap when making the rounds in Raleigh. With the help of his old supervisor at the state Commerce Department, Albert developed a step-by-step plan to pave his way to respectability.

Step one was to become a reliable political contributor. Step two was to become a vocal advocate for the causes most important to the politicians he supported. Step three was to increase the flow of money necessary in steps one and two. Step four was to affect an air of piety and social consciousness. This last step was the stumper. Albert was already a member of the most vibrant church congregation in the area, though not its most conscientious attendee, but to become a man of consequence demanded more than mere membership.

In due time, the new 1,200-seat Sanctuary and Assembly Hall of the Everlasting Kingdom Pentecostal Church and World

Mission, known to Albert's friends as the House of Waters, welcomed another stray lamb back into the fold with broad Clorets-laced smiles and meaty double handshakes all around.

Albert had held many jobs in his fifty-five years, but the most valuable, the one that had set him onto his current path, was as a rural labor advisor for the state of North Carolina. This was a fairly low-level state job within the North Carolina Department of Commerce, described in the state literature as "an individual responsible for assisting and advising the agricultural community in finding suitable employees to work in the planting and harvesting of crops." In other words, a position created to help farmers find cheap seasonal labor. And where was the best source for cheap, seasonal labor? Mexico and Central America.

The headquarters for NCFC was located in a large, nondescript metal building at the end of Main Street. It was, in fact, directly in front of where a newly arrived bus from Mexico was now parked. All of the recently arrived workers were now assembled inside the building awaiting transportation to their final destinations across Eastern North Carolina.

The two men who had taken turns driving the bus to Beulah were sitting on a bench in front of the NCFC building smoking cigarettes when a six-foot tall balding man wearing a particularly sour expression approached them.

"Well, lookie here, Dumb and Dumber! Listen, you two shit-for-brains assholes, you better get your heads outta your asses and start payin' attention. When I give you a list of names of people coming to Beulah, you better fuckin' read it and do what it says."

Jose "Junior" Vasquez, the man driving the bus when it last stopped for gas, tried to protest, but Jimmy "Bubba" Ross held up his hand.

"Stop! I know what you're gonna say, shit maggot, but listen to me. Unless you hear it directly from me, I didn't say it. If I tell you to bring someone to Beulah, you fuckin' do it. I don't give a shit what Luca Castro or anybody else says. When I said for you to bring the Puente girl to Beulah, I wasn't askin', I was orderin'. You fucking understand?"

Junior nodded, then said, "Yes, I understan', Mr. Jimmy, but when I say that to Luca, that we suppose' to take the Puente woman to Beulah, he show me a pistol and say he call you and you say okay. I no argue with no pistol."

Jimmy Ross, still agitated, said, "Okay, maybe I don't blame you. Anyway, when exactly did Luca pick up the girls?"

Junior pursed his lips and looked up at the sky before speaking.

"I no remember for sure, but it when we at the Kiger Store in Goldsboro."

Bubba scratched what was left of his fading red hair and looked at the bus. After a big sigh, he said, "Okay, try to remember, what kind of vehicle was Luca driving?"

Jose paused for a moment, then said, "It a white van with no window. It have a slide door an' two or three seat in the back. The long seat."

"Was there anything on the door? Any writing?"

"I don' remember, but maybe jus' plain."

"Okay, you two get some sleep in the dorm. Paco, you're driving a load of pickers north tomorrow morning, so you'll need to get outta here by five or six. Take the blue and white activity bus, the old Everlasting Kingdom one. You got it?"

Paco nodded as he got up and walked toward the NCFC warehouse entrance, and to the upstairs dormitory used by the drivers and in-transit workers.

Monday

7:45 p.m.

Maria sat on a moldy, tattered mattress with her knees pulled up and her arms wrapped tightly around them. Leaning against a damp, wooden-slat wall in a dark, cramped room, Maria listened to Julietta, her only companion, mournfully crying as she lay, bruised and beaten, on a cot against the far wall.

Julietta, who Maria guessed was a few years younger than she, had said very little in the white van on their trip from the gas station in Goldsboro to this fetid, run-down house, and even less since arriving, opting instead to lie mourning on her cot and moaning in pain each time she turned over.

The older woman, who had earlier beaten and humiliated Julietta, was in another part of the house plotting with Luca Castro, the apparent manager of the human-trafficking business in which Maria was also now entangled.

Fear, anxiety, and dread had conspired to crush Maria's spirit, but strangely enough, the emotion foremost in her mind was fury. How dare these people threaten her on her way to a new life and bright new world.

She dropped her arms to her side, leaned forward, and cursed in a whisper, "You're not going to beat me, you trash! I haven't come this far and worked this hard to be stopped by the likes of you."

In the back of her mind, she knew this was a boast she might not be able to fulfill, but it was one she was willing to fight for because she knew it was God's truth.

After parking the white van behind the house, Luca had come in to talk to the old woman, whose name, Maria had learned, was Valeria, a name too noble for one so repugnant. Based on the volume and level of anger that Valeria's and Luca's conversation had taken, Maria guessed that her kidnapping had created a serious problem for Luca.

From what she could hear, Luca's bosses were none too happy about his decision to bring her, along with Julietta and Valeria, to the farmhouse. When the shouting and name-calling finally stopped, she heard Luca say to Valeria, "You stay here with the girls. I need to check my other house and then see if I can straighten this whole fucked-up mess out. I'll be back tomorrow morning."

Maria hoped he was successful.

When she finally gathered herself together, Julietta sat up and wiped her tears. She looked at Maria the way a child would look to a comforting parent, so Maria walked over and sat down next to her.

"You want to talk about it?" Maria asked.

Julietta nodded. "I'm sorry you have been dragged into this. It's my fault. My stepfather said I was to come to America to make money for the family; to be a cook for the men in the camps. He told me that that horrible woman, Valeria, was a friend of his and was to be a cook also.

"I should have known he was lying. He is a bad man and mean to Mama and me. He has been after me for a long time, and it is only my mama that has kept him away, but she is beat up and tired, so she says for me to go to America to at least get away. I never know what he does in Mexico, but now I understand that he runs some whorehouses and that Valeria is a madam in one of them.

"She comes to America to make a business with the Castro man and his bosses. She tells me that my stepfather sent me to America to work in the whore business. I say, no, he sent me to cook, but now I know she is right. He sent me to be a whore."

Maria could not think of how to reply to such a terrible revelation, so she patted Julietta on the shoulder and said something about waiting to see how things work out. Of course, she wasn't at all sure how things would work out. What had started out as a life-changing trip for her, too, had become just that, but in a negative, dangerous way rather than in a good way.

The thousands of young men and women who come to the United States each year to work in its fields and warehouses are often forced to live in small, cramped, and poorly maintained work camps. Some enlightened farmers provide food service to their employees, and thus use native cooks imported to work in the camps. This was what Julietta expected would be her job.

Since most of the workers are young men, female companionship is something in high demand; thus, enter Luca Castro, Valeria, Jimmy Ross and their collection of traveling prostitutes. Luca was in charge of the business operating out of a series of small, well-hidden farmhouses, such as the one in which Maria and Julietta now found themselves. This particular house was Luca's most recent addition and not yet renovated to the same extent as his other properties. Not being a citizen, Luca couldn't own the houses, but then he didn't need to. In all cases the buildings were rented from some wealthy local farmer who needed multiple work camps and recognized, without ever admitting it, that his workers would welcome Luca's services. This run-down house was owned by a man named Jasper Upchurch.

The Upchurch family owned or leased over seven thousand acres of prime land in Eastern North Carolina, the biggest part of which was in Jackson County, where Jasper and his wife, Sara, along with his oldest boy, Jasper Jr., and his family lived. Upchurch Farms, Inc. was probably the largest customer of Albert Waters and NCFC, but Buddy Waller's farm wasn't far behind. In order to house the workforce necessary for such a large operation, the Upchurch family maintained ten labor camps spread over a five-county area. At peak season, Upchurch Farms employed over two thousand migrant workers. They grew berries, sweet potatoes, cucumbers, melons, pumpkins, and tobacco, all of which demanded massive amounts of near-slave labor. They also had large acreages in corn and soybeans, but these crops were highly mechanized, so didn't need much manual labor.

The berries needed picking in the spring; tobacco needed to be topped in the summer and primed in the fall; sweet potatoes and pumpkins needed to be gathered and graded in the fall; and the melons and cucumbers needed picking all the summer and into the fall. This meant that the Upchurch labor camps were full most of the year.

Soon after Luca's departure, the locked door to the small room opened and Valeria stepped in, holding a tray with what looked like a couple of sandwiches and two bottles of water.

She said, "You two need to eat something. We can't have our assets depreciate."

Maria looked over at her. "I'm not your asset."

Valeria replied, "No, you're not. You're our liability, but not for long."

Julietta, who was again lying on her cot in a fetal position, gave no indication that she heard her.

Valeria continued, "Anyway, see if you can get our young friend to eat something."

She put the tray down and relocked the door. Julietta was no longer crying but made no reply. Maria waited a minute and then stood up and walked over to the tray. "Julietta, come on, let's eat and drink something. She's probably right. You'll need your strength."

Julietta sat up but didn't move off the cot.

"What for? So I'll be a good little whore for her and that horrible man?"

"No, so you'll have the strength to escape with me."

For the first time in two days, a spark, a look of hope came into Julietta's eyes and spread to her face.

"Do you have a plan? Have you seen something that can help us?" She looked around the room. It was the first time she'd paid any attention to where they were, to any escape opportunities.

Maria sat down on the cot and handed Julietta a sandwich and bottle of water. She unwrapped her own and began to eat.

"No, I haven't seen anything yet, but I will. There's always something—some way out somewhere. Besides, I know my family is looking for me right now. They know I'm missing because they know I got on the bus two days ago. I'm sure my Aunt Marianna called Uncle Tomás and told him I was on the bus, so I know he's looking for me now."

"How do you know?" Julietta asked.

"I know because I am like his daughter. He has been like the father I never had."

"But I thought you are from Mexico. That your mother put you on the bus. I saw her."

"She's my aunt, the sister of my mother and my Uncle Tomás.

She raised me ever since my mother was killed. I never knew my father. He died just after I was born. Aunt Marianna and her husband, Uncle Luis, raised me with the help of Uncle Tomás, who lives not far from here. He is a rich man who has a business in Mussel Ford. He sent money for food and clothes and paid for much of my education at the special schools. Believe me, Julietta, he is looking for me, which means he's looking for you too."

Tuesday
September 24th
DAY THREE

Tuesday

11:00 a.m.

Tomás Delgado was worried. He had expected that by this time his niece, Maria Puente, would be settled in his neat four-bedroom house on Franklin Street in Mussel Ford. Isabella, Tomás's nine-year-old daughter, could barely contain herself. So it was with great effort that Tomás managed to keep his calm and even demeanor.

After repeated calls to the offices of Martin Agribusiness, where Tomás had secured a job for Maria, he still had no idea where she was. She was supposed to have arrived in Beulah on an AmTex bus late Monday or early Tuesday morning, and then been driven to Hogg County and Mussel Ford in one of AmTex's in-state vans.

The office manager at Martin Agribusiness, Vonda O'Brien, said she called NCFC Monday evening and again early Tuesday morning to find out where Maria was, but after a lot of "we're checking" replies, was told by Jimmy Ross, the operations manager at NCFC, that Maria never got on the bus in Mexico.

Isabella and Tomás knew this was a lie because Marianna had called on Sunday after dropping Maria at the AmTex parking lot in Monterrey.

"Hank, this is Tomás Delgado. You have a minute to talk?"

Henry Odell Grier Jr., known to everyone as Hank, was the

chief deputy of Hogg County and the son of Odell Grier Sr., Tomás Delgado's employer and eventually his friend as well. Hank had known Tomás ever since he was a young boy, even before he could legally work in any of his father's businesses. Hank hung out in the garages of Grier Tire and Auto and begged Tomás to let him work on the cars and trucks that were awaiting engine maintenance or rebuild. Under Tomás's watchful eye, he learned how to rotate and balance a set of tires, and eventually how to tune an engine.

Tomás was a patient teacher, a man who began his career as an engine mechanic in an Arco Industries factory in Nuevo León State, Mexico. When Arco, a producer of tractors, harvesters, and related equipment, decided to build a factory in the US, they picked a location outside Raleigh. Since Tomás already spoke English, he was a perfect person to send to the new factory. For Tomás it was a match made in heaven.

Being a bright man and hard worker, as soon as he got to North Carolina, Tomás began researching educational opportunities that could increase his credentials as a premier mechanic. He attended classes at two community colleges in the Raleigh area and took several courses at State.

After a few years of hard work and dedication, Arco assisted Tomás in applying for and getting a green card, proof of permanent residency status.

A year later, while attending a seminar at NC State on management innovations, Tomás met Odell Grier Sr. from Mussel Ford. Odell was attending the seminar for the ostensible purpose of learning ways to improve his management skills, but was really there to find a qualified manager for a new venture he was planning.

Odell wanted to expand his auto parts and tire business by

adding a body shop and a fully equipped engine maintenance and rebuild facility. His time was already taken up with running five gas stations and twelve automated car washes, so he needed someone who could dedicate himself to the new venture. Tomás Delgado was the perfect choice.

One conversation led to another, and within three months Tomás Delgado was the new manager of the Grier Tire and Automotive Company. It became one of the largest and most respected in the region, and finally established Odell Grier's reputation as the most successful black businessman in Eastern North Carolina.

Hank smiled as he heard Tomás's voice. "Of course, Tomás. I always have time to talk to you. I'm in my car right now, so I don't know how long I'll have good reception. If we get cut off, I'll call you from the office. What's up?"

Tomás quickly explained what had happened, and why he was so concerned. He begged Hank to do something.

"Please, Hank, Maria is like my own daughter. I have helped Marianna with her ever since my second sister, Maria's mother, was killed. I know that the NCFC people lie and I'm afraid why."

Hank slowly shook his head when he heard "NCFC." His face tightened as if he'd just stepped in something rotten. Like many in Eastern North Carolina, he was well aware of Albert Waters's reputation, as well as the collection of toadies and yes-men who worked for him. Few were fooled by Albert's newfound piety—only the recipients of his largess. He had a loyal following among the mass of Carolina farmers he'd recruited as members of NCFC because they desperately needed Albert's cheap Mexican labor.

Hank waited to reply until he had fully digested what Tomás had just told him.

"Tomás, of course I'll help, but I'll need to know more. We'll talk when I get to my office."

"Okay, please call me when you can."

What Hank really needed was advice on a matter for which he had no experience. Only Will Moser, the high sheriff of Hogg County and Hank's boss, could help him. Hank had known Will from the time he was old enough to remember anything; in fact, Will had inspired Hank to go into law enforcement.

Hank decided to call Will even though Will had cautioned all his deputies to minimize sensitive conversations on their cell phones—too dangerous if hacked. And easy to hack.

"Will, it's Hank. I'm on my way back to the office. You got a few minutes?"

"Sure. What's up?"

"I just spoke with Tomás Delgado. Something has happened to his niece, Maria Puente, who was coming to live with him… She's missing."

"Missing from what?" Will asked.

"Missing, as in, they don't know where she is."

"Okay, back up, Deputy. What's this all about?"

Hank put his phone down to make a turn, then continued, "Will, I'm about ten minutes out and think we need to talk in person. You know what you said about cell talk."

"Okay, see you in a few."

Hank parked his patrol car behind the Hogg County Administrative Offices, which included the Sheriff's Department, and charged up the back stairs. He passed Janice's office and knocked on Will's door without stopping.

Will was on the phone and pointed Hank to the sofa in front of his desk. As he hung up, he looked at Hank and said, "You've got my attention. Shoot."

Hank took off his Stetson, put it on the sofa beside him, and said, "About five months ago, Tomás Delgado called Oris Martin about a job for his niece in Monterrey and the possibility of getting her a long-term work visa. Since Oris has lots of contacts at NCFC and Tomás had done many favors and overtime work for Martin Agribusiness, Tomás figured Oris owed him a favor.

"As luck would have it, Oris was in desperate need of some help in his computer and accounting department. By hiring Maria, who is fluent in English and has a degree in computer programming, he could, A, do a favor for Tomás, thus insuring future favors from him, and B, fill a needed staff position with someone who is highly qualified and would probably work cheap. The latter being his primary motivation.

"But now Maria has disappeared. She was supposed to be on one of the AmTex buses arriving in Beulah on Monday or early today, but she hasn't shown up. According to Jimmy Ross, Albert's bagman, she never got on the bus in Mexico."

Will shifted in his chair. "Did anyone call Mexico to see if she did get on the bus?"

"Yes. In fact, Tomás's sister, who raised Maria, called Tomás and Isabella right after she dropped Maria at the AmTex parking lot in Monterrey. She told them when and from where the bus left. Not only that, she described the bus."

Will nodded slowly and looked at Hank.

Hank knew Will so well that he read his silence as a sign to shut up and let him think. Will tilted back in his chair and looked at the ceiling.

After a minute or two he said, "I'm trying to think of a way we can avoid calling Garland Hoots or Albert Waters. I assume Jimmy Ross doesn't fart unless Albert gives him permission, so calling him would be pointless, and Sheriff Hoots is little more than Albert's paid stooge.

"I talked to Albert a few weeks ago about our unidentified man found on Pee Dee Road, and as you know, he feigned complete ignorance. If something has happened to the girl and Albert or the sheriff are involved, I don't want them to think we don't believe their story about Maria not getting on the bus."

"How about calling Oris to see if he has any suggestions?"

Will frowned and thought about this. "Maybe, but maybe Oris is too tight with Albert. I can't say. I gotta think about that one. In the meantime, we need to talk to Tomás. Why don't you give him a call."

Hank nodded as he got up to leave the room, but out of habit paused at the office door.

Without noticing that Hank had stopped, Will got up, arched his back to relieve the arthritis that had increasingly begun to affect him, then walked over to the windows behind his conference table.

He leaned against the sill and gazed out, thinking about Tomás and his niece, and how he would feel if his own daughter, Grace, was missing. The very thought gave him a chill. His back still hurt, so he turned and walked over to the sofa in front of his desk. Ever since the hip surgery that had removed the shrapnel from Viet Nam, he had been bothered by arthritis-like symptoms.

When he saw Hank still standing in the office door, he said, "What? Why you still here?"

"Just waiting to see if there was anything else you wanted me to do. When you start pacing and looking out the window, I can hear your mind turning, and figure that something else might occur to you."

"No. Just call Tomás," Will smiled.

Hank nodded and left.

Still smiling and shaking his head, Will sat down on his sofa and leaned back, spreading his arms out across the pillows. He closed his eyes and again pictured Grace—how dear she was to him and Lana.

When he opened his eyes, he found himself staring at an 8" x 10" photo on the wall behind his desk. It showed him, Lana, and Grace at the county fair. Grace must have been about five or six at the time. It was the kind of photo that always brought a smile to his lips. Next to it was a picture of Will with Lana and her first husband, Paul Reavis, one of Will's closest childhood friends. Paul had died, or rather been murdered, in a workplace argument.

Standing between Paul and Lana was their son, Paul Jr., and his best friend, Hank Jr. Young Paul had died when the waste lagoon on a local hog farm had ruptured and swept him and Hank into a nearby creek as they were playing pirates on the Mississippi. Young Paul had died, but Hank had survived.

The rest of the wall was covered with a mixture of photos, citations, and awards. Most of the pictures were of Will standing with notable people in notable places, but there were also pictures of his parents, friends, and group photos with his deputies. Mixed in with these were citations from the Boy Scouts, Chamber of Commerce, and other civic organizations, but more important than any of these were the photos of him and his fellow soldiers as young men in the streets and rice paddies of South Viet Nam.

The top row held his most valued awards. The Silver Star for bravery, Bronze Star with "V" device, Purple Heart, and a series of other medals that attested to his courage and quality of service, and, of course, his commission as an officer in the military police.

Will knew that he was cut out to be a lawman from the first time someone asked him, "What do you want to be when you grow up, William?"

"I wanna be a policeman," he said straight out. He also remembered the smiles and laughter that followed, along with the indulgent pat on his head, "And I bet you'd be a good policeman, William."

According to the people in Mussel Ford, as well as to his own father, there was only one thing that William Moser the third would be, and that was president of Moser Hardwoods Corporation, one of the state's largest specialty lumber companies. When he finally convinced his father that he had no intention of going into the family business, it brought down the final curtain between them. William Jr. never understood why William the third would turn his back on the family business. Even when Will was awarded the Silver Star in Viet Nam, the nation's third-highest award for valor in combat, his father barely acknowledged the rare achievement.

His mother eventually came around to accepting Will's decision and, he liked to think, even took a great deal of pride in the job he did and the respect the people of Hogg County and Eastern North Carolina had for her son.

As his eyes continued to scan the wall of photos, they came at last to a picture taken in Raleigh. It was one of the notable-people-in-notable-places pictures. He was with a group of men in front of the Capitol Building. Standing in the middle of the group was the Governor of North Carolina, and around him were various elected officials and prominent business leaders from Eastern North Carolina. Will's cousin, Dooley Marshall, president of what was now Moser-Mansfield Corporation, stood on Will's right, and on his left was Oris Martin Jr., president, owner, and founder of Martin Agribusiness, Inc., the company that had hired Maria Puente.

Martin Agribusiness was a diversified agricultural sales and service company with multiple operations in Eastern North Carolina and parts of South Carolina. The genesis of the business was Martin Farms, Inc., a massive hog-breeding and contained-feeding operation started by Oris Jr.'s father. It had become one of the premier companies in North Carolina until an outbreak of hog cholera shuttered the whole operation and bankrupted Oris Sr.

Up to the time of his death, Oris Sr. was convinced that he had been the victim of foul play, the target of some aggrieved enemy; however, without proof of a crime, he was left only with free-floating bitterness and anger. Most of his suspicions had fallen on Lana Moser, Will's wife, since her first husband and son had both died at or near a Martin Farms facility.

Oris Sr. decided that, out of revenge, Lana had somehow engineered his demise. He had no proof, but desperate for an explanation of his downfall, Oris kept his suspicions and hatred alive until his death from a stroke exactly two years after the collapse of his business.

The phoenix that rose from Martin Farms was Martin Agribusiness, Inc. There were no disease-susceptible creatures owned or cared for by Martin Agribusiness; rather, it was a feed producer, seed brokerage, cotton gin operator, farm manager, and consulting business. Oris Jr. wanted nothing to do with cows, chickens, turkeys, and especially pigs. He'd sell 'em food but didn't want to own any. Not a one.

Hank knocked on Will's door.

"Yeah?" Will said as he looked up.

"Tomás said he needed to go to the doctor and then pick up Sofia at the factory this afternoon."

Will looked at his watch and said, "I have a meeting at two with the commissioners. Call him back and see if he can meet us here first thing in the morning."

Hank nodded and turned to walk down the hall.

Ten minutes later Hank returned and sat on the couch across from Will's desk. Will put down the papers he was reading, looked at Hank, and said, "And?"

"And, Tomás will be here at seven thirty a.m."

"Good, so let's go over again exactly what Tomás told you."

Hank nodded and took a deep breath. "Okay. Tomás called me this morning while I was in my car and told me about his missing niece, Maria Puente. He said he'd gotten her a job with Martin Agribusiness as a translator and computer programmer, but now she's missing. She was supposed to arrive in Beulah and then Mussel Ford on Monday evening or sometime today, but she hasn't shown up. He said he paid NCFC fifteen hundred dollars to help her get her H-1B visa.

"I asked who he dealt with at NCFC, and he said he never spoke to anyone there because Oris took care of the whole thing. He said his sister, Marianna, called two days ago and told him that she'd dropped Maria off at the AmTex offices and parking lot in Mexico. She even described in detail the bus that was loading to bring Maria to North Carolina. She said it had some writing on the side, something like 'Texas Barstools.'"

Will nodded and said, "I've seen that bus. It used to belong to a fellow named Tex Montgomery. I even heard him and his band, the Barstool Boys, at a concert in Greenville a while back. Pretty good. I'm guessing that when Tex hung up his guitar, he sold the bus to Albert or to somebody who modified it and then sold it to Albert. I'm told Albert has a whole fleet of buses bringing pickers by the thousands into North Carolina. Anyway, go on."

Hank shook his head, "That's all I know. When the girl didn't show, Tomás and Isabella called Oris's office. The office manager, a woman named Vonda O'Brien, told Tomás that she'd called the folks at NCFC, but they kept saying that they were checking to see where the girl was and would let her know.

"Finally, Jimmy Ross called Ms. O'Brien and said that Maria never got on the bus in Mexico. Tomás says they're lying. Based on what I've heard about Ruff Waters and Jimmy Ross, he could be right."

Will nodded, then picked up the papers he'd been reading. "Okay, let me know if you hear anything tonight. If not, I'll see you here at seven tomorrow."

Tuesday

11:40 a.m.

Jimmy "Bubba" Ross sat staring at Luca Castro without moving a muscle or saying a word. He was pissed that he had to come to the house in the first place, much less try and figure out a solution to the problem Luca had created for him and Albert. Nor did he did try to disguise the fury that was etched in every inch of his face. Luca could no longer be trusted.

Finally, Jimmy cleared his throat and said, "So, tell me again, Luca, why the fuck you felt it necessary to take the Delgado girl when you knew she was meant to come to Beulah."

Luca fidgeted in his chair and rubbed his hands together as if washing them. "Like I told you, Jimmy, when Valeria told me that the Delgado girl had heard everything that went on in that bathroom, I knew I couldn't leave her there. I don't mean leave her in the bathroom or in the gas station, I mean I couldn't let her get back on the bus. I mean…" Luca, stuttering and repeating himself, was out of ideas.

Jimmy held up his hand. "Luca, shut the fuck up. You're babbling like a fool."

Luca took a few deep breaths, then said, "Okay, listen, I wanted to protect the business. I couldn't see any way to do that except to bring her here. Anyway, I called you as soon as the bus left."

Jimmy still hadn't moved from the chair opposite Luca, nor had he softened his glare. "Yeah, you called me, and exactly what the fuck do you think I was supposed to do about it then? You'd already sent the bus on. Tomás Delgado started calling Martin yesterday afternoon wanting to know where his niece was.

"I pushed them off with a lot of bullshit about the bus being held up, but eventually that couldn't work anymore. I mean what if somebody saw the goddamn bus sitting in Beulah and called Tomás or Oris Martin? I had to tell them something, so I gave 'em that horseshit lie about her not getting on the bus in Monterrey. I guarantee that nobody believes that. And where does THAT put us, Luca?"

Luca sat forward in his chair 'til he was right in Jimmy's face. "Jimmy, there ain't no way it'uh been better to let the Delgado girl get back on the bus and tell everybody that Valeria was really a hooker on her way to Jackson County and that we was kidnapping the Lampe girl to make her one, too."

Jimmy changed his glare to a lecherous smirk, "Maybe, maybe not. After all, the other passengers were just a horny bunch of young men on their way to Eastern North Carolina without wives or girlfriends. They might have taken up a collection to make sure the girls got to Jackson safely. Who do you think your clients are, dipshit?"

Luca bowed his head, then slowly looked up. "I had to stop the yelling, plus the bus was waiting. Maybe I should have let it wait while I called you, but I still think taking her was the only choice."

"Luca, we don't pay you to think. Perhaps I could have talked to the girl on the phone and told her to come on to Beulah without saying anything unless she wanted to screw up her chance to live in America. Maybe I could have said that I was sure she didn't want anything bad to happen to the Delgados. I don't know what she might have agreed to, but I do know that you left me no choice but to lie to Oris and her family! And saying that she never got on the bus in Mexico is already causing us major problems. Major!"

Luca leaned back in his chair, exhaled, and looked at the ceiling. "Okay, so what do you want me to do now?"

Jimmy stood up and moved his chair to the table in the center of the room. "Where's the old woman?"

"She went to the house on the Willis place to tell the other girls that we're slowing things down for a while. That we'll pay them while we wait for things to cool down."

Jimmy ran his hand over the table while he thought. "Okay, I'm gonna send someone to guard the two girls here. When they come, you go and tell Valeria that we're gonna find another house, probably in another county, maybe the house on the Elliot place, and relocate everyone there for a while. In the meantime, I've gotta figure out what to do with these two girls."

Luca nodded then said, "Listen, Jimmy, I've got this. I promise you that with a little breathing space, we'll be back in business just as soon as you give me the word. This Valeria woman is sharp, and she has some good ideas about how we can grow the business. Tell Ruff he ain't got nothin' to worry about."

Jimmy didn't look at him, but as he left the room he said, "Luca, don't do anything stupid for a while. Just lay low. I'll get back to you."

Maria backed away from the door in the dark and silently shuffled across the uneven, decaying floorboards until she bumped into the cot and mattress against the far wall. She turned and sat down, her gaze still fixed on the door. But her mind was on the two men in the next room. She didn't say anything until she saw Julietta looking at her expectantly, and then only in a quiet voice more to herself than to Julietta she said, "Okay, so this Jimmy is the one who Luca called from the bus stop and the one who's really running the prostitution business. Others are involved, but he and Luca seem to be the main ones. I hope to God Mr. Martin didn't know about any of this, but based on what Jimmy said, I don't think he did. This is all Luca's doing, the stupid bastard."

She stood up and stretched her back. As she leaned forward, Maria noticed that Julietta was looking up at her and starting to cry again. She smiled ruefully, realizing that like the conversation she'd been listening to, she'd been speaking in English, so Julietta hadn't understood a word. She took a deep breath, then started over again in Spanish. "Lo siento, Julietta. I was thinking in English, so I forgot you couldn't understand, but I think I know what's going on here, now. The man in charge of this whole whore business is Jimmy and some rough guy. That bastard Luca is just a little soldier.

"The company that Jimmy works for, the farmers collective, got you and me the B visas, the ones for jobs not in farming. Most of the others on the bus have A visas, the ones for pickers. When Valeria told you about being a prostitute and you got so upset, Luca, the one who brought us here, heard you and Valeria yelling. When he knocked on the door to the bathroom and asked what was going on, Valeria said that she had it under control, but then she realized I was in the bathroom all that time. When she told Luca, he freaked out. He knew I had discovered their prostitution business and was afraid that I'd tell, so he brought me here along with you and Valeria. We're both captives.

"The other man out there, the one Luca called Jimmy, is his boss, and the one he phoned after the bus left. When I didn't show up in Beulah and then Mussel Ford, Jimmy told Uncle Tomás and Mr. Martin that I never got on the bus in Mexico. They weren't supposed to take me off the bus with you and Valeria, but now they're afraid I'll tell someone about the prostitutes. That's why they're holding me."

Julietta asked through her tears, "What are they gonna do with us? Where will we go?"

"I don't know. Jimmy said they're moving the whores to a house somewhere else for a while and that they're stopping the whore business until things cool down. I'm guessing they'll move us to that house, too." Julietta didn't say anything, only lay back on the mattress.

Maria stood up again. She needed to think. She didn't want to scare Julietta, but she needed to figure out if there was something she could say to Jimmy to assure him that she would keep quiet. She knew that Aunt Marianna would have called Uncle Tomás after she dropped her off at the bus parking lot, and she was sure he would go to his friends in Mussel Ford and tell them that the story from Jimmy was a lie. Surely they were looking for her now, but she had to buy them enough time to find her.

Anyway, Julietta, Luca, and Valeria were in big trouble. She just got caught up in this whole mess by accident. Jimmy had to know that Mr. Martin and Tomás would suspect that they were lying; so maybe she could convince him that they would be better off by saying that they got some bad information, that she had gotten on the wrong bus in Monterrey. She would go along with this.

She could say that she was on a bus going to somewhere like Florida and that she didn't have any money to call. Jimmy could say that they had just gotten a call from their representative in Florida and that Maria was safe. They could wait a few days and then bring her to Mussel Ford. She needed them to believe that she could be trusted. She'd be silent if they took her to Uncle Tomás.

"Maria, where do you think they will take us?" Julietta said, her voice beginning to crack.

Maria shook her head and focused on Julietta again. "I don't know. I'm trying to remember everything Luca and Jimmy said. Let me think for a few minutes more."

The more she tried to rationalize her planned silence, the

more foolish it seemed. They wouldn't trust her to keep silent; why should they? And for Julietta, that plan was a death sentence or at best a short life of servitude, prostitution, and an early death. There had to be a better way out. If only Uncle Tomás and his friends could hurry up and find her.

"Maria?"

Maria forced a slight smile and said, "Okay, I think from what I heard that they will probably move us to another house. I get the feeling that Luca is in trouble because Jimmy seemed really angry for the whole time they talked. Jimmy said for Luca to go to the house where Valeria went and that he would tell him where to take the other girls.

"Someone is coming here to guard us while Luca is gone, but like I said before, Julietta, I know that Uncle Tomás and his friends in Mussel Ford are looking for us. We just need to stay as calm as we can. We need to think. We need to look for opportunities to escape, okay?"

Julietta nodded pitifully, rolled onto her side, and pulled her legs up. She pressed her face into the mattress to muffle the sound of her crying. Maria sat down again on the cot, then patted Julietta's shoulder and whispered, "It'll be okay. We're survivors. Look! We're alive *now*, and that's a gift."

Slowly the frightened girl turned to face her. "I can't do what they want, Maria. I'm not a whore. I'd rather die than be one of those women. You have to help me. Take me with you if you find a way—please."

Maria gently stroked her arm and back. She couldn't just forget about Julietta. Valeria and that scum Luca could roast in hell for all she cared, but she had to help Julietta if she could. She also had to save herself.

As Julietta softly sobbed, Maria also began to tear up. By instinct, she reached into her pocket for her handkerchief. It was still there. She took it out, wiped her eyes and handed it to Julietta, who wiped her own tears away.

"Thank you," she said as she gave it back.

Maria took the handkerchief, looked at it, and then handed it back.

"You keep it, Julietta. A present from me to you. A symbol of our pledge to each other to survive—and be strong through this."

Julietta took the small white handkerchief and turned it over. Embroidered on the corner were the initials MPD.

"What do these stand for?" Julietta whispered.

"Maria Puente Delgado. I got a dozen for my Quinceañera. My aunt who raised me is named Puente, and when my mother died, I took my aunt and uncle's last name. My father died when I was a baby. Delgado is my mother's maiden name."

Julietta, the tears still bright in her eyes, said, "Thank you, Maria. You're my friend—and my only hope."

Tuesday

1:00 p.m.

Jimmy Ross looked at his watch. He was early for his meeting with Albert, so he walked over to Blackie's and got a Coke and a pack of cigarettes. Albert said to meet him at the NCFC offices in Beulah at one thirty, but since he was already in town, it seemed a waste to drive home after talking to that dumb ass, Luca Castro.

He was still pissed. How the hell Luca figured that kidnapping the Delgado girl—and it would be seen as kidnapping—made any sense was beyond belief. Then again, kidnapping might not apply to a foreigner. Maybe Albert could find out the answer to that.

He lit a Marlboro and started walking over to the office. Albert was sitting behind his desk when Jimmy walked in.

"Ruff, how you doin'?"

Albert Waters looked up. "Don' know. Why don't you tell me how I'm doin', 'cause I'm thinkin' we ain't doin' so fuckin' good."

Jimmy forced a smile, took off his hat, and sat in the wooden armchair in front of Albert's desk. He looked at Albert, then moved his gaze to the large painting of a Mexican hacienda on the wall behind Albert's desk. He'd practiced what he was going to tell Albert about his meeting with Luca, but now that he was sitting in front of the man, he needed to compose himself. Albert was famous for his short fuse and even shorter attention span, so Jimmy didn't want to launch into something without planning his opening line. Albert rocked back in his chair and waited.

"Ruff, I think we need to find Mr. Castro a new line of business. It's been over an hour since I was with that fool and I'm just now coolin' down. The only word that comes to mind is 'stupid.' He's just plain stupid, and the problem is that..."

Albert held up his hand. "Stop, Bubba, you don't need to tell me the man is stupid, I already figured that one out. Just tell me what you two talked about. What happened?"

Jimmy took a deep breath, exhaled, and then spent the next five minutes describing in detail everything Luca had said about the events in the Goldsboro convenience store. He said how sorry Luca was, how he wished he'd called before sending the bus on to Beulah, and how loyal he was to their operations. Albert was by now leaning back in his chair, clearly bored, so Jimmy closed by saying that he told Luca they were gonna move the girls to another house, maybe the Elliot place, and that...

Albert slammed his fist on the desk so hard that his lamp crashed to the office floor, spraying glass shards all over Jimmy, who put his hand over his eyes and pushed back so fast that he almost fell over. Albert, his face red and twisted, was now standing.

"Talk about stupid! Where the fuck were those girls while you two dimwits were talking and making plans?"

Jimmy, his mouth open, stammered, "What... what do you mean? What girls?"

"What girls? You gotta be dumber than that moron Luca. The Delgado girl, dumb shit, and the Lamply or Lampe or whatever the hell her name is. Who the fuck do you think I'm talking about?"

Jimmy gripped the arms of his chair and hung his head. After a few seconds he looked up and said. "In the back room, I guess. Yeah, they were in the back of the house, locked in a small dark room."

"So they heard everything you and Mr. Castro said, right?"

"I guess they could have, but if they did, they didn't understand. We weren't talking in Spanish."

Albert rocked his head back, put his hands on his hips and looked at the ceiling, gathering himself. When he looked down, and right into the eyes of Jimmy Ross, he said calmly, "Bubba, think about it. We helped Oris Martin get a 1B visa for the Delgado girl. A 1B because he needed a computer programmer and a TRANSLATOR." Albert paused, leaning forward, "Now concentrate, Bubba... This means she can speak perfect ENGLISH, you stupid shit."

Jimmy's expression said everything. He had been focused on what Luca had been describing in Goldsboro, not Maria Puente. Though he would never admit it to Albert, he hadn't even thought about the two girls while he and Luca were arguing. He'd only felt anger and hate for Luca. Then only at the end, when he said for Luca to go and find Valeria, had he realized that someone needed to guard the girls.

"Ruff, you're right. I was so pissed at Luca that I forgot the Delgado girl could speak English." He took a deep breath. "Maybe she didn't hear everything. I mean they were in the back of the house and we were in the front room, you know..."

Albert held up his hand. "Stop. We have to assume that she heard everything. I haven't been to that house, but I feel pretty damn sure we're not talking about Tara from *Gone With the Wind* here. I was raised in a small farmhouse, probably a lot like that one, and I could hear my brothers fart two rooms away. No, Bubba, she heard it all."

Albert sat down and rocked back in his chair, slowly turning until he was facing the hacienda painting on the wall behind him. Jimmy gripped the arms of his chair and waited for Albert to say something.

With his eyes closed and his breathing returning to normal, Albert let his anger slowly wash away. He needed to be as calm as possible. He needed to think. How could they support their lie and protect themselves at the same time?

The Delgado girl's family in Mexico undoubtedly called Tomás up here after putting her on the bus, and Tomás undoubtedly contacted Sheriff Moser about her disappearance, and the sheriff has probably called or visited Oris Martin; so we have to assume that a bunch of anxious people are now looking for her.

Albert shook his head and, turning to face Jimmy, said, "It isn't bad enough that Luca took the girl off the goddamn bus, but then he takes her to one of his whorehouses, where the two of you talk about plans to move the other whores to the Elliot place. Now, thanks to you and Señor Castro, she knows names, places, and plans."

Jimmy didn't say a word. Albert paused for a minute then said, "Jimmy, how many people know what happened in Goldsboro? What all the yelling really meant?"

Jimmy thought a minute, "Umm, Luca; Valeria; the bus drivers, Jose Vasquez and Paco Diaz; and," he hesitated to make sure there was no one else, "And that's it. The two men who are guarding the girls don't know shit. All they know is that they are supposed to make sure the girls stay where they are."

Albert turned his chair around and looked at Jimmy, who was sweating.

"Okay. So, Luca," Albert paused, turned his head back to the painting behind him and, more to himself than to Jimmy, said, "I'll take care of that one."

When he returned his gaze back to Jimmy, he said, "How about Valeria? Have you met her?"

Jimmy nodded.

"And?"

"And she is glad to be here and will do anything that we want her to do. She's no pal of Luca's, but she sees lots of opportunity here. She ran a bunch of whorehouses in Monterrey for the Lampe girl's father. She was vetted by our friends down there, and she sees this as a way for her to be more than just a madam. Given her age, she ain't got a lot of options for a new life."

"So, you can probably buy her silence by offering her a job and place to live."

"I guarantee it," Jimmy said.

"What about the bus drivers, Jose Vasquez and Paco Diaz?"

"No problem. They've been driving for us for years and wouldn't do anything to screw up their chances of staying. I think they're both married with a couple of kids. Most of the people they know and hang out with work for the company. I don't think they'll be a problem."

Albert said, "Bubba, let's let me do the thinking from now on."

If Jimmy felt the insult, this wasn't the time to show it.

Albert continued, "That leaves you and me. I certainly won't talk. I'm guessing you won't. That leaves the two girls. The Lampe girl was sent by her stepfather, who is, I'm told, a close associate of our friends in Monterrey, right?"

"Right."

"So, we can assume that anything that happens to her is no problem since her own stepfather sent her off to be a whore. And by the way, you gotta be one shitty father to send your own stepdaughter off to be a whore, but then he does own a whorehouse."

"Two," said Jimmy.

"Well, excuse me! Two whorehouses, a man of means."

Albert, energized by his witty comeback, started walking around the room, talking more to himself than to Jimmy.

"So, that Delgado girl is the problem. By now Will Moser and his colored deputy, Henry Grier, are spreading their nets trying to find out what happened to her since there's no way they believe our story about her not getting on the bus."

Albert suddenly stopped walking and, his anger red and obvious in his face, turned and looked at Jimmy. "Bubba, for sure it's Luca who put us in this shit hole, but I gotta tell ya, your ill-considered story about her not getting on the bus has added a big pile of shit to the hole."

Jimmy stammered, "Ruff, what the hell was I supposed to do? Oris Martin's girl and Tomás Delgado were calling nonstop. I put them off as long as I could."

Albert, disgust dripping from every word, said, "You could have called me, Jimmy, instead of pulling that bullshit story out of your ass. You could have let me decide how to handle Oris and Tomás. You…" He couldn't continue without losing control, so he leaned his head back and looked at the ceiling while tapping his forehead with his fingers, then started pacing again. "Anyway, I'll take care of Luca. Now we gotta figure out what to do with the girls. I'm thinking that moving them back to Mexico and dealing with them there is our only option. If the Delgado girl's body is found in Mexico, that proves she never got on the bus, and as far as the other girl is concerned, she's just collateral damage.

"We have plenty of vehicles and can coordinate with our partners in Monterrey to pick the girls up in either the US or Mexico, then let *them* handle it. One thing's for sure, we gotta move on this. The more time it takes, the deeper Will Moser will dig into our operations. We need to move them to another safe house and not one full of jabbering whores." He again stopped walking and closed his eyes as if in prayer.

After a minute of silence, his eyes popped open and, prayer answered, he said, "Of course! I've got a small piece of land in Redmond County. I bought it out of foreclosure. It's off any main road and sits between two huge pine forests owned by Georgia

Pacific, so there ain't no houses around. It's perfect. It's got a trailer on it and a little barn. Nobody's lived in it for months, but it's got water and electricity and a phone. I'll go over there this afternoon and make sure the power is still on and the phone works. If everything checks out, we'll move the girls tomorrow. You'll need to get that whore you brought from Mexico to stay with them."

What concerned Albert the most was the possibility of his being publicly connected to the sex-trafficking business. He'd taken great pains to impress his political patrons in Raleigh with his local philanthropy and community service and, coupled with his considerable political contributions, had created a mantle of respectability that hid the true nature of his businesses.

NCFC and AmTex, along with Manpower Solutions, his Mexican recruiting company, were throwing off millions of dollars a year by providing cheap seasonal labor to thousands of farmers as well as to non-farm businesses across the US. This whole sex-trade business was more or less forced on him by his partners in Mexico, and while it could generate considerable revenue, it also increased the possibility of negative exposure.

Albert had never wanted Mexican partners, but Jared Hill, the man who ran Manpower Solutions, had convinced him that trying to recruit workers in Mexico and Latin America without the powerful Mexican cartels wanting a piece of the action was impossible. While the cartels had enormous financial and political resources, they also had an unquenchable thirst for more.

The visa program was a clean and relatively easy business, one the authorities showed little interest in bothering, but the sex-trade business had no friends; still, if he wanted to grow his visa business, he'd have to appease his partners in Mexico by facilitating their sex-trafficking business. His challenge was to continue supplying the farmers and small businesses of America with cheap labor while avoiding any negative publicity.

It's one thing to bring people into the country who have no alternative but to work in the fields for minimum wages, but quite another if those people are made to work as prostitutes. Young girls were daughters, and whether Mexican or American, daughters, like Albert's daughter Silvia, were sacred. The idea of young girls being forced into prostitution would anger the public even more than drugs, another proposal the Mexicans had thrown on the table and that Albert had to deal with, but not, thank God, one that he'd discussed with Jimmy. He'd told Jared that he didn't want any part of drugs, but when Jared relayed this to their partners down south, they just shrugged and said something like, "We'll see."

Albert refocused his gaze on Jimmy. "Bubba, I got talked into setting up this mobile whorehouse scheme because it could help our recruiting operations in Mexico, but you and Jared and our partners down there promised I wouldn't have to be involved in any way. Now I'm sitting here trying to figure out how to avoid a possible charge of kidnapping and perhaps involvement in a sex-trafficking ring."

Albert's eyes got darker and darker, fury contracting his face into a hate mask like none Jimmy had ever seen. Jimmy needed to calm Albert down before he took a course of action that put Jimmy in his cross hairs.

"Look, Ruff, let me take care of this. I might be able to talk the Delgado girl into keeping quiet. She has family. She wouldn't want anything to happen to her uncle and aunt. She wants to stay in America. She has no loyalty to the Lampe girl. She didn't even know her until Luca brought them to the Upchurch farm."

Albert interrupted. "Jasper Upchurch doesn't have any idea about any of this, does he?"

"Of course not, but I can tell you that Jasper is delighted to have his farm workers happy. I'm guessing he knows what goes on but is willing to turn his head in order to stay out of it."

"Maybe so," Albert said, "but let's not test him. Like I just said, we need to get those two girls moved off his place. They could start trouble for us, Jimmy. I'll call you after I get back from the trailer and you organize transportation. Wait until dark. Night is our friend.

"And by the way, your idea of talking the Delgado girl into staying silent… total bullshit. Do you really think that even if we came up with a convincing way to cover the lie, that she won't say something to her uncle or Will Moser or somebody in Mussel Ford about the whores? I need to talk to Jared, see what he thinks."

"Why him? I can handle this. He needs to stick to gettin' more pickers from Mexico."

"Jimmy," Albert said with disgust, "Just do what the fuck I tell you. I don't pay you to think. In the meantime, I'll call Oris and say that our people in Mexico are trying to find out what happened to the girl. I'll tell him that perhaps she got on the wrong bus or got grabbed by some bad guys while waiting for her bus. I'll make it sound like we're just as upset as he is and doing all we can to find out what happened."

Albert paused. "Now that I think about it, did any of the men on the bus hear or see what went on in the store?"

Jimmy shook his head. "I asked Jose exactly that and he said they couldn't have since none of 'em were in the store at the time. The only thing somebody might have heard was the Lampe girl crying, but if they did, they didn't talk about it; plus, no one asked him about it when they got to Beulah. If they saw or heard anything, they're not about to fuck up their own situation by running their mouth, especially Jose."

Albert didn't say anything, but it was clear he was still worried. His faith in Jimmy had taken a big hit.

"Maybe," Albert said, "but make sure Jose and his buddy remember the old saying, 'Silence is golden, but talking's bloody red.'"

Jimmy didn't disagree.

Wednesday
September 25th
DAY FOUR

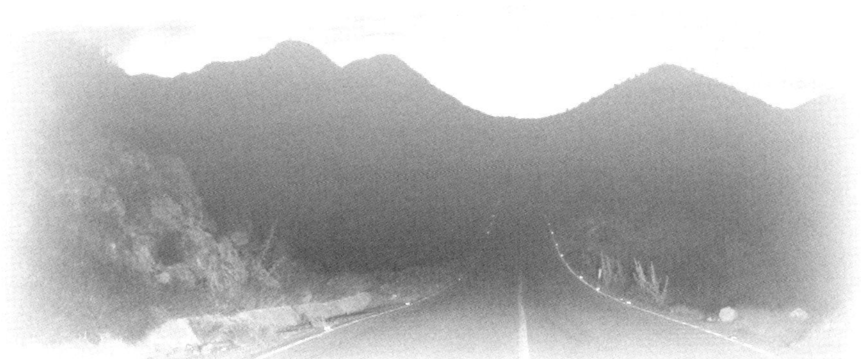

Wednesday

7:30 a.m.

Will and Hank were just finishing their first cups of coffee when Will's phone rang. "Will, Tomás Delgado is here."

"Okay, show him in, Janice."

Janice opened the door and showed Tomás into the room. He nodded at Hank and shook hands with Will. Will motioned toward one of the chairs in front of his desk.

"Thank you for seeing me, Will. I know Hank has told you that my niece, Maria, is missing."

"Yes, Tomás, Hank filled me in last night. I'm sorry, but please know that we'll do everything we can to find out what has happened to her. What we need to do now is understand what the facts are and who is involved. For starters, we need to know exactly what your sister said when she called. We need to know anything, no matter how small, that can help us."

Tomás put his Grier Tire and Auto cap on the desk and took a deep breath. For the next five minutes he recounted everything he could remember about Marianna's call. When he finished, Tomás leaned back in his chair and said, "Sheriff, Maria is as much my daughter as Isabella is. Not my real daughter, of course, but I have helped raise her since my sister was killed many years ago. Maria is family. I must find her and I need your help. So, what do we do now?"

Will looked from Hank to the ceiling and back to Tomás. After a minute, he turned to Hank and said, "You know, I'm thinking we need to call Oris first. Find out what he said to Albert about getting a visa for her and what Albert said to him. Then maybe take a trip to Jackson County to see their asshole sheriff, Garland Hoots."

Hank said, "Will, instead of the sheriff, I know a deputy in Jackson, black guy named Wimbley Johnson. We played ball against each other in high school and I run into him occasionally. He's a good man, and based on a few conversations we've had, not a big fan of Sheriff Hoots. If the sheriff is involved, Wimbley might have heard something. I can call him and see if we can't meet somewhere.

"He's well connected in Jackson County. In fact, I've heard that he might be thinking of running for sheriff himself one day. Probably just wishful thinking since Garland's got Albert Waters's money behind him. I think I remember hearing that Sheriff Hoots is kin to Albert somehow.

"Anyway, Wimbley is a Democrat and they haven't elected a Democrat in Jackson for some while. I reckon the only reason Garland hired him is that Jackson County is over forty-five percent black, so Garland figures he needs some black deputies. Redmond County has a black sheriff as does Smith County, so there might be a door opening for Wimbley."

Will smiled at Hank, "So what are you telling me, Deputy? You think Hogg County needs a black sheriff?"

Hank laughed, "Not yet, Sheriff, but someday when the old man who's now sheriff retires."

"That might be sooner than you think, young man."

Tomás listened patiently as the two bantered back and forth, but finally his patience ran out.

"If you don't mind, Sheriffs, I need to find my niece."

The two men looked at Tomás. Will said, "Sorry, Tomás. You're right. What we need to do right now is find Maria."

He looked at Hank and said, "When you meet Deputy Johnson, make sure it's someplace private and preferably not in Jackson County. I'll call Oris, and depending on what he says and what Wimbley says, we can decide whether to call Garland or maybe even Albert Waters. It doesn't much matter since both are liars.

"You remember our conversation yesterday about that unidentified dead man found near a Buddy Waller farm?" Hank nodded.

"As I said, Albert denied knowing anything about the man. He said he'd have no way of knowing about the death of an NCFC recruit unless it was reported by the man's employer. But I guarantee you he knows, because as sure as I'm sittin' here our Juan Doe was recruited by Albert Waters and NCFC."

Will turned to Tomás. "Tomás, if your niece did get on the bus, and I'm sure your sister is being accurate, then something either happened in Mexico after your sister left Maria, or something happened in the US. If something happened here, then I guarantee you Albert is either responsible, or at the very least, knows something about it.

"Go home, call your sister, and see what else she remembers that she might not have thought to tell you. See if she saw Maria get on the bus and then watched it leave, or whether she just dropped Maria *at* the bus and then went home. See if she remembers anybody else that was on the bus. Did she recognize anybody? Was there anything unusual about anybody? Is there anything she can remember that could be helpful? I want times, names, anything she remembers, then call me or Hank."

Tomás got up and walked toward the door. Before leaving, he turned and said, "Sheriff, if I call her now, I can get her before she goes to work. Can I use a phone here?"

"Sure. Hank, let Tomás use the phone in your office, and Tomás, make sure to take notes."

Hank came back to Will's office after showing Tomás to his. "Will, you think it might be better for me to call Oris?"

Will took a deep breath, looked at Hank for a few beats, then said, "No, I'll call him. It's been a long time, and success has a way of dulling any hard feelings from the past. We've had plenty of pleasant conversations and even worked together on a few projects. It's not like I'm asking him for a favor. I just want some information to help us find Tomás's niece—and his future employee. So it's in his interest, too, and Oris'll see that right off."

Wednesday

9:00 a.m.

"Martin Agribusiness, how may I help you?"

"Morning, Doris. It's Will Moser. Is Oris in?"

"Yes, he is, Sheriff, but he's busy right now, and I don't think he can speak."

"It'll only take a minute, and it is important," Will said.

"Okay, let me see." Shortly, the receptionist came back on the line, "Sheriff, Mr. Martin said to take a message and that he will get back to you. He is very busy right now."

"Doris, I need to speak with him now. It's official business."

"Well, I…"

Will interrupted, "Official business, Doris, so that means now."

Within a minute Oris got on the line, "Will, I'm sorry, but this is a bad time. I have two more calls to make this morning, and then a meeting with some men from out of state who are here to discuss a very big opportunity for us."

Will replied, "Oris, I wouldn't be asking if it wasn't important. I'll just need twenty or thirty minutes, but I do need them, and I need them right now."

Oris thought about asking for a warrant or some official order, but decided that intentionally getting in Will's face wouldn't be a good plan. He was more than familiar with Will Moser's reputation for getting what he wanted, when he wanted.

He remembered the anger and antagonism his father felt

toward Will following the Paul Reavis investigation. Then there was the death, or murder as his father called it, of his friend Eugene Winslow by the sheriff. Finally, there was the bankruptcy of Martin Farms that Oris Sr. attributed to Lana Moser, Paul Reavis's widow.

Oris Jr. was young at the time of his father's bankruptcy and thus never knew the whole truth about it, but he had over the years heard enough stories to realize that his father had not been totally honest about his own complicity in the events leading to his bankruptcy. In any case, Martin Agribusiness was a prosperous company, now providing Oris Jr. a sturdy, public platform from which to rehabilitate the Martin family reputation. He had no intention of damaging that.

"Okay, Sheriff, come on over. I'll rearrange a few things."

"Thanks, Oris, and I promise I won't take up too much of your time."

Wednesday

10:00 a.m.

Martin Agribusiness was housed in a modern four-story office building in the center of Mussel Ford. It stood out from the other buildings along Roanoke Street for many reasons: it was new, well maintained, and built to impress. Between the first and second floors were two parallel flagpoles anchored at forty-five degree angles. An American flag hung from one, and a North Carolina state flag hung from the other. Beneath the flags and immediately above the front door was the name of the business, Martin Agribusiness, Inc., spelled out in backlit, two-foot-tall raised letters.

Oris wanted to make it clear that this was now the most important business in Mussel Ford and even in Hogg County. It had always been a sore point with his father that Moser Hardwoods, Inc., the business started by Will Moser's grandfather, had been viewed as the premier business in the region and that he and Martin Farms were considered Johnny-come-latelies. He always resented that the Mosers were held in such high regard while he and his family were seen as upstarts.

Of course, had the Martins ever tried to participate in the life of the community in the same way the Mosers had, things might have been different. But Oris Sr. had no social skills, and, in fact, was a man believed to be guilty of or complicit in numerous illegal acts. The collapse of Martin Farms and the continued growth of Moser Hardwoods left Oris Sr. a bitter, angry man; a man who would believe or invent any story that showed him to be the aggrieved hero.

After the merger of Moser Hardwoods and Mansfield Pulp and Paper, Dooley Marshall, Will's first cousin, took over as the CEO of the new corporation. Dooley had become president of Moser Hardwoods after the death of Will's father, and since Moser Hardwoods was the larger of the two merging companies, he was chosen to head the new corporation. It was decided to move the corporate headquarters to Wilmington since the offices of Mansfield were larger, and the city more accessible. It was also a more attractive place from which to recruit staff; however, the company still maintained a major presence in Mussel Ford.

Dooley was the only child of Will's Aunt Clara and was an MBA graduate of the Fuqua School of Business at Duke. While Will was the largest shareholder of Moser Mansfield, he was more than happy to let Dooley handle the day-to-day management of the business.

Will parked his car in one of the several visitors' parking places at the side of the main building and walked around to the front door.

"Good afternoon, Sheriff. I'll tell Mr. Martin that you're here. He's expecting you."

"Thanks, Doris," Will replied.

Will assumed that Oris would keep him waiting for a fuck-you amount of time, so he took a seat on one of the three very expensive sofas in the reception area. Surprisingly, as soon as he picked up a magazine and started to read about the wonderful world of corn blight, Oris appeared from the back hallway.

"Hey, Will. Come on back and we'll talk in my office. Doris, hold my calls for a while."

The two men shook hands and walked back to the elevators. Oris's office took up most of the fourth floor.

"Four floors ain't much of a height to get a view, but this one ain't too bad," Oris said as he sat down in a large leather wing chair. Will stood in the center of the office looking through a massive plate-glass window at one of the most impressive views of the Roanoke River basin he'd ever seen. Oris motioned for Will to take a seat across from him.

"Very impressive, Oris—quite a view. You've done a great job with this building. It really has dressed up the downtown."

"Thank you, Will. You want any coffee, soft drinks, anything?"

Will smiled and replied, "No, thanks. Lana has taken Cokes off my permission list."

After a few more pleasantries, Oris leaned back in his chair, crossed his legs and looked at Will with a so-what-is-this-all-about expression on his face. Will put his white Stetson on the nearby sofa and said, "Oris, I have a missing-person situation that may turn out to be a kidnapping."

Oris made a small "humh" sound, then said, "You're talking about Tomás Delgado's niece, right?"

Will nodded. "How much do you already know?"

"Not much. Vonda told me about Tomás's call after the girl didn't show up. She said she called NCFC and they told her that the girl never got on the bus in Mexico. That's what I know."

"I assume then that you haven't spoken to anyone at NCFC."

"Right."

Will searched Oris's face for anything unsaid. None registered.

"Well, thing is, Oris, Tomás's sister, the woman who raised Maria, says she personally dropped Maria at the AmTex lot in Monterrey, Mexico. She gave the time, place, and description of the bus. In fact, I've seen the bus. It used to be a tour bus for Tex

Montgomery and his band but is now used by your friend Ruff Waters to bring pickers from Mexico to Beulah. The question is, who do I believe—Tomás's sister or Ruff Waters? I imagine you know the answer to that one."

Oris smiled, "True, but the real question is, how do you *prove* which one is lying and which one is telling the truth?"

Will took a deep breath. "That's why I'm here, Oris. I was hoping you might have an answer."

Oris shook his head, "All I know is what I've just told you, and, by the way, Albert Waters is no friend of mine. I've only spoken to the man maybe a dozen times; three or four when we were doing work for NCFC and then a few months ago when I called him about a visa for Tomás's niece. NCFC has been a good client of Martin Agribusiness, but we worked mainly with his operations people. And, by the way, that's one damn big operation."

Will shifted in his chair and waited a moment before replying.

"Oris, what can you tell me about NCFC that might be helpful? Most of what I know about Ruff Waters and NCFC is based on rumor or hearsay, and most is not very complimentary. For example, I know that the farmers in Eastern North Carolina need a lot of seasonal labor. Based on what my daughter Grace says, a lot of that labor is illegal. I know that NCFC was created to supply *legal* temporary visas for workers it recruits in Mexico. I know they charge a lot of money to both the workers and the NCFC members. What am I missing?"

Oris looked out of the window and then back at Will. "Will, you will of course appreciate that I can't discuss anything about NCFC that is confidential or the result of our work for them; however, I can give you some general observations that we've made on the whole migrant-worker situation in the state, and perhaps some insight into Albert Waters and his associates."

Oris spent the next ten minutes explaining the ins and outs of the visa program as set up under the 1986 Immigration Reform and Control Act; the numbers involved; the federal, state, and local inspection responsibilities; the loopholes within the laws; the pressures to keep regulations at a minimum; and the enormous profits that NCFC and its affiliates bring in.

"Will, the thing is, NCFC provides a service to the farmers in our part of the state that is essential for their survival. It's not a watchdog or a regulator or even a decent citizen, but it does have the power of thousands of farmers behind it even as it screws them with high fees for dubious workers."

"How are they dubious if they have valid visas?" Will asked.

"Well, let's just say that some of the farms for which Albert gets visas don't raise crops that need a lot of field workers. I mean if you raise soybeans or corn, why do you need pickers the way you would if you raised, say, cucumbers? Answer, you don't. I have a seed customer who says that NCFC applied for fifty workers for him and all he raises is corn and soys. Anyway, I'm not in the business of giving legal advice to my clients. The work we did for NCFC was totally centered on their computer operations, which, by the way, are extensive, and, thanks to us, in good repair.

"At their headquarters in Beulah, they have records on every individual they've ever brought into the country. There's also a company in Monterrey, Mexico, called Manpower Solutions that recruits and documents prospective workers for NCFC, but it doesn't appear on any of the org charts at NCFC, and whenever we tried to access their computer system to coordinate it with the NCFC operations here, they would just say, 'Don't worry about that one.'

"I imagine Albert owns Manpower or some part of it, but if

he does, it's silent. A fellow named Jared Hill used to run it, but he moved back to North Carolina from Mexico a year or so ago and now works in Beulah at the NCFC headquarters. We dealt with him on a number of computer issues involving worker documentation, and he's the one who kept the wall up between the US operations and the Mexican operations.

"There's also a company called AmTex Transportation, Inc., which you apparently already know about. So, the bus that Maria was supposedly not on belongs to Albert Waters. Normally, I'd suggest that if you wanted to know who was on the bus, you should ask to see the trip manifest, but I doubt they'd show it to you without some kind of court order. Even if you got it, it wouldn't do you any good because if they want her record gone, it's gone. You'd spend months if not years trying to get NCFC to turn over any records. Plus, you'd have to have proof that a crime may have been committed. I doubt the county has enough money to fight Albert on such flimsy evidence.

"Look, I'm no fan of Albert Waters or NCFC, but they do provide a real service to a lot of my customers. The state and federal governments ignore any discrepancies in documentation because they have to. There are too many farmers out there who depend on both legal and illegal laborers, so they aren't about to screw with new regulations, much less enforce the existing ones. Face it, this country lives on cheap migrant labor but isn't about to go into a confessional and admit it. I don't know what's happened to Tomás's niece, but I like Tomás and Odell Grier, so if I can help without betraying confidential material, I will.

"The fact is, I do need Maria's skills, and I spent a lot of time following the procedures for getting her a visa. As you know, or may not, we applied for a H-1B visa. This is quite different from those held by most of the migrants on Albert's buses. He mostly gets H-2A visas, the ones for temporary agricultural labor.

They're short-term and expire after the picking season, when the visa holder is supposed to return to Mexico.

"Maria's visa, unlike the seasonal visas, is for three years. It's issued for nonagricultural jobs requiring special talents and skills. We had to post a notice for her position in the company as well as in the local papers. We had to fill out an application that specified her credentials, education, and our need. The position required a college or associate degree, advanced computer programming skills, and a special language talent.

"We do a lot of work for Hispanic companies or companies involved with Hispanic companies, so I need someone who can interact with these businesses easily in their primary language. The main reason I used Albert and NCFC is their relationships with all the government agencies that handle visa applications. Getting an H-1B visa is difficult, so having an organization on our side that understands the ins and outs of government bureaucracy and deals with it on a daily basis is essential. They made the important introductions and helped expedite Maria's application. We would have wasted a lot of time without their help. One thing you have to say about Albert Waters—he knows what he's doing in this inscrutable area of governmental regulations."

Will nodded, then picked up his hat as he stood. "Oris, I appreciate your time and your offer to help. I don't yet know how to proceed, but I'll figure something out, and if I need you, I'll call." He paused before putting on his hat and looked at Oris.

"Thanks for the information and tutorial, and yes, I do understand the need for large numbers of temporary workers. I guess it's just the nature of the business and the careless way these migrants are treated that pisses me off.

"You might have heard about an incident that happened a week or so ago. A Hispanic man was found dead near a Buddy Waller farm. We found his body beside Pee Dee Road after it had cooked in hundred-degree heat for the better part of a week. Bob Velez, the M.E., said the man probably died of heat stroke, but it could have been a heart attack. Since the condition of the body precluded a definitive conclusion, he wouldn't state a cause of death, but he doesn't think it was a heart attack. The man was too young for that to be a logical cause of death. I called on Albert Waters to inquire about the man, but as you might guess, Mr. Waters was less than helpful. Anyway, I'll call you if I need help, but I won't put you on the spot with your customers if I can avoid it."

Oris stood, shook hands with Will and walked him to the elevators. As they stood in the elevator lobby, Oris said, "Will, don't worry too much about me and my customers. I can always find a channel into touchy places without making waves."

As the elevator doors opened, Will stepped in, then turned back, holding the door open. "Oris, I appreciate everything you've done for the girl, but right now this is a serious problem. I'd like to keep our conversation just between us, if you don't mind; but I would appreciate a call if anything occurs that you think might be helpful in finding her. I'm guessing that getting any information out of Jackson County will be tough, if not impossible. Truthfully, I don't feel comfortable calling Sheriff Hoots, and while we're on that subject, I've heard that he's related to Albert Waters, or if not, is especially cozy with him."

Oris smiled, "Will, as far as our conversation goes, don't worry. What was said here stays here, and as far as Garland and Albert being related, I don't have a clue. But as far as being cozy... Let me put it this way: Sheriff Hoots's nose is so far up Ruff Waters's ass that it could qualify as a proctoscope."

Wednesday

1:30 p.m.

"Hank, it's Will. Where are you?"

"I'm on my way back to Mussel Ford, maybe ten minutes out. What's up?"

"We need to talk."

"Yes, we do. I need to tell you about my lunch with Wimbley Johnson."

"Good, and I had a surprisingly productive meeting with Oris Martin."

Will understood from Oris that very little went on at NCFC that Albert didn't know about. If Albert's computer systems were sophisticated enough to store the names and vital statistics of every worker he'd ever gotten a visa for, then he undoubtedly knew what happened to Maria Puente. Still, Will wasn't sure that bringing Oris Jr. into the investigation wouldn't get back to Albert one way or the other. Calling Oris back would only be his punting decision.

Hank parked in the back of the building and came in through the doors used to bring prisoners into the Sheriff's Department. He wasn't wearing his uniform and didn't want to raise any questions about where he had been or what he'd been doing. He took the stairs up to the second floor and Will's office.

Janice Morgan, Will's assistant, was on the phone when Hank came into her office adjoining the sheriff's, so she just waved him toward Will's door without pausing her conversation. When Hank knocked on the door he heard, "Come on in, Hank."

Hank closed the door behind him and sat on the couch against the wall opposite Will's desk.

"How'd you know it was me, Sheriff?"

Will smiled, "Nothing wrong with my sense of smell, and I smelled barbeque."

"Bullshit. You been spying on me!"

Will gave him a sly grin and said, "Perhaps you forget that our cars are all fitted with LoJack. Even our personal cars. How was lunch in Cranston?"

Hank smiled and said, "Excellent. Elmer Banner has the best barbeque in Eastern Carolina."

"So how was Mr. Johnson?"

"Fine. I really like Wimbley. He'll make a great sheriff one day."

Hank leaned back on the sofa and stretched. "Since you know where we ate lunch, I'm sure you'll agree that being in Smith County instead of Jackson was important. I was out of uniform as was Wimbley, and since Pete's is black-owned, it seemed unlikely that any deputies from Jackson would be there. There were two Smith County deputies in the place, but I didn't know either one. Wimbley knew one, a fellow named Nathan Holliday or Holloway, something like that. They took a course together at Elizabeth City State on courtroom procedures. Seemed like a nice guy. I think Wimbley stayed and talked to him after I left."

Will shifted in his chair and put on his stop-the-bullshit-and-get-on-with-it face. Hank sat forward. "Word is that Jimmy Ross, Albert's operations guy, and Albert have had a bit of a falling out. Wimbley doesn't know the reason and doesn't seem to think that Garland does either, but something's up. Albert has been holed up in his office for a day making phone calls to Mexico."

"How does he know that?" Will asked.

"'Cause one of the girls who works in the NCFC office is a friend of Wimbley's wife, Cora, and she heard Mr. Waters and Jared Hill, Albert's Spanish-speaking partner, on the phone to Mexico for an hour yesterday. At one point she heard Albert tell Jared to tell the Mexican guys to call him and only him, and that he would fill Albert in. Jimmy Ross has been Albert's number two for years, and so leaving him out of the picture is odd. Something has changed."

"Anything else?"

"Yeah, Wimbley says that Garland told all the deputies that if anything comes up about NCFC or any of its people, to call him and let him take care of it. It's been made abundantly clear to all the deputies, white and black, that NCFC is off limits to them. I didn't want to put Wimbley in a tight spot, but I had to tell him something about what we were investigating. So I told him we were looking for a young girl who was supposed to be on one of the AmTex buses this week but never showed up. She has a job waiting at Martin Agribusiness and they're trying to find out what happened to her.

"Wimbley said he hadn't heard anything, but he would keep his ears open. I told him to keep the particulars between us. He said he figured it was something important and confidential when I asked him to meet me in Cranston out of uniform.

"I gotta tell you, Will, Garland ain't real popular with most of the deputies in Jackson County, white or black. They all see the crap he does for Albert and the rewards he gets for it, but don't ever see any of that generosity flowing their way.

"Wimbley said that if he heard anything, he'd call me at home. I told him to use landlines and not a cell."

Will nodded as he stood up and walked over to the windows behind the conference table. He stood there for a minute then turned to Hank, "Our friend Oris was reasonably forthcoming about his relationship with NCFC and Albert Waters, but it's not something I want to test unless we have no other choice.

"What I did learn is that Martin Agribusiness has done a fair amount of consulting work for NCFC in their computer operations department. Oris says that NCFC has one hell of a sophisticated data system and maintains records on every person they've ever gotten a visa for.

"I think that if we need help from Oris, it'll be in this area. I figured he could search their records to find Maria Puente's information, but he said—and I have to agree—that if Albert or Jimmy had a hand in her disappearance, then her records have long since been pulled." He sat back down and looked at Hank.

Hank waited then asked, "Have you talked to Tomás yet? Do you know if he talked to his sister in Mexico?"

Will shook his head.

"You want me to go over there?" Hank asked.

"No, let's call him first."

Will went to Janice's door, opened it, and motioned to Janice to come into his office. She came in, closing the door. Will leaned against his desk and when the door closed, said, "Janice, see if you can get Tomás Delgado on the phone. He's probably at the body shop, but if not then I imagine he's home." Will looked at Hank. "If he has talked to her, you think we should have him come here or maybe meet somewhere less public?"

"Somewhere else," Hank replied.

"Okay, Janice, see if you can get him on the phone."

After a few minutes Janice came to the door and said, "He's at home and asked if you could come there."

"Tell him yes. We're on our way."

Wednesday

2:20 p.m.

Franklin Street was a quarter-mile long and lined with long-leaf pines and moss-covered live oaks. The neighborhood was what a realtor would call "transitional." Mid-range homes a step above starter but not in the "gracious home" category. Tomás and Sofia's house was on a corner lot with a large front yard and a backyard with a very productive vegetable garden. The house itself was known as a "two-story rancher."

Tomás was the beneficiary of a generous profit-sharing plan that Odell Grier had set up years before. Odell understood that to keep loyal employees, he had to pay them well and treat them with respect, something he understood from experience.

Will and Hank drove Hank's personal car to Tomás's house in order to be as inconspicuous as possible. Tomás was standing outside his garage when they arrived.

"Hey, Will. Hank."

"Afternoon, Tomás. Busy day, huh?" Will replied with a tight smile and quick turn of his head toward the house.

Tomás nodded as he turned to enter by the kitchen door. "Sofia is at work and Isabella is still in school, so we have the place to ourselves," he said, looking over his shoulder.

The three men came into the kitchen and then into the living room, an airy space of bright colors with a Mexican-Carolina mix of furniture and paintings.

Will took off his hat and said, "You and Sofia have really done a great job on this place, Tomás. It's beautiful and comfortable at the same time. I also envy the garden out back. You could stock the Piggly Wiggly produce department with a garden that size."

Hank smiled and said, "Well, Tomás, Daddy and Momma might rival you on gardens, but Maya and I can't come close."

Tomás acknowledged the compliments, then asked, "You want something to drink?"

Will shook his head, "No, but thanks for the offer."

Will sat in a Lawson chair beside the sofa, and Hank on the sofa next to Tomás's chair.

Will put his hat on the floor and cleared his throat.

"Okay, so, Tomás, your sister in Mexico."

"Yes, I have talked with her this morning. She is very upset and tell me to thank you for your help to find Maria." Tomás took a deep breath. "Marianna say she take Maria to the bus parking place on Sunday morning, three days ago. Maria have one big suitcase and a small one that she carry on the bus with her."

"Did she describe either of the suitcases?" Will asked.

Tomás shook his head, "No, I don't ask her that."

Will said, "Sorry, it may not be important, but I just thought about it. Go on."

Tomás continued. "Anyway, when they get to the parking place for the buses, there is maybe twenty or thirty men who go on the bus, the one with a band name on the side; plus, there is a woman and a young girl, but she not recognize them. The girl is maybe Maria's age, but the woman is much older.

"She say she not pay much attention to the men at the bus, but away from them was three men who talk by themselves. She say that one of those men look familiar to her. When she ask Maria if she recognize him, she say maybe. She think maybe he was in school with her."

Will asked, "Did Marianna give you a physical description of the women or the man she thought they recognized?"

"She not describe the women except to say how old, but the man she think they know have red hair and light skin, more Anglo than Hispanic. She say he was with another man who is older and bigger, but also have light skin and maybe red hair, but she can't tell because he have on a hat. She say the man with the hat have shaved hair on the side, like a soldier have. The two Anglo men talk to another man, a more Hispanic-looking man."

Will started to speak but pulled back and turned his gaze to Hank. Tomás stopped talking, thinking that Will was going to comment. After a brief pause, Will looked at Tomás and said, "Sorry, Tomás, I was just thinking—please keep going."

"Marianna say when the man from the bus company tell the people to get on the bus, she leave. She say the two Anglo men leave also, so she not see the bus leave. She say she and Maria have tears in their eyes and that she not remember anything else."

"Okay, Tomás, if you will, please call her back and ask if she can remember anything about the two women… height, weight, hair color, clothing, anything that could help. Also see if she can find out a name for the young man that Maria may have known from school."

Tomás nodded, then said, "Will, Maria is a good girl. She has worked very hard to help pay for her school since she was a little girl. She is a very beautiful woman now and have made a lot of money working as a model for advertisements and clothes companies. She also has made money teaching other students. After I get my green card, I go to Monterrey to see her and my sister. Sheriff, she is family!"

Will smiled and nodded. "I understand, Tomás, and we'll find her." He leaned back in his chair, paused a minute, then said, "Okay, we know that Maria wasn't the only woman on the bus. There was an older woman, name unknown, and a younger woman, name also unknown. It was the Tex Montgomery bus, and there were at least twenty or thirty men, young and old, standing around waiting to board.

"There were three men standing apart and talking among themselves, two of whom were Anglo-looking, one of whom Marianna and Maria may have recognized. The two Anglo men left when Marianna did, and the third man, the more Hispanic one, apparently went on the bus. Finally, Marianna left when Maria got in line to board the bus, so she didn't see the bus leave.

"I think we have two options. Number one: Maria got on the bus and something has happened to her in route. Number two: she never got on the bus or did get on and for some reason either got off or was taken off before it left. Knowing what kind of woman Maria is and how hard she has worked to start a new life with you and Sofia, Tomás, it seems impossible that she would change her mind without telling someone and even more unlikely that someone would take her off the bus with so many witnesses around. She certainly wouldn't have gone silently if they had tried."

Tomás, a look of anger rising in his face, said, "You are right, Sheriff. Number two is impossible."

Will said, "Then I think we all agree that Jimmy Ross and Albert Waters are both liars. Hardly a surprise. Have I left anything out?"

The two others shook their heads.

"All right, Hank, let's go back to the office and figure out our next steps. Tomás, do you have any connections with any of the groups that help migrant workers?"

Tomás thought for a minute and then said, "The priest at St. Leo's work with some of the groups who help the farm workers. Miss Grace know him and work with him with some of her friends from Duke. I will talk with him."

Will said, "Okay, but don't say anything about us searching for Maria. Just see if he might have heard about anything unusual concerning the bus or any of the people on it. There is something fishy going on, and I don't want to alert Albert or Jimmy that we don't believe their bullshit story, even though they'll probably assume we don't. I don't know if finding one of the women or a man from the bus will matter, but we have to assume that Jimmy and maybe Albert have lied to us for some reason. If we can find someone from the bus, maybe they can point us to Maria. We'll see."

Will got up to leave, but then turned around. "Tomás, there's another thing that you might be able to help me with. About ten days ago we found the body of a man, a Hispanic man, out on Pee Dee Road. There was no identification on the man, so we have no idea who he was. When you talk to the priest at St. Leo's, see if he has heard anything about a missing man."

Tomás nodded. "I will ask him."

Wednesday

6:00 p.m.

Valeria unlocked the door to the small back room, then stood in the doorway as her eyes adjusted to the darkness. When she saw where the two girls were, she said, "Time to go! It's moving day and you're going to another house a few counties away." Neither Maria nor Julietta moved from their cots. Maria looked at Valeria with a flat, hateful glare while Julietta stared at the far wall as if in a trance.

"Okay. See, when I said it was time to go, that meant for you to stand up and walk this way. So, stand up and move your asses outta here."

"Go to hell," Maria replied, continuing to sit on her cot.

Julietta started crying.

"Nice mouth, bitch, but I'm not impressed," Valeria replied.

"I'm not trying to impress, only letting you know I'm not going anywhere with you."

"Very brave, but you have no choice. You can either go peacefully, or we can tie you up and drag your ass out of here."

Julietta got up and slowly walked toward the door. "Come on, Maria, we got no choice. I know this woman and she's not kidding. She would murder her own father if there was a peso in it." Valeria stepped aside and let Julietta pass.

"Señor Ross, they are coming," Valeria said in English.

Jimmy Ross put his head in the room, looked at Maria still

sitting on her cot and said, "It don't look like that one is coming."

Valeria smiled, "Then get some rope, tie her hands, and drag her out."

Maria didn't move or give any notice that she understood what Valeria had just said.

"I'm not going," Maria continued in Spanish.

Jimmy Ross walked over, bent down, and looking at her face to face said, "Enough with the Spanish, asshole, I know you speak good English."

Maria smiled, and this time in English, said, "Yes I do, asshole, so I'll translate for you: I'm not going."

Jimmy grabbed her by her hair and yanked her to her feet, then spun her around and pulled her arms behind her.

"Have it your way." He started to tie her hands, but she countered, "Okay, okay, I'll go. No need for the rope."

Jimmy, Valeria, and the two girls walked out into the dusk. At the bottom of the front steps was a dirty blue van, nothing like the large clean white one that had brought them to the house. This one was old and beat up without any logo identifying a business. A pair of step ladders and two long plastic tubes were lashed to the top, showing its previous use as some kind of maintenance or construction vehicle. Standing below the steps and beside the van were the two men chosen to drive the girls to their new prison house: Jose "Junior" Vasquez and Paco Diaz, the same men who had driven the bus from Monterrey. Albert told Jimmy to move the girls with as little notice as possible, so to wait until it was almost dark before shipping them off.

Paco was the shorter of the two men, maybe 5'5", and in his mid-to-late thirties, while Jose was over 5'5" and in his mid-forties. Paco was wearing a red Washington Redskins hoodie, and Jose a blue-jean jacket with a Mexican flag on the back.

Jimmy said to Valeria, "These men are going to drive the girls to their new house. You go back to the Elliot farm and make sure all the women there are settled in. I'll come over after I close up here, and we can discuss our plans."

He turned to Jose and Paco, "When you get to the trailer, call me and let me know that you got there all right. Mr. Waters says that everything is working, but that there was a problem with some of the plumbing. It really doesn't make a difference since you're not gonna be there long. There ain't any food, so you might want to stop and pick up something on the way. Keep it brief and don't ever leave these two alone in the van. It's almost six, so there'll still be some country stores or convenience stores open. I'll be up in the morning." Paco nodded as he got into the driver's seat. Jose pulled back the door on the side of the van and stood outside waiting for the girls. Jimmy walked them down to the van and pointed to where they were to sit.

Valeria followed them down the steps, looked into the van as they sat down and said, "See you two later," then smiled at Maria, "Or maybe not…"

Maria slowly raised her hand, middle finger extended.

Maria figured they'd been driving for about forty-five minutes. She couldn't guess how far they'd gone since they appeared to be using narrow, bumpy back roads to avoid notice. She tried talking to the two men to convince them that what they were doing was wrong and possibly dangerous, but neither would respond. They'd obviously been told to say nothing to the girls or even to each other. The only time either man spoke was when Paco needed to verify the directions. Jose was sitting in the back of the van with the two women.

Since the vehicle had apparently been used for some type of construction work, perhaps plumbing or electrical, there were shelves and bins along the far side opposite the sliding door. As a work van, it had never been fitted with seats in the back, so the seats put in for the girls and Jose were loose and ill-fitting.

Maria and Julietta sat on a narrow seat that looked like it had been taken from the back of an SUV. Jose sat in a low aluminum lawn chair. Maria guessed they were using the work van rather than the large white passenger van in order to be less memorable on the road. Julietta kept quiet, but occasionally she began to cry and tremble. Maria put her arm around the younger girl to steady her whenever she seemed to be breaking down. In truth, it steadied them both.

The road had become quite curvy, causing the seats in the back to sway and rock more than before. After a while, Julietta began again to tremble and then to gag. Maria hugged her tighter and asked, "You all right?" Julietta didn't say anything but leaned over like she was going to throw up.

"Stop the van!" Maria shouted. "Can't you see that she's going to be sick?"

Jose shouted, "Paco, pull over. The girl is going to puke, and if she puke, I puke." Paco slowed down and, seeing a turn off for a small dirt road on the right, pulled over. When the van stopped, Jose stood up and pulled the side door open. Paco looked over his shoulder and, as he started to open his own door, said, "Jose, you stay with the other one. I'll watch the sick one."

Before either man could react, Julietta jumped from the van and started to run. When Jose saw her running, he jumped from the van to catch her, but Maria tripped him, knocking him forward. As he fell, he hit his head on the side of the van's open door and dropped, dazed, to the ground. Paco leapt from the driver's seat and raced after Julietta while Jose struggled to his feet. Angry and bleeding, Jose lunged at Maria, hitting her in the face with his fist so hard that she fell back, her left eye closed and her nose bleeding into her mouth and down her neck.

Even though it was getting dark and she was having trouble focusing with one good eye, Maria could make out Julietta running wildly up the road with Paco in pursuit. The road was narrow with thick stands of pines on both sides. Through her good eye, Maria saw Julietta fall as she looked back over her shoulder. Paco was closing in on her.

Julietta managed to get to her feet, then, still looking back over her shoulder, darted across the road just as a pickup came through a wide curve up ahead. Julietta didn't see or hear the truck, even when the driver honked his horn and slammed on his brakes. The sounds and sight of the collision was something Maria would never forget. She turned her head and screamed, "Noooooo!" as she vomited out of the open door.

Jose was standing beside the van looking up the road when Maria vomited onto his pants. He jumped back too late, then, gagging himself, leapt forward and struck Maria again in the face until more blood, mixed with vomit, covered the floor of the van.

By this time, the driver of the pickup truck was out of his vehicle and kneeling in the road beside Julietta. Paco, assuming that Julietta was either dead or close to it, raced back to the van motioning for Jose to get back in. "Now!" he yelled. Jose pulled the door closed as Paco leapt into the driver's seat and in one motion started the van while accelerating into a U-turn, racing down the road in the opposite direction.

Wednesday

8:15 p.m.

Jared Hill was finishing his beer when Albert came in from the kitchen.

"Albert, I thought Jimmy was gonna call you when his guys got to the trailer in Redmond." Jared said.

"He was supposed to. Maybe they got lost or delayed somehow. I told Jimmy to tell those two tacos not to draw attention to themselves and to only drive the speed limit. 'Course they could've dropped off for a cerveza or two, fuckin' beaners."

Albert sat on the sofa and was turning on the TV when the phone rang.

"Finally," he said, as he hit the speaker button. "Speak to me, Bubba!"

A panicked Jimmy Ross, his voice trembling and ten decibels higher than normal, said, "Ruff, the girl's dead. She jumped outta the van and she's dead. Those two fuckers let her out to..."

Albert shouted over Jimmy's panic. "Jimmy, stop yelling! Calm down. I can't understand what the fuck you're saying. Just shut up and get hold of yourself."

Jimmy stopped talking, took a deep breath, and started over.

"Albert, there's been an accident. Jose Vasquez called me from the trailer and told me that while they were driving the girls to the trailer, the Lampe girl said she was about to be sick, so Paco pulled over to let her get out to throw up. When Jose opened the door of the van, she bolted and started to run, but when he jumped up to stop her, the Delgado girl tripped him, and he smashed his head on the side door of the van. Paco jumped out and ran after the girl, but before he could catch her, she ran across the road and right into the path of a truck coming the other way.

"Paco stopped when the driver of the truck got out and ran toward her. Since he couldn't get to her, Paco ran back to the van and drove away as fast as he could. They don't know for sure, but they think the girl is probably dead. That's all I know."

Albert sat, mouth open, staring at Jared. His expression was one of anger, panic, and hatred, but he knew that what was most important was action. Who else knew about the wreck? Which Sheriff's Department was in charge? Was the girl really dead? Did Jimmy or either of those two dumb fucking Mexicans call anyone else? Jared tapped Albert on the shoulder and motioned toward the hold button on phone.

Albert said, "Jimmy, where are you now?"

"I'm at home. I told Paco and Jose to stay with the Delgado girl until they hear from me. They have her locked in a bedroom at the trailer. They said that after she tripped Jose, she puked on him; so he hit her and knocked her unconscious. She doesn't seem to be totally with it yet, but she's okay otherwise."

"Jimmy, hold on a minute. Someone's at the door. Let me get rid of them."

When he hit the hold button, Jared asked, "Albert, weren't Jose and Paco the ones who drove the bus that brought the girls to the US?"

"Yeah, so what?"

"So this is the second time they've been witness to one of Jimmy's fuck-ups. It's time for a reduction in force. Time to cut our losses. We gotta get rid of both of those guys and maybe Jimmy as well."

Albert nodded without agreeing. "Let's get a little more info, first." He hit the hold button again. "Jimmy, you still there?"

"Yeah. Who's at the door? Is anybody else listening?"

"UPS, and no, it's just me." He looked at Jared, putting his finger to his lips. "Listen, where did the accident take place?"

"Smith County, they think."

"They *think*?"

"Hey, Albert! We're not talking Lewis and Clark here! It was dark. They were on back roads. They were panicked. They were lucky to even *find* the trailer."

"Okay, I'll call Garland and have him find out where the accident was and where they took the Hispanic girl. I hope to fuck they're right and she was killed at the scene or at least DOA at the hospital if they took her to one. If not, then we've got some real shit to deal with."

"They said she got knocked maybe twenty yards down the road. They're pretty sure she didn't survive."

"Pretty sure?"

"Well, it was getting dark and they had to get out of there. They don't think she survived."

"No comfort there!"

Albert leaned back on the sofa and looked at Jared, then at the ceiling. He had to come up with something fast. Before he could figure out what his next steps should be, Jimmy interrupted his thoughts.

"Albert, you still there?"

"Yeah, I'm here. I'm just trying to decide what we gotta do now. Give me a minute."

He looked at Jared, who mouthed, "Paco and Jose," then pulled his hand across his throat. Albert nodded, this time in agreement.

"Jimmy, listen. This is the second time those two beaners have been a witness to one of your fuck-ups. It seems clear that we need to get rid of both of them as soon as possible. You don't have to be involved, I'll take care of it."

"Ruff, wait a minute! The families of both Jose and Paco know that they're doing a job here, in the area. If they don't show up tonight or tomorrow, their families will raise hell and who knows what might happen. I know that if they call Garland he'll keep a lid on it, but what if they call the state highway patrol or start yelling to their neighbors or church friends?

"I know the sheriff in Hogg County is out looking for the Delgado girl, and if these guys show up missing, that's just more commotion. Why don't we send Paco and Jose to Mexico on the Friday morning bus and tell their families that they're making a run to Mexico to get more pickers? If something happens to them in Mexico, there won't be an inquiry."

Jared pursed his lips and nodded, then took pen and paper and started writing a note.

As he watched Jared writing, Albert said, "Jimmy, as far as them looking for the Delgado girl, Garland spoke to Will Moser and Will said that they aren't looking for her now but are still trying to find out what happened to her. If that's the case, then your solution might solve one of our problems, but you gotta make sure that neither of those guys talks to anybody before we get them to the bus. You hear me, Bubba?"

"Yeah, I hear you. Like I told you, I already told them to stay put and not go anywhere or talk to anyone until they hear from me."

Albert rolled his eyes and said, "Why do I not feel all warm and cuddly with that?"

Jimmy closed his eyes and twisted his head around to get the tension out of his neck. He knew Albert and knew that his own neck was on the line. If he fucked this up, he'd have more than sore muscles to worry about.

Jared handed Albert the note: "Tell him to pick up the big white van at NCFC headquarters and drive to the trailer tomorrow afternoon to pick up Jose and Paco. Tell him to wait until dark, then drive them to the reception building in Beulah to spend the night before getting on the bus Friday morning."

Albert nodded, then gave Jimmy his instructions.

"Jimmy, you know the big white van that Luca used to bring the girls to the house on the Upchurch place?"

"Yeah."

"Come to the reception building tomorrow morning and get the van… I'll meet you there. Drive to the trailer and wait until it's almost dark, then drive Jose and Paco back to Beulah. Stay in the dormitory with them, then put them on the bus Friday morning."

"What if they don't want to go?"

"What they want is not our concern. Tell them we need to get them out of town until things calm down. Tell 'em there are cops already asking questions about the Delgado girl, and now there'll be a lot more investigating after the Lampe girl's accident. Tell them we'll take care of the Delgado girl, but for them to keep their mouths shut."

Jimmy didn't say anything, so Albert said, "You hear me, Bubba?"

Jimmy sat with his eyes closed slowly shaking his head. How the hell could this have happened to him? Everything was going along fine until that dumb shit Luca snatched the Delgado girl, and now Albert was pissed and clearly blaming him. He had to redeem himself.

"Albert, I'm thinking I should pick up the van tonight and go to the trailer. I don't trust those two to keep their cool. I also want to make sure the Delgado girl is secure and not still passed out or in some other trouble."

Albert looked at Jared who shrugged and nodded.

"Good idea, Bubba. I'll meet you at the office in thirty minutes."

Jared got up from the couch and started pacing. After a few laps around the living room mumbling to himself, he walked into the kitchen and got another beer from the fridge. As he came through the kitchen door, he said, "Okay, Ruff, let's see how this can play in our favor. First off, we don't have to deal with getting rid of the Lampe girl. She's probably already dead or close to it, but you still need to have Garland call around to confirm that. Let's hope so.

"Next, we have no alternative but to get rid of Jose, Paco, and Jimmy, and it's gotta be permanent. Finally, as you've said before, we need to get the Delgado girl back to Mexico so we can get Will Moser off our ass and cover our lie."

Albert, looking peeved, said, "So, how are we gonna do that, Mr. Genius? I don't think shipping her back on one of the buses is gonna cut it, and stuffing her in the luggage compartment won't work unless she's already dead—and that seems to defeat the purpose. Plus, when they check at the border the stink would be a giveaway."

Jared shook his head, "I haven't figured that out yet, but I have a few ideas."

Albert, his annoyance clearly apparent, asked, "And those are?"

Jared smiled. "Remember when I told you a while back that Gabriel Materos, the guy in Monterrey we spoke to the other day, wanted one of their guys to come to the US to look over the prostitution operations and check on a possible distributor for a future drug deal?"

Albert didn't reply. He just stared at Jared.

"Hello, Albert? Do you remember?"

Albert rolled his eyes, and with barely concealed anger said, "Yes, I fucking remember. I'm just waiting for the twenty questions to stop."

Jared, seeing the anger on Albert's face, said, "Ruff, I'm sorry. I should have filled you in yesterday, but we were both so busy that I just forgot. After our call the other day with Gabriel, when we told him about Luca's fuck-up, he called me back and said that they're sending one of their top guys to see if he can help. I think they feel bad since Luca Castro was their choice to start the prostitution business.

"Anyway, a guy named Dante Sandoval is getting here some time tomorrow or early Friday. He's taking a plane from Monterrey to Toronto and then to Charlotte. I told him that if he'd let us know when he was getting in, we'd pick him up at the airport, but he said no, that he'd get a car. He's traveling under the name Robert Major.

"I know you haven't been keen on the prostitution business, Albert, and especially their ideas for drug distribution, but I think when he explains what they have in mind, you'll be more enthusiastic."

Albert replied, "I doubt that. And busy or not, you should have told me about some hotshot cartel guy coming to town. I still run this fucking show, in case you forgot."

"You're right, Albert. I'm sorry and I know that it's your show, but you need to understand the pressure I'm under in dealing with these people in Mexico."

The more Jared discussed the Mexican connections and the drug distribution idea, the more nervous Albert got. "Jared, you know how I feel about this shit. I never wanted to expand our visa program into prostitution, much less drugs. I don't know why you insisted on these businesses!"

Jared took a long swig of his beer, then sat down opposite Albert, looking him in square in the eye. "Albert, I've told you all this before. It's not me. You gotta understand Mexico. At the top of the heap, you have about a dozen major corporations that control everything from oil to telecommunications to food to heavy manufacturing to pharmaceuticals and to technology. The owners and managers of these monopolies effectively own the government. They control who will run for office, who wins, and what they'll support when elected.

"Next you got the cartels. These control all the illegal drugs, prostitution, and human trafficking in the country, and they're damn near as powerful as the corporations. The difference is that the guys who run these businesses didn't go to Harvard Business School. They're stone-cold killers and are afraid of nothing. They maintain their power in Mexico and Latin America the same way Stalin did in Russia—murder, intimidation, blackmail, and purchased loyalty. The Mexican citizens, who are, by their nature, patriots and decent people, are terrified for their lives.

"The big corporate guys isolate themselves behind heavily armed private armies, but even they have to deal with drug money and the dealers at some point.

"Albert, we started Manpower Solutions in order to meet the demand for cheap labor here, but I couldn't do that without the help of some well-connected people. Only one group in Nuevo León State has the right connections and the muscle necessary to maintain them, and they're the Olmecs. They control a large part of the State of Nuevo León and a good part of Tamaulipas State. For me, an Anglo, to find pickers in the numbers we need would have been impossible without local partners; so, I formed a relationship with the Olmecs.

"According to Gabriel, Dante Sandoval, our future guest, grew up in Nuevo León State near Monterrey and even went to school for a short while in McAllen, Texas. Gabriel says that Dante had a rather privileged childhood since his father was a federal judge in Monterrey; but like a lot of government officials, the judge was co-opted by the cartels, and then his greed got the best of him. He lost his judgeship but is still involved with the cartel as a private lawyer.

"After high school and two years at a professional military institute, Dante enlisted in the Army and very quickly rose to the rank of Major in the Special Forces; probably the reason he is using Major as his current alias. His progress in the Army wasn't hurt by the fact that he had strong family connections and a better-than-average education. He even got some special warfare training in the US at Fort Bragg and Fort Benning.

"When it became clear that Dante couldn't have the lifestyle he wanted on a major's pay, he offered his services to others. He speaks excellent English, as does his little brother, Germaine; is educated, knows the ins and outs of government; is trained as a killer; and is ruthless. In other words, he has the perfect resume for a job in one of the cartels! It turns out that Judge Sandoval already had some sub-rosa contact with the Olmecs, so it was an easy decision for Dante to join the organization.

"He's been a member of the leadership for almost ten years but isn't yet the final authority. The head guy, the Patron, is a fellow named Romero. His nickname is 'El Ejecutor,' the executioner, and he wasn't given that name lightly."

Jared paused a moment and looked at Albert with a slight smile. "And Albert, don't take offense, but you didn't get the nickname Ruff Waters because of your middle name. You've been a kick-ass kind of guy for a very long time. Time to be kick-ass again!"

Albert, looking grim, said, "Jared, I've had to fight for everything I've ever got, and you're right, I didn't get the nickname 'Ruff' just because of my middle name, but this ain't Mexico. We got our share of crooked politicians, but I don't see it runnin' from the top down. I deal with a lot of people in Raleigh, but I'm damned careful about who I wink at and who I don't.

"We got us a bought sheriff here in Jackson County, but I doubt he'd kill anybody for money, and I'd never ask him to. If someone needs killin', then I'll get it done my own way, but I gotta tell you—I'm nervous about Jimmy's plan to ship Jose and Paco to Mexico."

Jared sat down and put his feet up on the coffee table. After finishing his beer, he looked at Albert, smiled, and said, "I agree. Too many things can go wrong. We need to solve that problem sooner rather than later. So, as I just said, we need to permanently get rid of the beaners as well as Mr. Jimmy Ross. Jimmy is getting shaky, and even though he hasn't been part of the new drug-distribution discussions, he probably knows something is going on. Jimmy would crack like a pecan if confronted by a badge."

Albert shook his head. "Jared, I've known Jimmy for a long time, and while he's not the sharpest knife in the drawer, he's been loyal. How about sending him to Mexico to work at Manpower and then bring him back in six months or a year?"

Jared said, "Albert, if we send him to Mexico, the Olmecs will have him cut up and cooking in a fifty-gallon oil drum within the week."

"Well goddammit, just tell them to leave him alone."

Jared didn't say anything, only looked at Albert with an expression whose most optimistic interpretation would be read as "Good luck with that."

Neither man said anything for a long time. Finally, Albert got up, walked over to the window, and said, "Okay, Mr. Genius. What's our next move?"

Jared took a deep breath. "Ruff, I think I've got an idea that is perfect and can be done quickly.

"I was out at the Ellis farm the other day talking to Jimmy Ellis about his labor needs for this summer. I asked him how many men he would need for his crops, then whether he needed help at the quarry. He said he shut the quarry down last year. He said he's selling all the equipment, and when I asked if there was anything we might want or need, he said not unless we wanted a Barber-Greene rock crusher. He did say that there was a ten-ton dump truck still there, and that, while not in the best of shape, it still runs. I thanked him but said we had no need of something like that."

Albert was clearly getting impatient and started to speak as Jared held up his hand. "Just hold on, I'm not finished. Does the white van have a LoJack tracking device on it?"

Albert nodded.

Jared smiled, clearly enjoying what was coming next. "I'm thinking that tomorrow night when Jimmy is driving Jose and Paco to Beulah, a terrible accident will occur. I think that Garland Hoots, sheriff of Jackson County, will report Friday morning that a large dump truck full of gravel was stolen from the Ellis farm, and that the thief or thieves, in their hurry to get away, smashed into a van coming in the opposite direction, killing the driver and two passengers. That the driver of the truck is nowhere to be found, and that the families of the three men, upstanding Jackson County citizens all, have been notified. He will add that every effort is being made to find the perpetrators of this cowardly deed."

Albert listened without saying a word or showing any emotion. It was clear that, while distasteful, eliminating Jimmy was necessary to protect the businesses that had taken Albert so many years to create and grow. Albert's loyalty went only so far as the register of his checkbook would allow.

"Okay, but what if the Delgado girl is in the van as well? We could say that Jimmy and the two Mexicans came up with a plan to kidnap and ransom her. That we are just as shocked as everyone else. We could…"

Jared shook his head. "Forget it, I thought about that, but

nobody would believe it. I mean, who would pay ransom for a girl that was sure to be killed? And who would believe that Jimmy Ross, who has worked for you for twenty years, plus two semi-legal Mexicans, were smart enough to carry off something like that?

"No, finding her in the wreck would be disastrous. First off, it would prove that Jimmy lied about her never getting on the bus in Monterrey. In addition, you expanded the lie. 'Oris, we're investigating her disappearance with our folks in Monterrey. A terrible thing. We're just as upset as you.' That ring a bell, Albert? Plus, nobody would believe that you weren't involved. The whole world knows that Albert Waters runs NCFC and that little Jimmy Ross doesn't shit without your permission."

Albert, a look of disgust on his face, said, "I just wish that was true. The dumb fuck made up that story without even calling me until it was done."

Jared continued, "Regardless, I guarantee that Will Moser hasn't quit looking for the girl. The fact is, finding her body in an NCFC van would bring down the wrath of not only Will Moser, but the SBI and probably the Feds too, on NCFC—and on you in particular. If it's your van, it's you, and like it or not, Sheriff Moser is a real power in this state. He was twice president of the State Sheriff's Association; he's one of the wealthiest men in the state, and you'd need a crowbar to separate him from the governor. You wouldn't have a friend left in Raleigh. Even with our solution for Jimmy and the two beaners, the prostitution operation and any thought of a drug distribution plan would have to be put on hold until things cooled down."

Jared got up and walked into the kitchen, saying over his shoulder, "Ruff, I understand your concerns, but like you said, our only real option is to get the Delgado girl back to Mexico as soon as possible. We need to talk to Dante and see what ideas he might have."

"What if he says to kill her here?"

"Then we say no. We remind him that this is our operation, and we are the ones who are at risk here, not him. We say that for us to continue supplying the thousands of workers needed in this country, that we, NCFC and Manpower, need to have clean skirts and proof that the girl never got to the US. The Mexican police need to find her in Mexico and possibly have witnesses who saw her get killed. Dante might even arrange for the blame to fall on a rival cartel. With the death of the Lampe girl, things are gonna heat up, so we need to move quickly… quickly—but carefully."

"So how do we do it. How do we get her back to Mexico?"

"I don't know, but I'm sure Dante will have some suggestions."

When Jared saw Albert's head starting to shake, he said, "Ruff, don't worry so much! We can find a way to move her, my friend. What we need to do now is make sure she's kept secure, and with that in mind, you need to tell Jimmy to get that madam over to the trailer to stay with the girl. If she can't figure out how to get there on her own, then have Jimmy go and get her tomorrow morning and bring her to the trailer. She only has to be there for a couple of days. At least until we have a plan. I'm thinking we need to shoot for some time this weekend."

Albert shook his head. "Goddammit, Jared, this is exactly what I was afraid of. Son of a bitch, it's getting too fucking messy. And by the way, who the hell is gonna drive the dump truck? I ain't doin' it—Jesus!"

"Leave that to me, Ruff. You don't need to know. Just know that the driver will never be found out… or even found, for that matter!"

Albert stood up and put on his jacket. "I've got to meet Jimmy at the van. Stay here until I get back. Motherfucking Mexicans!"

Jared followed him to the door. "I agree with that, but stop worrying. It'll work out, plus it might make us all a whole lot richer."

Wednesday

9:30 p.m.

"Will, it's Hank. I just got a call from Wimbley Johnson in Jackson County, and he just got a call from his friend Nathan Holloway in Smith County. He's the deputy Wimbley and I saw at lunch yesterday. Anyway, it seems there's been an accident. A young Hispanic girl was hit by a truck tonight and is in the hospital in Cranston. She's in critical condition, but Wimbley says she's still alive. I think we need to get Tomás and get over there damn fast."

"Does anybody in Jackson County other than Wimbley, know about this?" Will asked.

"No. Wimbley hasn't said anything. He knows we're looking for a missing girl, and he knows to keep quiet about it. There's no reason for him to tell anyone in Beulah about some accident in Smith County."

"Okay, I'll call Tomás then go by his house and pick him up. You go to the hospital in Cranston and make sure they keep a lid on it for at least a few hours. Maybe you can call Sheriff Haines and see if he can meet you there. Tell him that I'm on my way over."

"Right. See you there."

The hospital in Cranston was small but equipped to handle emergencies until transportation could be arranged to Greenville, North Carolina, and the much larger medical center there. East

Carolina University was in Greenville, and its hospital had 900 beds and a medical school.

Hank walked through the emergency room doors of the Cranston Hospital and asked the attendant how to get to the intensive care unit. When she started to say something about admissions and authorization, Hank held up his hand.

"Miss, I understand procedure, but there is a young Latina woman who was hit by a pickup truck tonight and brought to this facility. She may be a person of interest. I just spoke with Sheriff Haines, who is on his way here along with my boss, William Moser, the high sheriff in Hogg County. We're looking for a young woman who we believe was kidnapped two days ago. I don't know if the young woman you have in intensive care is the one we're looking for, but if she's still alive and conscious, I need to see her."

"Wait a minute, let me call intensive care and get a status."

Hank walked over to the doors leading into the emergency room and then looked back at the attendant. She was still talking on the phone. He started to walk back to the desk when a doctor wearing scrubs and a face mask came out of the emergency room.

"Are you the deputy inquiring about the young girl who was hit by the truck tonight?"

Hank turned around, "Yes. I'm Deputy Henry Grier."

The doctor took off his mask. "I'm afraid she didn't make it. She died ten minutes ago." Hank stood looking at the doctor, then said, "Doc, I've got a man coming over who thinks that maybe she's his missing niece. Did she have any ID on her?"

"Nothing. She had a few personal items in her pocket but no papers or ID."

"We'll need to have this fellow take a look at her." Then more to himself than to the doctor, Hank said, "Tomás, for your sake I hope this ain't Maria."

The doctor turned around and said, "When is this fellow coming? We may need the space."

"He'll be here any minute," Hank replied.

"Okay, we'll put her in a back cubicle until he gets here. There's already a deputy from Smith County in the back. He's been talking to the truck driver who hit the girl. As you can imagine, the guy's pretty shook up."

"What's the deputy's name?"

"I think he said it was Nathan Holloway. Something like that."

"Can you take me to him? I need to talk to him."

Will waited until he got behind a slow-moving vehicle before turning on his lights and siren. No need to keep it on all the way from Hogg County to Cranston. Tomás hadn't said a word but was clearly agitated and worried. As they arrived at the hospital, Ed Haines, high sheriff of Smith County, was just getting there as well. Will parked outside the ER and followed him in.

"Hey, Ed, thanks for meeting us here. This is Tomás Delgado." Ed shook Will's hand and then Tomás's. "No problem, Will. Good to see you." He waved at the attendant, "Hey, Joyce. Is Nathan in the back?"

"Yes, Sheriff. He got here 'bout an hour ago. There's another deputy back there with him. Think he said he was from Hogg County."

Will nodded, "That would be Deputy Grier. I told him to come ahead."

The three men went through the ER doors and were directed to a cubicle at the back of the ICU. Tomás stopped before going into the cubicle. He needed to catch his breath and calm down. He crossed himself then pulled the curtains back and walked through.

"Hank and Nathan were standing on either side of the bed. Tomás stopped at the foot of the bed and waited. After a brief pause, he looked at Hank and nodded. Hank pulled the sheet back, keeping his gaze on Tomás's face. He knew the minute Tomás looked at the girl that it wasn't Maria. The air returned to the room as Tomás shook his head and whispered, "It is not her."

The four lawmen plus Tomás gathered in a small conference room down the hall from the ER. While they were relieved it wasn't Maria lying in the cubicle, they also realized that she was still missing, thus there was more work to be done. Plus, someone had to investigate the tragic death of the young woman lying in the ER. Such an investigation was not only a legal requirement, but might lead to information about Maria too.

Will looked at Tomás, "Tomás, I'm of course relieved that the young woman isn't your niece, but that also means we still have work to do. I've filled Sheriff Haines in on our situation, and he's agreed to give us all the help we need." Will looked at Sheriff Haines, "Thank you, Ed. We can use the help."

Hank and Nathan sat beside each other facing their respective bosses across the table. Tomás was at the end of the table.

Hank cleared his throat. "Okay, Nathan and I have been talking, and I think we all need to hear about his conversation with the truck driver who hit the young lady. I think we can definitely say that it was an accident. Nathan."

"Thanks, Hank, and yes, it was definitely an accident. Ed and Will, I spent about an hour with the fellow who was driving the pickup that hit the young girl. He is really shook up, as I imagine any of us would be.

"The basic facts are these: it was almost dark when the accident occurred. Otis, that's the driver, Otis Chambers, was coming home from work when he came around a sharp curve out on Balsam Road." He looked at Ed, "It was about a mile west of Moreland's Store, Ed, right in the middle of a pine forest."

Ed Haines nodded.

"Anyway, it was almost dark out; plus, tall pines were blocking any light that was left. When he came out of the curve, he saw something dart in front of the truck. At first he thought it was a deer, but as he slammed on his brakes and started to skid, he saw it was a person. He said he wasn't going too fast by that time, maybe thirty or thirty-five, but still too fast to avoid the collision.

"He swerved to the left and hit the girl on the right side of the truck, at his right headlight. She was knocked about ten to twenty yards down the road. He said he jumped out of his truck the minute it stopped, and ran to the girl. He knew it was bad. He tried to put pressure on the bleeding, but it didn't seem to help."

"Did he see anything else? Any other cars or… anything?" Ed asked.

"He said when he looked up, he saw a man running down the road away from him. He yelled at the man, but he didn't turn around. The guy got in a blue van about a hundred yards down the road, wheeled it around and drove off like a bat-outta-hell in the opposite direction."

Will said, "How does he know it was a man?"

"'Cause he could make out the outline of the figure. He had short hair, and Otis said he ran like a man."

"What else? Could he tell how big the guy was? What he was wearing?" Ed asked.

"The man was wearing a Washington Redskins hoodie and was short."

"How short?"

"Maybe five-foot-four or -five."

"So how'd he know he had short hair?"

"'Cause his hood was down."

"How could he see all that in the dark?"

"He said he saw the yellow Redskin mascot's head on the back of the hoodie, and when the guy got in the van, he kinda hopped up to get in."

"What else?" Will asked.

"I asked him if he could identify the van, but he said there were no business logos or markings that he could see. He knows it was blue, kinda between a Carolina blue and a Duke blue. He couldn't make out the license plate but is pretty sure it was North Carolina, and—oh yes, he said that the van had step ladders and some plastic tubing on the top and stickers on the back windows, a round Marines sticker on the left back window, and a round NRA sticker on the right window."

"How the hell could he see those and not the license?" Ed asked.

"'Cause he's got the same two stickers on the back window of his truck."

Hank stood up and walked over to the credenza against the side wall. He turned around and said, "I asked the doctor if the girl had any ID, and not surprisingly, he said no, but she did have a few personal belongings in her pocket." He took an 8" x 10" manila envelope out of a drawer and emptied its contents onto the table.

"One Chap Stick. One pair of gold hoop earrings. One small tube containing three Bayer aspirin. And a lady's handkerchief with a bit of blood on it and the initials MDP."

With this, Tomás, who hadn't said a word since coming into the room, leapt to his feet and walked down to the other end of the table. He picked up the handkerchief and stared at the corner with the initials. When he looked up it was with a horrified expression. No one said anything.

"This is Maria's handkerchief! These are her initials! She get this for her Quinceañera…"

After digesting this information, Will said, "So, maybe this is the girl Marianna saw getting on the bus in Monterrey with the older woman. So much for Jimmy Ross's bullshit story, now a provable lie, that Maria never got on the bus."

Ed looked over at Will. "You're undoubtedly right, Will, but if you confront Albert Waters or Jimmy Ross with this, they're gonna deny knowing anything about the girl, or the older woman, or Maria. They'll say that a young girl getting killed is a terrible thing but has nothing to do with them. As of now, I can't see anything material tying them to the van or the girl. As far as the handkerchief goes, maybe Maria and the girl were friends in Mexico and exchanged gifts there. We got nothing but supposition."

Will sat staring at the ceiling. Ed was right, nothing tied Albert or Jimmy to the girl's death, but it also seemed clear that Maria was on the bus from Monterrey. Meaning that she might be, at this very moment, nearby or at least in a neighboring county.

"You're right, Ed. We can't prove that Albert or Jimmy are tied to this girl's death, but as far as the handkerchief goes, let's look at the facts. One, there's a dead Latina girl lying in the cubicle down the hall who had a handkerchief belonging to Maria Puente on her body when she was killed. Two, Maria doesn't have any friends in America or any friends in Mexico who have recently come to America who might have gotten a handkerchief from her. Three, if the dead girl was on the bus with Maria and they had known each other before, why didn't they greet each other at the bus parking lot? Finally, I don't give a shit about what we can prove. I give a shit about what we all damn well know, and that is that Maria Puente is in North Carolina, and the dead girl in the cubicle down the hall got that handkerchief from Maria sometime in the last day or two. In fact, I'd be willing to bet that Maria was in that blue work van tonight."

No one in the room spoke. Tomás carried the handkerchief to his seat and sat down while holding it to his face. Will waited for a few minutes, then said, “Hank, we need to track down that van, and we need to find a man, a short one, who wears a Redskins hoodie.” He turned toward Sheriff Haines, “Ed, if you have a spare man, we sure could use some help.”

“We’ll do whatever you need, Will,” Ed said as he got to his feet and walked over to the credenza, looked at the items from Julietta’s pockets, then leaned against the table while crossing his arms.

“So, what do you think’s going on, Ed?” Will said.

Ed stared at the items taken from Julietta’s pocket as he rubbed his hand over his mouth.

“Could be that they were taking the girl, or maybe girls, to some safe house. You’d think that if they’d decided to get rid of the girls here in North Carolina, they would have already done it. The fact that the girl was still alive and being driven somewhere in a nondescript blue van—and we should assume that the girl got out of the blue van that the truck driver saw speeding away—means that the kidnappers may have something else in mind, like getting rid of the girls some other way. Then again, maybe the man or men in the van were taking the girls to some swamp or disgusting landfill to kill them. But I’m guessing they intend to send them somewhere else, maybe back to Mexico where they could solve their problems much easier. If this is true, then they were probably driving them to some place where they could keep them hidden until they had a way to ship them out.”

He looked over at his deputy, “Nathan, you take whoever you need and start going to every gas station, convenience store, body shop, restaurant, and anywhere else you can think of, and see if anyone has seen a blue work van with ladders on the top and the stickers on the back.

“Don’t say anything about a missing girl. Say only that we’re investigating the death of a young woman hit by a vehicle and are looking for a van that may have been involved. I need to write up a report on the accident, but I'll keep it vague and still in the investigation stage.

"I guarantee you, Will, that we'll get a call from our buddy Garland in Jackson County, inquiring about the accident. So make sure you all tell folks that I'm the only one allowed to speak about this. Nathan, tell the driver of the truck to keep quiet and talk to nobody but you or me. And tell him not to worry, that he's in no danger of being charged with anything.

"Also, we should assume that Albert believes Will and Tomás are looking for Maria, but he doesn't know about the accident in Smith County, at least not yet."

Will stood up and walked over to where Ed was standing, then turned and said, "As a matter of fact, gentlemen, I already got a call from our buddy in Jackson County. Garland said he'd heard about Tomás's niece missing the bus in Monterrey. He said he'd heard we were looking for her and wanted to make sure I knew that Albert was aware of the problem and had either already called or was going to call Oris and tell him that Tomás's niece never got on the bus, and that he has called Mexico to have his people down there find out what happened to her. He said that there was no reason for us to get all worked up about searching for the girl since she isn't in the States, or at least not that they know.

"I told him we've been inquiring about the missing girl, but when we heard she hadn't gotten on the bus in Mexico, we slowed up. I did tell him that we're still trying to find out what happened to her, and that we'd appreciate any help they can give."

Ed smiled. "You think he believed you?"

"I think it's what he wanted to hear, so, yes, I think he believed me. I don't know if Albert will believe him, but he might. At least it might be enough to calm Albert down a little. Still we need to focus on the business at hand."

Will looked at Hank and Tomás. "Tomás, since you're in the body shop business, can you quietly inquire about the blue van?" Tomás nodded.

Hank said, "I'll get a couple of Latino guys I know to snoop around in Beulah to see if they can spot a short guy wearing a Redskins hoodie. I'll also call Wimbley and see if he's seen such a person around town, but I think we should be careful to not get Wimbley too involved. I don't want to put him in danger with Sheriff Hoots. Crooked or not, Garland ain't somebody you want to fuck with. Will, you think we should put a tail on Jimmy Ross?"

Will shook his head. "No. If Jimmy or Albert think they're being followed, they might panic and do something that can't be undone. We need to hunt down the van and the short guy. Ed and Nathan will be looking in Smith County. We need to check out Jackson County and maybe some of the other surrounding counties. Ed, can you call Sheriff Pierce in Redmond County and have a quiet man- to-man?"

Ed nodded. "Yeah, I can call him and fill him in. He hates Garland Hoots and probably Albert, so he'd love to stick it to 'em."

Will said, "Don't tell him more than necessary, but enough so that he knows you and I are working on this together, and that it's urgent we find the missing girl. No need to tell him her name or that she's Tomás's niece. We don't want Albert to find out that three adjacent counties are looking for the girl. After my call from Garland, Albert might be more comfortable thinking that we are still curious about what happened to Maria but aren't actively looking for her. That might buy us some time."

Will stopped talking and turned toward the credenza. After a brief pause, he turned back around, looking at each man in the room.

"Gentlemen, what I am going to say now is very confidential, and I'd like it to *stay* in this room. Does everyone agree?" All in the room nodded in agreement.

"This afternoon I spoke to a friend of mine high up in the SBI about getting some help. After filling him in on our situation, he said that unless I had something more concrete to work on, he didn't know what they could do. He said that kidnapping is handled by the FBI, and unless we had something tying our case to human trafficking, his hands were tied, but he would nose around. Again, I don't want anyone to know that a high-up in the SBI is helping. I haven't called the FBI since all we have right now is an uncle's worry, no ransom note or even sure knowledge that our supposed victim is in this country, plus a statement from a prominent, politically influential businessman who says he has no knowledge of a missing girl, at least not in this country.

"It appears that this one is on us, gentlemen. My friend in the SBI also said that if what we fear is true, we probably don't have but a day or two to find Maria. I hope he's wrong, but let's go on the assumption that he's not."

As Ed and Nathan got to their feet to leave, Ed turned around and said, "Will, Tomás, if she's in Smith County, we'll find her."

Thursday
September 26th
DAY FIVE

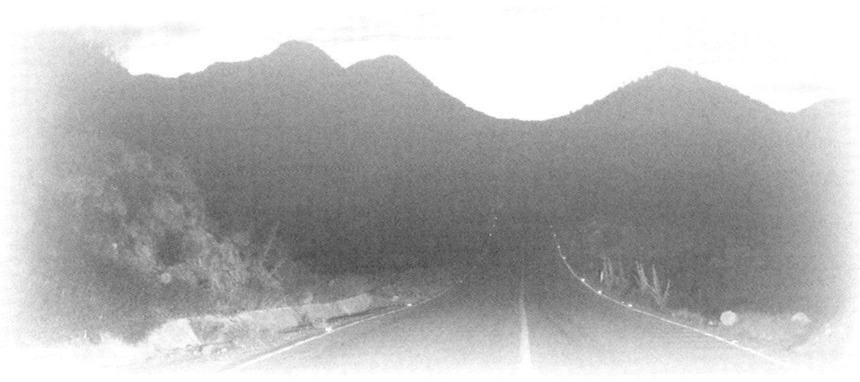

Thursday

11:00 a.m.

Maria rolled onto her back. Her headache was gone, but her left cheek and eye still throbbed. When she tried to open her eyes, the right one opened right away, but her left, still swollen and watering from where Jose had struck her, needed some gentle massaging before it could open, and even then, it only gave her an unfocused, blurry image.

She slowly sat up and, through her good eye, looked around the small bedroom in which Jose and Paco had locked her the night before. The lumpy, damp mattress on which she had slept lay on the floor without a frame. A straight-back chair stood to the right of the door, and a table with only three good legs rested on its side next to the chair. The broken fourth leg lay on the chair's seat. A single window at the end of the room showed a badly broken blind hanging from one corner.

She had no idea when they had finally gotten to this hot, smelly trailer, but she did sense that both Jose and Paco were in a panic and afraid for their own safety. Just after they arrived, she heard Jose talking so loud and fast on the telephone that the person on the other end must've told him to slow down. When he did, he recounted the accident, how Julietta got away, the fact that she was probably killed instantly, and it being almost dark, that they surely couldn't be identified. The man on the other end of the line must've told them to get rid of the van, which she assumed they did right after they hung up. Maria guessed from the conversation that the van was now at the bottom of a nearby lake or snake-infested swamp.

It was overcast outside, but at least the temperature was now bearable. She slowly stood up and walked to the bedroom door.

Pounding on the door she yelled, "Hey, Shit-heads, I need to use the bathroom!"

When no one replied she pounded on the door again.

"Anybody out there? I need the bathroom!"

At last she heard movement and someone shuffling to the door. A key slid into the lock and the hollow-core door swung open with a harder-than-necessary push. Outside the door, a sour expression on his face, stood Jimmy Ross.

"Go piss and hurry up."

Maria paused for just a moment then said, "Well, well. Look who the cat dragged in. Come to make sure you killed the right girl?"

Jimmy didn't change his expression. "I come to make sure you were locked up."

"Well, congratulations! Your two attack dogs did what you told them to do."

Pointing toward the bathroom, he said, "Shut up and do your business."

Maria turned and walked into the bathroom, pushing the door closed behind her, but as she did, Jimmy put his foot out to stop it from closing.

"Leave it open."

"Why? You need to get your early-morning thrills by watching a woman pee?"

"Like I said, shut up and do your business."

Maria spit on the floor at Jimmy's feet then put the seat down and dropped her pants.

"Having fun yet?"

Jimmy didn't reply but did turn his back to the door.

When she finished, she pulled up her pants, walked back to the door and said, "How about something to eat? I haven't eaten in days. The last meal I had, is, I assume, still on Jose's pants."

"There ain't no food here. I'm going out to get something this morning. Until then you just keep quiet and get back in your hole."

"While you're out, how about some ice for my face?"

"I'll think about it," he said, then pushed Maria back into the bedroom and locked the door.

Maria walked over to the window. A large white van was parked in front of the trailer. It looked like the one that had brought her and Julietta to the first house. After a few minutes, Jimmy walked out to the van with Jose close behind him. The two men were arguing until Jimmy opened the van's door, pointed toward the trailer, then drove off. Jose stood for a few seconds watching the van drive away, then yelled something at the departing van that Maria couldn't hear but assumed wasn't wishes for safe travels.

Thursday

1:50 p.m.

It was almost two when Will got back from lunch. He parked the patrol car, took his Stetson off the seat, and started across the asphalt lot to the back door of the sheriff's office. Days like this always reminded him of those miserably hot afternoons in the Mekong Delta; afternoons when his jungle fatigues stuck to him as if they'd been painted on. It wasn't supposed to be this hot here in September, but the drought and lack of rain was turning Eastern Carolina prematurely brown.

As he opened his office door, Hank Grier called down the hall, "Hold the door, Sheriff, I need to talk to you."

Will left the door open and walked over to his desk. Hank came in and sat on the couch.

"So, what's up, Deputy?"

Hank took off his hat and leaned back. "Okay, I talked to Tomás this morning, and he said the only lead he's gotten on a blue van was from one of his mechanics. From time to time, he's worked on a blue van owned by a plumber in Redmond County. When Tomás asked him to describe the van, the guy said it was a Chevy, about ten years old, and had a huge NC State sticker on the back. Nobody else in the shop has seen or knows of any other blue vans around."

"Did anybody ask why he wanted to know?"

"Yeah, one guy did, but Tomás just said that Odell had told a guy who drove into one of his gas stations to bring his van into the shop 'cause it needed some muffler work. Tomás said he was just wondering if the guy ever showed up. He didn't mention the accident."

Will twisted his neck to the left and right, then closed his eyes and exhaled in a long, drawn-out release of air and frustration.

"Any word on the short guy in the Redskins sweatshirt?"

"Nothing. I called Wimbley to see if he'd seen a short Hispanic guy wearing a Redskins hoodie, but he hadn't. He did say that his wife, Cora, told him that her friend at NCFC said that Mr. Waters was in a pretty nasty mood these days. She said Albert and Jared Hill have been in some pretty heated discussions in Albert's office. Something is going on, and I'll bet they're trying to figure out how to cover their asses. I wouldn't want to be Jimmy Ross if he said something that Albert didn't approve of. Do you think that Jimmy is that stupid? "

"Oh, yeah," Will laughed.

Will waited a few minutes, then added, "She said, he said… Sounds like we know about as much now as we did yesterday, namely nothing. I talked to Ed Haines and he said that Nathan and two other deputies had been all over Smith county this morning and even last night. Nobody has seen a blue work van. He has to file a public report about the accident today but has told his deputies and office staff that if they get any questions, he's the only one authorized to speak. His report will say that the victim hasn't been identified yet and that they're still investigating. He figures that will buy some time and make Albert rest easier. He also called Sheriff Pierce in Redmond County and is meeting with him today."

Hank said, "You want me to go to Redmond and talk to Tom Pierce as well?"

"No, Ed can handle it. He knows how delicate this is. I just wish we had something more concrete to go on."

Will got up and walked to the windows behind the conference table. He stood there, arms crossed, trying to imagine what Albert must be thinking. How scared was he? Was he scared at all? Based on what Wimbley's wife's friend said, Albert was obviously concerned, but that didn't mean he was panicking. He might just be having problems in Mexico finding workers. He might be having problems in Raleigh with the State Department, or he might just be pissed at Jimmy for being stupid about something.

Will turned around and said, "By the way, while I was at lunch at the Roanoke Diner, Oris Martin came over and asked how the search for Maria Puente was going. Without filling him in on the accident in Smith County, I said that we were checking on some leads but still didn't have any answers as to what happened to the girl.

"I said that regardless of what Jimmy Ross said, we know that Maria got on the bus. Then, almost like he wasn't sure he wanted to tell me, Oris said that Albert had called him yesterday afternoon. I didn't say anything, so he looked around the restaurant and then sat down at the table.

"He paused, then said, 'Will, Albert Waters called me yesterday to say that he personally called the AmTex offices in Monterrey to see what happened to the girl. He said his people in Monterrey told him that the girl got off the bus before it left. They said that Jimmy had misunderstood them and thought they said that she never got on the bus when what they really told him was that she got on the bus but then told the driver that she needed to get off. He said he talked to the driver and the man confirmed what the AmTex people had said. The driver said that the girl told him to let her off just as they were leaving the AmTex parking area."

Hank said, "Does Oris believe him?"

"He said he doesn't, but he didn't tell Albert that. Albert also told him that he should call Tomás and tell him that they're trying to find out where she went, but Oris said he wasn't going to call Tomás since it would just upset him. He said that if I wanted to call Tomás and tell him what Albert said, I could, but I'm not gonna do it. I mean why tell Tomás something that we both know is a lie?"

Hank looked at Will. "Boss, they've done something to that young woman, and they're trying like hell to cover it up. I got nothing to back that up except that little voice you're always talking about, and it's telling me that Maria Puente is in trouble. We gotta find her. Tomás Delgado is, along with you and my daddy, one of the men in my life that truly matters, and I ain't leaving this until we find out what happened to Maria."

Will smiled, "Deputy, you surely know how I feel. I owe the man, and by God, no matter what, we're gonna get to the bottom of this."

Thursday

5:00 p.m.

After what she guessed was four or five hours, Maria heard the van return. She got up from the mattress and walked to the window. She saw Jimmy Ross get out of the van then step over and pull the side door open. Stepping out, looking angry as always, was the hated Valeria. What the hell was she doing here? Maria felt like crying, but knowing how that would please Valeria, she took a deep breath, wiped her eyes, and worked on ginning up enough bile to get her through dealing with that miserable woman again.

Jimmy picked up several bags of what Maria hoped were groceries and some ice for her face. As the front door to the trailer closed, Maria heard Valeria speaking to Jose and Paco in Spanish while someone fumbled around in the kitchen outside Maria's room. She was standing by the window when the door opened and Jimmy looked in.

"No ice, but I did get one of those chemical ice packs for your face. I also got you a burger and fries."

He threw the ice pack and the takeout bag of food onto the mattress.

"What's that whore doin' here?"

Jimmy smiled, "I thought you might like some female company."

"That's no female. That's a heartless, diseased creature."

"Whatever. She's gonna be your keeper for a while. I'm taking Jose and Paco to Beulah tonight and I want to make sure that your every wish is met; so, I brought a heartless creature to visit with you."

"Gee, thanks."

After an hour of applying the ice pack to her face, the swelling seemed to be going down. She looked at her face in the mirror the next time she was allowed to use the bathroom, and while still puffy, it did seem to be better. It still hurt, but nothing like last night. As evening approached, Maria heard Jimmy, Jose, and Paco getting ready to leave. She went to the window, but rather than hearing the trailer door open, the door to her room opened.

Jimmy was standing in the doorway with a chain in his hand. "I've padlocked the other end of this chain to the base of the toilet. This end goes around your ankle. I need to make sure that while I'm gone you don't give Valeria any trouble. Don't try to resist, because I don't want to have to call the others in here to hold you down."

Maria looked at the chain, then at Jimmy. "You think that'll hold me?"

Jimmy smiled, "It should. It's two-aught double loop steel chain. It'll hold my Rottweiler, so it ought to hold you."

Maria walked over to the chair and put her foot on its seat. "It's not really my color. I usually wear gold chains around my ankle."

Jimmy grinned, "Sorry, this was the only color they had." He wrapped the chain around her ankle and locked it with a medium-sized padlock, putting the key in his pocket.

"You got enough chain to get from the bathroom to your mattress. Sorry you won't be able to watch television in the living room with Valeria, but you two can have a nice chat in the kitchen."

Maria didn't say anything, only took her foot off the chair, pushed the broken table leg back and sat down. Jimmy patted her on the head and said, "Be a good girl, and I'll see you tomorrow," then closed the door. Apparently there used to be carpeting on the bare floor of the hall and bedroom because the chain easily fit under the door when it was closed. At least he hadn't locked the door.

Maria sat on the chair and thought about her new situation. All the men were gone or were going, so she was now chained in the smelly trailer with only the old whore guarding her. But this might hold some promise for her escape. She put her left foot on the chain leaving about four feet between her left foot and her right ankle. She stood up and pulled on the chain. No way she was going to break that. She looked around the room for something she could use to cut, bend or break the chain. Nothing stood out.

She walked across the bedroom as far as her chain would let her, finding it far enough to see Jimmy, Jose, and Paco get in the van and drive away. She turned and walked back to the bedroom door to see how far into the trailer she could go, but as she reached for the doorknob, the door swung into the room. Standing in the opening, a twisted smirk on her face, stood Valeria.

"Well, well," Valeria said, "Look who's here, the smart-ass bitch from Monterrey."

Maria stood her ground, looked at Valeria, and said, "Correct. And who do we have here? Oh yes, the whore from Monterrey. One bitch and one whore, should be a hell of a party."

Valeria backed into the kitchen, then turned and walked to the cabinet over the counter beside the stove. She opened the cabinet, took out a bottle of Tequila, poured three inches of the strong alcohol into a glass, then looking at Maria, said, "Well, it appears only one of us will be having a party."

Maria walked through the doorway, but after only a few steps into the kitchen, she was pulled up by the chain. She looked at

Valeria, "You know what they say about someone who drinks alone, don't you?"

Valeria took a swallow, wiped her mouth, and said, "No, I don't know, and don't give a shit."

This could be good. Maria smiled at the thought of her guard getting so drunk that she would lose her ability to react to an escape attempt.

"Let me ask you something, Ms. Whore," Maria said.

Valeria didn't answer.

"Why do you let these men tell you what to do? Why do you let yourself be used in this way?"

Valeria finished her drink and poured another. She set the bottle down on the counter and looked over at Maria.

"You know something, you arrogant little shit, you got no idea what a woman like me has had to deal with. You have a family, an education, and a future," she paused, a smirk on her face, "Or used to have a future—so you think that allows you to judge me. Well, some of us don't get to choose our paths. Some of us have to claw and scratch our way to survive, even though sometimes survival might not seem worth it. But if you work at it, if you do more than just survive, life can provide some rewards, and believe me, perra, I'm ready for some rewards. It's a shame you got caught up in this, but shit happens, and when the wheel comes 'round, sometimes you get squashed. Live with it, or…" Valeria took another swallow of Tequila, "Die with it."

Maria didn't reply, only turned and said, "I'm gonna get some sleep."

Valeria pushed away from the counter, topped off her drink, and walked toward the living room. As she walked out of the kitchen, she said, "Sweet dreams."

Maria walked over to the chair, picked up the broken table leg, and sat down. What was the plan? How could she find something within her limited area of movement to break the chain? She got up, walked into the bathroom, and opened the cabinet doors below the sink. Nothing. Nothing in the drawers beneath the countertop. She lifted the back of the toilet to see if any of the pieces of hardware looked strong enough to break the chain. Again, nothing. She sat on the toilet seat patting her palm with the broken table leg. There had to be something.

She opened the bathroom door and walked to the end of her chain looking to her left. Valeria was nowhere to be seen. She leaned forward and put her left hand on the island in the middle of the kitchen. It was pointless because there were no drawers or cabinets on her side of the island; however, as she leaned against the island, she noticed some tools sitting on the counter next to the kitchen sink on the far wall. Apparently one of the men had worked on the faucet or maybe the drain under the sink.

A crescent wrench and two screwdrivers lay side by side on the countertop, but reaching them would be impossible, and it didn't seem likely that Valeria would give them to her.

She backed into the bedroom and sat down. There had to be a way. As she sat, patting her palm with the broken table leg, it came to her. She had a weapon. She had a 30-inch-long wooden club. She had never thought about clubbing another person into submission, but then she had never been in a life-or-death situation. Her decision was easy. She'd use the club against Valeria; but how? How could she get Valeria close enough but unaware enough to use the table leg? Valeria didn't give a damn about Maria's health unless it meant that she would be in trouble with her bosses.

It was a longshot, but it could work. She thought about all the ways it could fail, too. Her breathing became rapid. She had to calm herself down. For this to work, she needed to be in total control of her emotions. After getting her breathing into a steady rhythm, she stood up, turned around, and picked up the three-legged table. Holding it high over her head she took a deep breath, closed her eyes, and after saying a short prayer, slammed the table onto the floor in front of the bathroom. Then, getting on her knees, she pushed the table back into the bedroom and lay on the floor with the broken table leg gripped tightly beneath her body.

"What the fuck is going on in there?" Valeria yelled from the other room.

Maria didn't respond.

"Hey, bitch, what the hell is going on?"

Again no reply.

Maria heard Valeria get up and walk toward the kitchen and bedroom.

"You better not be trying to fuck with me, lady. I'm no one to fuck with."

Maria tensed up, gripping the table leg even harder.

When Valeria saw Maria lying on the floor she stopped.

"Hey, you all right? Hey, girl, speak!"

Maria said nothing and stopped breathing.

Just as Maria had hoped, Valeria bent down and touched her shoulder. When she didn't move, Valeria got on her knees and tried to turn her over. As she pulled on Maria's shoulder to turn her over, Maria pushed herself up, turned to face the hated woman, and swung the table leg as hard as she could. Her aim was true, and she hit Valeria in the head just above and beside her left eye. The older woman hit the floor with a thud. Maria dropped her club and rolled Valeria onto her stomach. The older woman was moaning but not fully conscious. If she was going to complete her plan it had to be now; so she climbed on top of Valeria and wrapped the chain around her neck.

She said a prayer asking for forgiveness, then tightened her grip on the chain and pulled back with everything she had.

Knowing that she was being strangled, the older woman began to move and fight the tightening chain, but Maria, being younger, bigger, and stronger, was too much for her. After a short struggle, Valeria went limp and lay still. Maria didn't loosen her grip until she felt sure that Valeria was dead. When she did, she immediately put her left finger against the older woman's neck while holding the chain in her right. She couldn't feel any pulse. She waited, still holding the chain around Valeria's neck, then checked the old woman's wrist along with another check of her neck. Nothing. No sign of a pulse.

Maria's breathing was rapid and her own pulse racing, but her enemy was dead. She dropped to her side and with her mission complete, broke down in tears that wouldn't stop. She had killed another human being, albeit a human being who would have had no problem killing her.

No time for pity, or self-pity, though. She had to get those tools and see if she could break her chain, but first she looked in Valeria's pocket to see if perhaps Jimmy had given her the key to the padlocks anchoring Maria's chain. No such luck.

She pulled the dead woman into the bedroom and sat on the chair to regain her composure. After some deep breaths, she stood up and, moving into the hall, looked at the tools on the counter. How far away were they?

How could she reach them? She took another deep breath and, looking into the bedroom, tried to identify anything that could reach the counter. She first looked at the dangling blind beside the window. She couldn't reach it, plus it was too short. She looked at the dirty sheets on the mattress. That's it. Tied together, the sheets would reach, but how could sheets be used to pull the tools onto the floor and over to her? A knot at the end! That could do it.

She pulled the sheets off the mattress and tied a large knot at one end. Holding the opposite end in her hand, she moved to the limit of her chain and threw the knotted sheet toward the counter top. It fell short, but only because she didn't extend her left hand far enough. She tried it again, and this time the knot hit the wall beside the sink. Very slowly she retrieved the knot until it touched the tools, then she yanked. The wrench and one of the screwdrivers hit the floor with a bang.

After other seemingly endless tosses of the sheet, she managed to pull the other screwdriver off the counter. Now the hard part. She needed to pull the tools across the floor to within her reach.

It probably took twenty minutes, but finally all of the tools were within Maria's reach. She sat on the floor holding them in her hands and began to cry again. To now be able to let her emotions out felt cathartic. She was alive! She could taste it… freedom, life, and perhaps a future. She held the tools in her hands as she studied the bonds that held her.

The chain was what Jimmy had described as double-loop steel. She had never heard of such a chain, but on inspection she understood the term. Each link in the chain had a double twist in the middle. It was as if the two ends of the link were pulled side by side and then wrapped around each other. She remembered seeing such a chain used on dogs, like Jimmy's Rottweiler. Unlike a welded link, these were not permanently joined, only twisted together. So she didn't need to cut the chain, only break it where the twisted ends met.

She guessed she could do this if she could figure out a way to twist the link until the two ends came apart. The screwdrivers were the answer. If she could anchor one end of the link, then she could twist the other end until it broke, or at least that was her plan. Maria went into the bathroom and looked at the Formica countertop in which the sink was placed. There were cracks in the Formica. She pushed the end of a screwdriver under the Formica and levered it up. The rotted material easily came up, revealing some equally rotted plywood underneath.

She lay the chain on the countertop near the edge and, putting the point of the biggest screwdriver through one end of a link, took her table-leg weapon and pounded the screwdriver deep into the plywood. This anchored one end of the link.

She pushed the other screwdriver through the other end of the link and by turning it in a 360-degree arc, managed to break the link in half. It took all of her strength to turn the screwdriver, but then there was so much adrenalin pumping though her that she could probably have bitten the chain in half. In any case, the two twisted ends snapped apart when she applied enough pressure.

Maria stood motionless, looking at the broken chain. She was free. She... No, she wasn't free yet. She was partially free. Now she had to escape. To get away from these terrible people and find her uncle.

She turned her head from side to side trying to ease the tension that gripped her neck, then put her hands on the front of the countertop, lowered her head, and closed her eyes. For the first time in days, she felt a sense of calm. After a deep breath, she waited a few seconds, then slowly let it out. When she raised her head and opened her eyes, she was looking into the mirror above the sink, but who was that person looking back? It wasn't Maria Puente. Maria Puente was a beautiful twenty-two-year-old woman, but the woman in the mirror was older, with lines in her face. The skin around her left eye was black and blue and the eye itself still bloodshot.

Where was the young woman who five days ago came to America to start an exciting new life? Dead, killed with the stroke of a table leg and a length of chain. The innocence that had always been a part of her beauty was gone. This wasn't how one's loss of innocence was supposed to be… not with murder. She started to cry, but then the woman in the mirror said, "Maria, stop your crying. It's time to survive. The death of innocence is the price we pay one day. Too many people love you and need you to let yourself be a victim. Stand straight. It's time to survive."

Maria smiled, saying wryly to the woman in the mirror, "Okay, if it's time to survive, then the first thing we need is a drink, and I know just where to find one." She wrapped the two-foot length of chain still locked on her ankle around her leg and walked into the kitchen. From the cabinet beside the stove, she took down the bottle of Jose Gold.

Pouring a healthy slug of Tequila into a glass, she remembered the hamburger that Jimmy had brought, so she walked into the bedroom and picked up the bag of food. She carried her drink and food to the front door and stepped out into the evening breeze, inhaling the warm, humid air, while twisting her head to loosen the tight muscles in her neck that had not yet returned to normal. The stars were out, and the full moon was just beginning its journey. She leaned against the doorjamb and let the Tequila settle her. She sat down on the step and ate the hamburger, throwing the now cold fries into the yard. When she had finished, she closed her eyes and thought about Julietta and Luca and the wretched woman who lay dead on the floor of the bedroom behind her. While she still had work to do, she had earned a few quiet moments, and found some solace in the fact that she had survived. She took another sip of Tequila and whispered to herself, "One day at a time, Maria."

After her brief rest, she stood up and began to look around the yard and the surrounding land. There were no houses within sight, at least she saw no lights anywhere. So the trailer had no close neighbors, much less any hint of civilization nearby. Jimmy and Albert would have wanted her and Julietta to be well hidden this time. It was too dark to get any idea of how much open land surrounded the trailer, but a spotlight on the corner of the trailer revealed a small shed or barn in the backyard.

It looked to be about thirty yards away, so she got up and walked toward it. It was an old barn that had clearly been ignored and allowed to fall into disrepair. In the front, the side closest to the trailer, there was a ten-foot-wide sliding door. Maria pulled on the door until it opened enough to allow her to walk through. The light from the trailer was not bright enough to light the whole of the inside, but it did allow her to look for a light switch or pull cord. In front of her and to the left was a small rope hanging down. When she pulled on it, a single bulb lighted the interior. Not well enough to see every corner but enough to understand the room.

An old tractor stood in the middle of the barn, a few pieces of farm equipment were on the right side, and some broken hay bales were piled behind them. On the left side and against the back wall was a large stack of wooden pallets, the kind used to carry tobacco to market. She realized that whatever they were, she could use them to make a hiding place. A pile of burlap bags and sheets of black plastic sat on top of the pallets.

Turning off the light in the barn, Maria started back to the trailer. The spotlight at the corner of the trailer shone in her face, so, deciding that darkness was her friend, she picked up a wooden stake lying on the ground in front of the barn door and broke the light. She had to presume that Jimmy's parting words, "Be a good little girl and I'll see you tomorrow," meant that she would be alone tonight.

Okay, she was alone, but should she stumble through the dark to find a road, and if she did, how could she be sure it would lead to some place that was safe? But what if Jimmy did come back tonight instead of tomorrow? She was inventing scenarios without answers, so took another swallow of Tequila to calm her nerves.

Calmer now, she decided that Jimmy would probably stick to his plan of coming back in the morning. Why would he want to return to that bitch Valeria? Still, staying in the trailer tonight would be foolish, but not as foolish as stumbling around in the dark trying to find a road.

She would make a space in the barn behind or under the pallets covered with the plastic and burlap, and, at first light, if no one was around, would try and find a way out. She was sure that sleep would be a fleeting luxury.

She finished her drink, gathered some blankets from inside the trailer, then walked back outside, pulling the trailer door closed behind her. As Maria walked toward the barn, she stopped and turned to look across the yard and the trees beyond. Her gaze moved upward to the bright white moon that had just crested the treetops.

"Julietta, I know revenge isn't looked on with much favor where you are, so tell Jesus that I'm sorry I killed Valeria, and I'm also sorry that I don't feel much regret. Tell him I'll seriously try to be a better person. And please ask him to help me a little bit more, since I'm pretty sure I'm gonna need more help. Descansa en paz."

Friday
September 27th
DAY SIX

Friday

6:30 a.m.

Not light, but the early morning songs of wood thrushes, mockingbirds, and small pine siskins roused Maria from unexpected sleep. She never thought she'd actually fall asleep, but as she slowly rose to consciousness, she was glad for it. Being cautious, she kept still, only rubbing her eyes to wake herself fully. She needed not to make a sound until she was sure that no one was in or near the barn.

After five or ten minutes of sitting and listening, Maria stood up from behind the stack of wooden pallets and burlap sacks. Now visible above them, she turned her head slowly from left to right, again listening for any sounds in the yard. Silence. So she slowly inched out of her burrow and tiptoed toward the partially opened barn door.

She peeked around the edge of it into the yard surrounding the trailer. No car or truck was parked nearby, no sounds were coming from inside the trailer, and no traffic noise, cigarette smoke, or smell of engine exhaust was in the air. That could be good or bad.

Maria walked out of the barn to the center of the overgrown and garbage-strewn yard. The scene outside the trailer was as disgusting as that inside, reminding her of the body she hoped still lay on the floor of the bedroom. She thought about looking inside to be sure but decided against it since she didn't want to see or smell Valeria again. She already had enough images of the dead woman in her memory.

Realizing that she was standing out in the open, and thus was visible from a long distance, Maria moved to the back of the trailer where she saw a picnic table under a massive oak. From there she could study the area surrounding the trailer and barn without being seen.

In front and to the right of the yard was a large planted field. She had no idea how big it was or what crop was planted there, but it seemed to be ready for harvest. On the far side of the field was a vast wall of pines, standing in symmetrical rows and appearing to be the same age and size. She guessed they'd been planted by a commercial timber company. If she was in the middle of a plantation of pine trees, her chances of finding a nearby farmhouse were not good. One thing was certain, however; she couldn't stay at the trailer any longer, because Jimmy was likely on his way back here.

She thought about what she might need from inside the trailer. She doubted that Jimmy would have left a gun in the trailer. Why would Valeria need one if Maria was chained to the toilet? If Valeria did have a gun, why wouldn't she have brought it when Maria smashed the broken table to the floor? No, there was no gun, and the tools would be of no help.

She shook her head, stretched, and took a deep breath. Time to go. She decided that walking down the road in the middle of the planted field would be a bad idea since anybody coming the other way was sure to see her, so she decided to cross the field and walk just inside the rows of planted trees on the far side. If anyone came down the trailer road, she could duck down and hide in the pines.

She also decided that flagging down a car at any time would be risky, since she would have no idea whether the driver or occupants were friend or foe. Jimmy would surely sound the alarm as soon as he found Valeria's body in the empty trailer, and that meant he and his cronies would soon be swarming all over this area.

Since the line of pine trees paralleled the dirt road, she would be traveling in the same direction and thus would eventually come to another, perhaps bigger, road. After standing, looking, and listening, she began to jog across the planted field to the pine forest on the far side. Once there, she paused to catch her breath, then began walking toward what she prayed would be her deliverance.

Maria had no idea how far she'd walked when she finally came to the end of the planted pines, but as she suspected and hoped, she'd come to another, much wider road perpendicular to the trailer road. Looking to her left, across the field, she saw that the trailer road dead-ended into this new, larger one. She leaned against one of the pine trees to rest a bit, then picked the grass burrs and beggar lice off her pants and socks. After maybe ten minutes, she walked out to the road, looking first to the left and then the right—no cars or trucks in sight.

Having no idea which way to go, she laughed and said, "Maria, you have no idea where you are and no coin to flip, so just close your eyes, turn around and point." After two turns, her hand was pointing toward the barely risen sun. She'd go east toward the sunrise. She started walking and after a few hundred yards came upon a small metal building on her side of the road, surrounded by a ten-foot-high chain link fence. On the fence, a white metal sign read "Property of Georgia Pacific Corporation, Private—Keep Out." So, now she knew. The forest was owned by Georgia Pacific, the giant timber company.

A single gate provided the only entrance into the compound, and as she approached the gate, she saw that it was secured with a heavy chain and padlock. Even if she'd brought the wrench and screwdrivers from the trailer, there was no way to break this chain.

She considered climbing the fence but realized that even if she succeeded, she might only be imprisoning herself inside. As she turned to leave, she noticed that the lock was not fully engaged. The curved part of the lock, the part that fit into the base, was simply resting on the top, not pushed all the way into the base. A break at last.

Maria opened the gate, walked in, then put the lock and chain back the way she'd found them. Luckily the door to the shed was unlocked, so she opened it and stepped inside. There was a light switch to the left of the door, but she decided to leave the light off and use only the light provided by two windows. Seeing a light in the shed might get the attention of a passing car.

As she looked around the room, which was maybe 20' x 20', she saw chainsaws, hard hats, various pieces of clothing, a couple of water coolers—one of which was half-full—fuel tanks, some tools, and what looked like surveying equipment. A small table with three chairs around it suggested this was a place for the timber crews to rest and store their equipment. She sat down on one of the chairs and closed her eyes. It felt good. She was hidden in a building no one would suspect. If someone was on the road, the gate would look like it was locked, so unless they got very close and inspected the lock, they would assume the building was vacant. This didn't mean she could stay here for an extended period of time, because eventually one of Jimmy's men would stop and look around. She decided she would only stay for a few hours, at least until dusk when she could walk down the road and easily see headlights.

After her short rest, she opened her eyes and looked around the room again. On the wall opposite her chair, she noticed a small black box. What was that? Fuses? Generator switches? She got up and walked over to the box. Finding a latch on the side, she pulled it and a door opened. Damn, a phone. She picked up the phone and held it to her ear. Nothing. No sound. She pressed the receiver bar. Again, no sound. She shook her head and started to put the phone back on the receiver when she suddenly froze, then yelled, "Shit! Shit! Shit!"

She slammed the phone down and turned around, shouting to the empty room, "There's a goddamn phone in the trailer, you dumb ass! You heard Jose talking to someone when we got there. How could you be so stupid?"

She sat back down. Maybe she could go back. Maybe Jimmy would be late returning. Maybe… no. No maybe. No way could she go back. Jimmy and his boys would be swarming all over the trailer and the surrounding area any minute. She prayed that they didn't have tracking dogs. Sometimes these good ol' boys have dogs. Why'd she forget about the phone when she was thinking of what to take from the trailer? Stupid, just stupid.

Well, no point beating herself up. Stay calm, remain in the shed until evening, then try and get to some gas station or store or any commercial building with a phone. She didn't have a watch, but it couldn't be too late. She'd left the barn just before sunrise, and that couldn't have been more than an hour or two ago, if that.

She took a pack of crackers out of her pocket. She hadn't eaten or drunk anything since the Tequila and cold burger last night, so she was hungry. Fortunately, before she left the trailer, she'd also found a half-dozen packs of peanut butter crackers and a Snickers bar. Not exactly a well-balanced meal but enough to give her strength. Now, she just needed to stay calm and wait.

Friday

7:00 a.m.

Lana Moser shut the refrigerator door and, holding a pint of half-and-half, walked over to the coffee pot on the counter. She poured herself a cup of coffee then called to Will, in the dining room reading the paper, "Will, you want any more coffee?"

Will kept reading the *News and Observer* and didn't answer.

She called again, "Last chance, any more coffee?"

He looked up, "Yes, please."

Lana came into the dining room with the coffee pot and refilled Will's mug.

"I'm sorry Grace didn't come home this weekend. I had a bunch of things that I wanted to do with her and don't know when I'll have any time in the next few weeks. I've got to go to Raleigh next weekend to give a lecture to a bunch of grad students coming to the vet school. They're real interested in the work we've been doing on hip dysplasia. I thought when you spoke with her on Thursday that she was coming for sure."

Will put down his glasses. "I thought so too, but she says that they're having an SFFW meeting tonight and since she's new on the committee, she felt she should be there." Will leaned back in his chair, took another sip of coffee. "You know, Duke is the perfect place for her. I was hoping she would like Vanderbilt more. I sure loved it when I was there, but I can see that she made the right choice."

Lana smiled at him. "Yeah, but Vanderbilt is probably different now than when you were there. I mean what with cars instead of horses and buggies, television instead of the telegraph, it's a whole lot different."

Will smiled and began to make an obscene hand gesture but thought better of it when Lana raised the coffee pot above his head.

With the sound of the kitchen phone, she lowered the pot. "Saved by the bell," she said, then walked into the kitchen to answer it.

"It's Hank Grier!" she yelled.

Will got up, and as he walked out of the dining room and down the front hall, called over his shoulder, "I'll take it in my office." Midway down the hall, he turned to his right and opened the door to the library—his home office, but more importantly, his sanctuary.

He stood for just a moment breathing in the quietude that always permeated this room. A large picture window, bordered with stained glass images of the birds and flowers of Eastern North Carolina, provided light to the room as well as views of the Roanoke River to the south. Floor-to-ceiling bookshelves wrapped the rest of the room like the inside of a cocoon. Within these walls, Will Moser relived the imaginative adventures of his boyhood, recalled the heroics and tragedies of ancient warriors, and contemplated ideas that had challenged the mind of man since the beginning of time. "God must have invented libraries to soothe the savage breast," he thought, appraising his room.

He shut the door and picked up the receiver of the phone on his desk. "Good morning, Deputy. What's got you up so early?"

Hank, without any greeting or small talk, said, "I just talked to Wimbley Johnson. He said three men were killed last night in Jackson County when the van they were riding in was hit head-on by a ten-ton dump truck stolen from Jim Ellis's quarry. He said the quarry has been closed for over six months, but the thief or thieves still managed to fill the truck with a load of gravel.

"The wreck happened on a section of Highway 21 running through a stretch of bean fields. Everybody in the van was killed outright, but, can you believe it, the driver of the truck is nowhere to be found. Funny thing is, the road where the wreck occurred is as straight as a hard-shell Baptist, and the night was clear—with a full moon.

"Wimbley says the van looks like an accordion and is about the same size. The truck is smashed in the front, but otherwise has damn little damage by comparison. He says the truck must have been going at least fifty miles per hour."

Will was now sitting at his desk, staring at the bookcases on the far wall. When Hank had finished, Will said, "Okay, but what's that got to do with us?"

Hank, expecting this would be Will's reaction, said, "Glad you asked, Sheriff. According to Wimbley, the driver of the van was one Jimmy Ross, and the passengers were two Mexicans named Jose Vasquez and Paco Diaz."

Will whistled softly through his teeth, "Well, well. What *do* you know."

Hank continued, "Not only that, but it turns out that Jose was the driver of the bus that brought the load of workers to Beulah on Monday, and Paco Diaz is a short little fellow who happened to be wearing a Redskins hoodie when they pulled what was left of him out of the van."

"Holy shit! Did Wimbley say anything to Garland or any of the other deputies about us looking for a short guy wearing a hoodie? Do they know that we suspect Mr. Diaz as the driver of the blue van?"

"Absolutely not. But Wimbley did say it seemed to him like

Garland wasn't very surprised about the accident. He is issuing a statement that laments the deaths of three fine citizens of Jackson County while seeking information on the stolen truck. The thing is, Will, Garland has assigned only one deputy to finding the truck driver, and he's the sheriff's biggest kiss-ass deputy, hated by all the other deputies. Wimbley thinks those men were murdered."

Will said, "I think Wimbley's right, but I'm a little surprised at Jimmy Ross. He's been Albert's bagman for a long time. Things must really be getting hairy around Beulah about now. This might work for us."

Hank waited a minute before replying, "Well, yes and no. Now we got nobody who might know about Maria and the dead girl except Albert and maybe that fellow Jared Hill, and we ain't gettin' a thing from them."

Will took a deep breath and stretched his head from left to right. "Thanks for that little dose of reality, Deputy. I've gotta get another cup of very strong coffee and think about this. Hank, make sure Wimbley keeps quiet about the Diaz and Vasquez guys. I'll call Sheriff Haines and Sheriff Pierce and fill them in." More to himself than to Hank, Will mumbled, "Fucking Albert."

"What was that, Will?"

"Nothing, just talking to myself. Trying to figure out what the hell is going on. We got a dead girl, three dead men, all of whom work for Albert Waters, probably another body or two that we don't know about, and we still don't know whether Maria Puente is dead or alive. I'm running out of ideas, Hank."

"I know, Sheriff, but we can't give up. Tomás is desperate."

"You know me better than that. I've never given up on anything in my life, and I ain't giving up on this, but I am grasping at straws right now. I just need to focus. Call Wimbley and then call me back."

Will got up and walked back to the kitchen. Lana was standing at the sink and turned as he came in.

"What was that all about?"

Will didn't say anything as he poured himself another mug of coffee.

"Hello, Sheriff Moser. What was that all about?"

Will turned, "Sorry, Lana. I'm not with it right now. I'm trying to figure out what the hell is going on."

Lana got a cup of coffee and sat down at the kitchen table. "Sit. I'm pretty good at figuring stuff out. Fire away."

Will looked at his wife and smiled. "Yes, you are. Always have been."

He was right. Lana Moser had had a lot of things to figure out in her life, and most of the time she got it right. Will and Lana had known each other since high school. They had been sweethearts, but when Will graduated and went off to college, Lana fell in love with and married Paul Reavis, Will's best friend. After Vanderbilt, Will enlisted in the Army and became an officer in the Military Police. With Viet Nam consuming all the personnel the Army could produce, he was sent, after a year in the States, to the 18th Military Police Brigade attached to the 9th Infantry Division in the Mekong Delta.

When his war was over, Will came home and was hired by the Raleigh Police Department. After three years as a detective, a messy divorce, and a strenuous recruiting job by the then high sheriff of Hogg County, Will came back to Mussel Ford. By this time, Lana and Paul Reavis, after a couple of unfortunate miscarriages and a few years of difficult times together, had a son named Paul Jr. with whom Will became very close.

When young Paul was about eleven years old, his father was killed in what was called a workplace accident but turned out to be a case of manslaughter. As the chief deputy of Hogg county, Will Moser had been the one to uncover the truth behind Paul's death. To add to this tragedy, a year after Paul Sr.'s death, Paul Jr. was killed in the hog waste lagoon accident.

Understandably, Lana Reavis fell into a state of inconsolable grief. With both her husband and son dying at facilities owned by or associated with Oris Martin Sr., Lana's life became focused on how to get justice for her destroyed family. For years following a devastating outbreak of hog cholera and the subsequent bankruptcy of Martin Farms Inc., rumors abounded that Lana Reavis had been somehow responsible. No proof was ever found.

During all of the trauma surrounding the deaths of Paul Sr. and Jr., Will Moser became the rock on which Lana's life would eventually be rebuilt. Two years after the death of her husband and son, Lana and Will were married. Lana, who had worked for the local veterinarian while married to Paul, decided to go back to school and become a vet herself. Will was there to support her, so she finally earned her degree, with honors, from NC State School of Veterinary Medicine.

During her last year of school, she and Will had a daughter who they named Grace Reavis Moser, after Lana's mother and her first husband. A life like the one lived by Lana Moser made for a strong and determined woman, the kind of person whose advice and counsel were worth listening to. So Will Moser always listened.

Will took a sip of coffee and leaned back. "Okay, you know about Maria, and the bullshit lies Albert Waters and his cronies have spread all over, and I told you about the young Latina girl killed Wednesday night in Smith County who had a handkerchief in her pocket belonging to Maria. Now we add yet another chapter to this disgraceful tale.

"Last night, on a straight stretch of road in Jackson County, Jimmy Ross and two NCFC bus drivers were killed when a ten-ton dump truck full of gravel ran into their van. The van, according to Wimbley Johnson, a deputy in Jackson County, is now about the size and shape of a squashed accordion.

"Needless to say, all three men in the van were killed, but imagine this! The driver of the dump truck is nowhere to be found! Oh, and to add some extra spice to this farce, one of the men in the squashed van matches the description of the man seen driving the blue work van from which that young Latina girl escaped."

Will put down his mug and walked over to the counter to get a doughnut. "You want one?"

"No, thanks, and you shouldn't either. That's number three if I'm counting correctly."

Will smiled, "Hey, I gave up my beloved Camels. Cut me some slack." He sat back down and said, "So, Detective Moser, what do you think? Jimmy Ross, a possible connection to Maria, is now squashed. The man who was driving the blue van, squashed. And the Latina girl, who was probably on the bus with Maria, is in the morgue in Smith County. I feel like I've been squashed. Hence the doughnut—fair is fair."

Lana, holding her gaze on her husband, said, "Will, have you called Josh Cooper at the SBI?"

"Yep. I called him Wednesday afternoon. He said the SBI doesn't handle kidnappings, and the FBI would need something more concrete than Tomás's claim that his niece is missing and was supposedly on a bus that got to Beulah on Monday. Add to this the fact that the owner of the bus, Albert-fucking-Waters, and his bagman, Jimmy Ross, said she never got on the bus. A perfect case of 'he said, he said.'"

Lana got up and walked over to the coffee pot. After she filled her mug, she sat back down and took a deep breath, slowly letting it out as she poured herself some half-and-half.

"Sheriff, what we need here is some out-of-the-box thinking, coupled with some way-out-of-the-box action. When was the last time you talked to your old Army buddy, Elijah Kahn?"

Will put down his doughnut and leaned back in his chair, a smile spreading across his face.

"Now that *is* way-out-of-the-box. I don't know, maybe a year ago. What brought him to mind?"

"Well, based on what you've said about him and his operation, he probably has the personnel and information-gathering ability you need right now."

"Lana, Elijah operates on a different scale. His clients are international corporations and even governments. Finding a missing girl ain't his thing."

"Yeah, but you've said he knows how to get results 'one way or the other,' and you seem to need 'the other.'"

Will thought about this, then said, "I'd feel a little silly asking him to help with this. I mean, why would he?"

"Money. He's in business. This is business."

Elijah Kahn and Will had served together in Viet Nam. As part of the 18th Military Police Brigade, Will had been assigned to work with the 9th Infantry Division in the Mekong Delta as part of its riverine operations. Elijah had been a Special Forces captain who provided intelligence and forward support for the division. Since Will was responsible for security at a number of the bases, he and Elijah had many occasions to work together. Elijah was smart, ruthless, and always found a way to accomplish his mission, especially when that way tended toward "the other" way. While it seemed unlikely that Eli would have any interest in helping on a problem so small, Will was out of easy options. If Josh Cooper was right, though, he didn't have much time. He started to say something, but Lana cut him off.

"Will, I understand that you're not comfortable with this idea, but the fact is, we owe Tomás Delgado a huge debt. Comfortable doesn't mean shit to me. A debt is a debt, and whatever it takes suits me."

As he got up from the table, he looked at his wife and said, "So, Mrs. Moser, time to ride the tiger?"

"Carpe diem, Sheriff."

"Right, but you do understand that calling Elijah Kahn probably means giving up on normal legal channels?"

Lana replied, "Does it have to?"

"No, but it likely does, and if it does, I'll have a hell of a time tryin' to get off the tiger."

"You know, Will, sometimes Lady Justice needs to *raise* her blindfold to find justice."

"Your clever analogy aside, we're all bound by law, Lana. I won't call Elijah and ask him to help me find Maria by breaking the law."

"So, don't ask him to break the law. Just ask him to help you find Maria."

She was right, but she was also wrong. He was the law in Hogg County, and for Will Moser, that was a sacred duty. He knew that people referred to him as Dudley Do-Right, but that's who he was. He had sworn an oath to uphold the law, even under trying circumstances.

But Lana was also right. Will was now at a place where the law stood in the way of repaying a debt. He'd tried to get information and help from every source he had. He'd called people who knew people. He had the sheriffs in two other counties combing their counties for clues, but time was running out, and he was no further along than he'd been two days ago.

Will looked over at his wife. "Okay, I'll call in reinforcements, but get ready for the shit to hit the fan."

Lana smiled, "Hell, Sheriff. We've seen shit hit fans before. This ain't nothin' new for us."

Friday

8:00 a.m.

Will walked back to his office and closed the door. He looked in his Rolodex and dialed the number he had for Elijah Kahn.

"Good morning. Guardian Security. How may I help you?"

"Good morning. This is Sheriff William Moser in Hogg County, I'd like to speak with Mr. Elijah Kahn."

"Colonel Kahn is not here at the moment. May I take a message?"

"Yes, please. Have him call me when he has a moment. Tell him it's urgent. My number is 252-665-3000."

"May I tell him what this is about?"

"Yes, it's about something urgent."

The operator mumbled something and hung up. Will got up and stretched his back. His arthritis was acting up again, and his hip was probably due for its fifty-thousand-mile check-up. Ever since the doctors at Duke had taken out the last of his shrapnel and fixed his hip, he'd had these recurring pains.

He walked over to the bookshelves on the right side of the room and ran his hand across a row of titles. In the middle of the third shelf, he found *The Art of War* by Sun Tzu, Elijah Kahn's favorite book and the one he endlessly referred to. At one point in Viet Nam, Will had gotten so tired of hearing about *The Art of*

War that one afternoon he'd said to Eli, "Hey, Captain Kahn, fuck Sun and fuck Tzu, too."

But today, Will pulled the book off the shelf and put it on his desk. If Eli did return his call and perhaps came to Mussel Ford, Will wanted to have an ice breaker ready.

When the phone rang, Will sat down, stretched his neck, and looking at the receiver, said, "Okay, Moser. Time to uncage the beast."

Friday

8:15 a.m.

Albert turned his truck onto State Road 621 and pressed the accelerator to the floor. For a brief moment the huge truck spun its tires, throwing dirt and gravel into the air. After twenty or thirty feet the tires finally caught, rocketing him down the road. He didn't know why he was in such a hurry, but something was pushing him. Perhaps it was a sense of guilt. He should have felt something, some angst at being complicit in the death of his friend, Jimmy Ross, or his involvement in prostitution and drugs, but the truth was, he wasn't feeling anything at all, only the fear of being caught.

Luca was at the bottom of the Dismal Swamp with a cinder block around his waist, probably an entrée by now for some young alligator and a gang of snapping turtles. The white van was crushed into a mass of metal beyond recognition, yet he felt nothing. He slowed down as he got to the turn-off for his trailer.

Leaving the whore in the trailer alone with the Delgado girl was careless, a mistake he would not make again. Albert looked in his rearview mirror and said, "Ruff, you should've come out here last night. You shouldn't have left the whore in the trailer alone with that girl. As soon as you can, you need to get someone else out here to guard the girl and take that whore back to the Elliot farm."

The Ford Dually came to a sliding stop in front of the trailer.

Albert got out and walked to the front door, opening it without knocking.

"Hello! Valeria, it's Albert Waters!" No reply. He called again, "Yo, I'm coming in!" Again, no reply. Albert walked to his left and looked in the master bedroom. Nothing. He opened the door to the bathroom. No one there. He was starting to worry.

"Where the fuck are you, woman?" he yelled.

Walking into the kitchen, he saw the open Tequila bottle sitting on the counter beside the stove. "Okay, now I got it," he said. Assuming that Valeria was passed out somewhere, he shook his head and turned toward the two small bedrooms next to the kitchen, but first he opened the bathroom door that stood between the two rooms. He fully expected to see a passed-out Valeria on the floor, but nothing.

He knocked on the bedroom door on the left, expecting the Delgado girl, but heard nothing, so he opened the door and surveyed the room. Empty. What the hell was going on. He turned to his right and pushed open the remaining bedroom door, recoiling from the odor.

With the door now fully open, he could see Valeria lying face down on the floor beside the mattress, a puddle of urine and feces beside her. "Must have shit when she passed out," he said. Then looking around, "But where the hell is the Delgado girl?"

He walked over to Valeria and pushed her with his foot. Nothing. He knelt down beside her and reached out to give her another push. "Hey! Time to get up," he said. There was no reaction, so he grabbed her far shoulder and rolled her over. Her mouth was open, and her eyes, fixed and dull, stared straight at him. As her body flopped onto its back, it exhaled a foul stench. Albert rocked back on his heels and began to gag.

He stood up and took a few steps back. What the fuck

happened? As he looked at the red chain marks around her neck, it was obvious. The Delgado girl had somehow gotten the jump on the whore and strangled her. He turned and looked in the bathroom. Sure enough, there was a ten-foot length of chain on the floor and a screwdriver sticking into the counter top.

Goddammit! He didn't need this shit right now! He raced into the living room. No point in yelling for Maria, because with Valeria strangled and the chain broken, the girl was long gone. But when? Where? He walked into the master bedroom, picked up the phone, and dialed Jared.

"Jared. We got big problems. The girl is gone and the whore is dead."

"What the fuck happened?" Jared yelled.

"How the hell do I know, asshole!" Albert yelled back.

In a calmer tone, Jared asked, "Albert, what do you think happened?"

"I'm guessing the Delgado girl jumped the whore, got her down, and strangled her with the chain that Jimmy used to secure her. It wouldn't have been too hard since the whore was probably drunk. There's a half-empty bottle of Tequila on the kitchen counter."

Jared closed his eyes and mouthed, "Fuck, fuck, fuck."

"Albert, where are you now?"

"Where do you think? I'm in the goddamn trailer with a fucking stinking corpse. We gotta get that goddamn girl right now."

"We will, Ruff, but first you need to get the whore outta there."

"No shit, Sherlock. I'll load her into the back of my truck and find somewhere to dump her. But we need to find that girl before anything else."

Jared shook his head, trying to think. "Okay, listen, Albert, get rid of the whore first and I'll think of something. How many trucks and cars you got in Beulah that you can get your hands on?"

"I don't know, probably half a dozen."

"Okay, let's round them up. Oh, and I forgot to tell you; Dante Sandoval got here last night. He's staying at my place. I'll talk to him and see what he thinks. We need to put together a plan."

Albert yelled, "Really, a plan? You think so? *You* fucking need to put together a plan, 'cause this ain't something your fucking Mexican big shot can help us with!"

Jared waited a few beats to let Albert cool down. "Albert, relax. This is no time to panic. We can find the girl, but we need to cover a lot of territory in a county that's thirty minutes from here. We don't have a contact in Redmond County, and I don't think Tom Pierce is about to help. He might already be helping Will Moser. I mean you ain't the biggest advocate of progressive race relations, so I don't imagine that a black sheriff is gonna have much time for you today. Dump the corpse, then come on back, and I'll have a plan by the time you get here."

Albert put his hand to his forehead. Jared was right. They had to cover a lot of territory in a hostile county, and while NCFC had a lot of members in Redmond County, he couldn't contact any of them without the possibility of alerting Sheriff Pierce.

"Jared, I'll call the office and have Marshall Davidson get a bunch of cars and trucks together. I've got some boys I can trust to help us search for the girl. We need to find her before she can get to a phone. I doubt she left the trailer last night in the pitch-dark after killing the whore, but I guarantee she took off early this morning. By the way, cell phone reception in this county is spotty at best, still, we need to have 'em. I'll make sure all my men have one."

After what he thought was too long a delay, Albert said, "Jared, you hear me?"

Jared was staring off into the distance trying to organize his thoughts.

"Jared!"

Jared shook his head, "Sorry, Ruff, I'm just thinking. If you can get your men together and Marshall can get the transportation set, why don't we meet in Redmond County rather than you driving back here only to turn around and drive right back? After you dump Valeria, call me and tell me where to meet you."

"Okay, but right now I gotta get this stinkin' bitch outta here."

Albert hung up and walked to the back bedroom. The smell was overpowering, so he pulled his tee shirt up over his nose. He looked around for something to wrap the body in when he saw the pile of sheets Maria had used to retrieve the tools. He untied the two sheets then spread them on the floor beside the body. After wrapping her inside the material, he put the long end of the sheets over his shoulder and started pulling.

As he was dragging her out, he looked around the trailer for something heavy to help sink the body in the swamp. Nothing looked heavy enough, so when he got to his truck, he left the body and went into the barn. After a few minutes, he came out with some nylon rope and a piece of rusted metal off of an old disc harrow.

After throwing the body in the back of his truck and covering it with some of the black plastic sheeting from the barn, Albert got into his truck. Looking into his rearview mirror, he said, "Waters, remind yourself never to listen to Jared Hill again."

He started the engine and drove down the trailer road to 621. He thought about taking Valeria to the same place he'd dumped Luca Castro, but it was too far away and besides, he remembered passing a blackwater pond surrounded by cypress trees somewhere down 621. Hoping his memory was correct, he drove the same way he'd come. If he was right, the pond would give him the perfect place to dump Valeria. Acidic black water provided little to no visibility and the added benefit of enough acid to melt human flesh. He'd look for a flat-bottom fishing boat tied up against the bank. A lot of folks around these parts liked fishing in the swamp ponds even though most of them had a healthy supply of water moccasins and the occasional gator.

On the way out, he called Marshall and arranged for four pickups and two SUVs to be assembled behind the NCFC headquarters; then he had Marshall call the six men he wanted to help in the search. He told Marshall to tell them that it was something confidential and not to tell anyone where they were going or when they'd be back. He said he'd call and let them know where to meet him.

As he approached the intersection of 621 and Highway 17, he noticed a small two-pump gas station and convenience store on the right. It was maybe five or six miles east of the trailer turn-off and had a sign over the front door for Pete's Grocery.

Across the road, on the opposite corner, was a kudzu-covered, dilapidated restaurant with a crumbling curb-service wing on the far side. On the other corner was a dumpy little used-car operation with maybe five or six trucks and cars parked facing 17. A ten- or twelve-bay storage facility surrounded by a chain link fence was beside the used-car lot, and two or three small houses on 17 behind the store. He guessed that the folks living there probably owned the store and maybe the used-car lot. Probably coloreds. This part of Redmond County was almost all black.

Pete's was out of the way but easy to find since it was accessible from both Highway 17 and State Road 621. 17 was paved and ran north-south down through Redmond County. 621 was a hard-packed gravel road running more or less east-west. He called Jared and gave him a description of the place, who to collect, and directions on how best to get there.

"Jared, collect the six men I've recruited, and then meet me at Pete's in an hour. That'll give me enough time to get rid of Valeria... Jared? You hear me?"

"Yeah... I'll be there."

Friday

11:30 a.m.

Maria stood beside the window and slowly looked around the edge. It had been an hour, maybe two, since she saw the big pickup go down the road to the trailer, then return and drive east on the road in front of the shed. She didn't recognize the driver, but it wasn't the white van and it sure wasn't Jimmy Ross. They must have sent someone else to pick up Valeria, and maybe her, but if so, why was there only one man in the truck? If they were gonna kill her, why wouldn't they have done it already? Why bring that whore to stay with her if they planned on getting rid of her? She pulled one of the chairs over to the window and sat down. She had to stop thinking of whys and what-ifs. She needed to focus on what to do now.

Okay, they obviously hadn't planned on Julietta getting killed, so their plans had to have been changing, but changing how? They'd kept her and Julietta alive for a reason, but what reason? She could think of only one; they wanted to ship them both back to Mexico so they could get rid of them there. Once in Mexico, the same scum that had killed her mother would then kill her. If so, that meant there wouldn't be men with guns out looking for her, but men with ropes and nets. "They need to catch me," she said aloud.

She stood up again and looked out the window. She hadn't seen or heard any cars or trucks since the big pickup had come back from the trailer. What time was it? She looked at the sun and figured that it must be at least late morning. Maybe she could wait outside the shed and when she saw a friendly-looking vehicle, say, a service van or a car with a family, she could yell and flag them down.

Then she remembered the blue work van that took her to the trailer. That looked like a service vehicle but obviously wasn't. No, she couldn't trust anyone in a vehicle. She'd wait till dusk when she could see headlights far enough away to let her jump into the brush beside the road. She needed to get to a public place— a store or church or anywhere that had lots of people.

As she was forming her plan, she heard a truck. She pulled back from the window. Within just a few seconds, the large pickup that she'd seen go to the trailer flew past the shed in a cloud of dust and gravel. They had undoubtedly found Valeria. The question was who had found her? She figured she'd find out soon enough. Either she'd hear sirens and see police cars, or she'd see a lot of cars and trucks cruising down the road looking for her.

She looked at the gate. The lock was still in place but not fully engaged. What if someone drove slowly down the road and noticed the open lock? Would they get out and inspect the compound? Possibly. If she closed the lock, then how would she get out? Maybe she could find something in the shed to cut some of the chain link fence. She looked around the room. Where were those tools she'd seen earlier? She walked over to the corner of the far wall where she had seen the surveying equipment and began to look through the tools scattered on the floor. There was nothing that looked like it could cut through the fence. Maybe they wouldn't notice that the lock was open.

Maybe... She stopped moving and stared at the black phone box. What was that on the top? She walked over to the phone and, standing on her toes, took a large pair of pliers off the top of the box. Finally, some luck. The back part of the jaw was a cutter.

She went back to the window and looked out. She didn't see or hear anything, so she opened the door, looked up and down the road, then quickly walked to the fence. She said out loud, "Just cut one piece, Maria, to see if you can." It worked. The pliers were big enough to cut through the fence.

She decided that if she went to the back of the compound, she could make a two- or three-foot vertical cut in the fence next to one of the corner posts, and then a two-foot horizontal cut at the bottom. To anyone looking around the compound, it would be invisible, but when she needed to leave, she could simply push the fence out at the cut and slide through. First, she needed to close the padlock so that anyone stopping to inspect the shed would see that it was securely locked and thus empty.

After closing the padlock, Maria walked to the back fence and cut her escape route, then returned to the safety of the metal shed. As she sat down, she scraped the padlock and two feet of chain still wrapped around her ankle against the table leg. She'd forgotten about her ankle chain in the excitement of escaping; so, as she bent over and cut the chain from around her ankle. She smiled and said, "It might hold your dog, Jimmy, you miserable son of a bitch, but it didn't hold me!"

She needed to sleep or at least lie down and rest for a while. Last night she'd gotten little sleep, and she was beginning to run down. She found a smooth spot on the floor and started to lie down when she spotted some work coveralls hanging on the walls. It wasn't exactly a mattress, but three or four pairs of men's coveralls was better than a cold concrete floor. She at least felt safe now. If anyone came into the compound, they would likely be employees of Georgia Pacific, thus the answer to her prayers.

Anyway, she figured she had at least six or seven hours until dusk.

Friday

1:30 p.m.

Will was sitting at his desk in the library when he heard a knock at the front door, followed a minute later by a knock on his door.

"Yeah?"

Lana opened the door and said with a smile, "Will, there's a gentleman here who says he knows you. He says that when Lieutenant Moser was a struggling MP, he saved your, well, your rear end."

Will rocked back in his chair, pushed himself up, and walked to the door. Standing in the hall, all six-foot-three of him, stood Elijah Cothran Kahn.

Older, grayer around the temples, and sporting a few pounds never there in Viet Nam, Eli Kahn still looked every bit the fastidious officer he'd been years before.

"Well, well, Captain Elijah Kahn. Still alive, standing straight, and I imagine, cocky as ever."

Eli smiled and put out his hand. "Actually, Mr. Moser, it's Colonel. I was promoted once I got shed of a bunch of green ROTC officers."

As the two men shook hands, Will said, "Actually, Colonel Kahn, it's Sheriff Moser. I, too, was promoted once discharged from the monotonous routine of the Army."

Eli smiled and dropped his hand, "Touché, Sheriff. Anyway, it's good to see you."

"Thanks, Eli, it's good to see you, too. And by the way, you're looking mighty fit for a man of advanced years."

Eli looked at Lana and rolled his eyes, then back at Will. "I'm still working, so I'm still in training," he said as he patted Will's stomach. "Anyway, never fear, the cavalry is here!"

"Well, at least part of a cavalry horse is here."

"Witty as always."

The two men stood looking at each other for another moment, then Will said, "Eli, come on in."

Eli turned to Lana and said, "Lana, when I think of brave, I'll always think of you. How on earth you manage to stay married to this erratic, smart-ass cop is a mystery."

"Endurance, Eli, endurance."

Eli smiled, patted Lana on the arm, then moved into the quiet of the library. Will pointed to two large Lawson chairs in front of his desk, "Eli, why don't we make ourselves comfortable. I've intentionally kept this room sparse, but I do like having a warmer space where friends can visit. I put the two floor lamps behind these chairs because I don't like to read with the overhead light on, beautiful though it is." Eli looked up at the massive, stained-glass Tiffany fixture hanging from the ceiling.

Will continued, "All the walnut paneling in this room, in fact, all the wood in the house, was milled by Moser Hardwoods years ago. My father used this room as his home office, as I do now. He wasn't as interested in collecting books and manuscripts as I am, but he did love the calm serenity of a library. Solutions seem more inevitable here."

The two sat down, more or less facing each other, on either side of a small Queen Anne table between the two chairs. It was a warm, inviting space, especially if one happened to love books, which both men did.

"I must say, you have an impressive collection here. Must be close to a thousand books," Eli observed.

"Over eighteen hundred, actually. It's the result of a lot of reading and collecting over the years. First editions are one of my weaknesses. Some folks like fancy cars, I like a signed copy of *Huckleberry Finn* or *The Great Gatsby*."

Lana knocked as she came into the room with two glasses of iced tea, set them on the table between their chairs and said, "I thought you boys might like something to wet your whistles as you told each other lies."

Eli smiled and replied, "I only tell the truth, Lana, but I will try and restrain your husband."

As Lana saluted and shut the door, Will picked up his glass. Holding it as if making a toast, he said, "All kidding aside, Eli, it's good to see you again, and thank you for coming. I owe you."

Eli returned the gesture, took a sip of tea, then said, "We were just lucky that I was at Guardian and on my way to Raleigh today. I don't actually live in North Carolina now. I live in Alexandria and come to Guardian about once a month. Anyway, I'm glad I could come by! So, Will, what's so urgent?"

Will put down his glass, looked at the ceiling to collect his thoughts, then spent the next twenty minutes recounting every detail of the last four days. At the end of his story, he said, "So, the long and short of it is, I'm stuck. I don't know where to turn.

"I have a hostile sheriff in the next county, an organization called NCFC that systematically lies and, according to my contacts at the SBI, is possibly a criminal enterprise. Plus, I'm dealing with a man named Albert Waters who has surrounded himself with for-sale politicians and lawmen. I'm sure they've kidnapped and possibly killed the young woman, but I have no idea why. I'm also convinced that timing is critical and that we have little of it, thus the urgency.

"I don't know exactly what you do aside from running your training facility in Currituck County, but from what I've heard, Eli, your organization handles personal security and information services for a lot of very powerful people all over the world."

Eli leaned back in his chair. "Well, no reason to wonder or listen to gossip. I'll tell you what we do. About ten years ago after I left the Army, I was contacted by a man I'd worked with in the Middle East. His name is Adrian Gavalas and he has worked as a case officer in the CIA for his entire career. When he retired, he decided to do something that could benefit from the knowledge he'd gained while with the Company. Without going into a lot of detail, let me just say that we had the same objectives for our retirements, so we formed a company called Ares Security."

Will smiled, "Ares. How appropriate! The son of Zeus and Hera and the Greek god of war. Not very subtle."

"No, but then most people haven't read as much as you and know even less about history or mythology. Anyway, the first thing we did was create a subsidiary of Ares called Guardian Security, located, as you have noted, in Eastern North Carolina. We needed a lot of cheap land that was far away from prying eyes. We got it in Currituck County.

"Since I know you've sent some of your men to Guardian over the years, I don't need to tell you about the services or facilities. This was our original cash cow and financed our expansion into other areas of security. Our mission, outside of training law officers and other combatants, is fairly simple; we offer protective services to government officials and to private citizens of high net worth in countries all over the world; plus, we operate an intelligence service rivaling that of many governments. We keep our clients safe while giving them the information they need to conduct their own businesses. We operate in every area of the globe and have a transportation service that rivals some small airlines.

That's it. Simple."

Will leaned forward, "I'd say that your business is anything but simple."

Eli smiled, "I didn't say our operations were simple. I said our mission is simple."

Will took a sip of tea. "Eli, I realize that finding a missing girl isn't the kind of thing that Ares does, but I'm desperate, and I'm running out of time. If nothing else, I need to know what the hell you think I can do to find this young woman or at the very least find out what has happened to her."

Eli thought a moment, then said, "Will, I have an office in Mexico City to serve my Mexican and Latin American clients, and another in Houston from which I dispatch my Middle Eastern teams. The Houston office is my biggie, the one where Adrian spends most of his time. Adrian was born in the US, so has an American passport, but he was educated in Mexico as well as in the US. His mother is Lebanese and his father is Mexican, but, like Adrian, he was born in the US.

"Adrian speaks Arabic, Spanish, English, French, and Farsi, plus a smattering of Russian and German. What he is primarily responsible for are our intelligence operations. Since we do a lot of work for the US government, we have access to intel sources that the average company would never have; plus, we have aligned ourselves with a number of foreign organizations that are reliable sources of information falling outside normal channels.

"And you're right that finding a missing girl, at least a missing girl who isn't the daughter of some prince or third-world autocrat, isn't really in our bailiwick, but the good thing about owning Ares is that I'm able to pursue any job I wish— and in this case, I wish.

"So, let's get on with it. Since your problem originated in Mexico, Adrian is in the perfect place. If you can give me more information, I can run it through our systems and see what comes up."

Will thought a moment. "More information—like what?"

Eli got up and began to walk around the room. As he turned toward the bookshelves behind Will's desk, he spotted *The Art of War* sitting on the corner of the desk. He picked it up and turned toward Will.

"Really, Sheriff? You, the hater of Lord Tzu, putting the great book on the desk so I would see it?"

Will smiled. "I just thought it might serve as a kind of welcome-to-my-house gesture. I know how much you love Sun Tzu, so I invited him to join our conversation."

Eli ran his hand over the book, looked back at Will, and said, "I shall refrain from giving my usual lecture on the wisdom of the great man; however, I will note that in chapter one, titled 'Laying Plans,' Master Tzu extolls the virtues of good information and warns of the dangers of undue haste in planning one's strategy. Anyway, back to needed information."

Will got up and moved to his desk to take notes on what Eli would advise and need.

Eli slowly walked around the room, stopping and touching various books as he did. Without looking at Will, he said, "I'd like to know the name of the young man Maria recognized at the bus station. If his companion, the older man who was talking to the fellow who went on the bus, is in fact a family member, then knowing who they are might tell us whether there are any known bad guys involved. I suspect, from what you say about Mr. Waters, that there are *plenty* of bad guys in his businesses, either locals he's acquired over the years or cartel types who've discovered him to be a pushover and a conduit to the US market.

"Next, see if you can get your buddy Oris to hack into the NCFC computers and get a list of the passengers on that bus. I'd like for Adrian to cross-check the list against our inventory of cartel names. The Mexican drug cartels are neck-deep in the human-trafficking business, and I'm guessing that Albert Waters has had or may still have contacts with cartel personnel. If we see cartel involvement, then our strategies will be very different than if it's just Albert and a bunch of rednecks." He paused and took down a copy of Henry Kissinger's *Years of Upheaval.* "Really, you bought this asshole's book? What a wanker."

He put the book back on the shelf and kept walking. "Get me a list of the companies Albert controls both here and in Mexico, and see if you can find out whether he has a criminal record, and if so, what for? While we're at it, see if Jared Hill has one. Get me Albert's home, office, and cell numbers; plus, the same for Jared Hill. Just for curiosity's sake, ask Oris if he knows how Jared Hill got involved with Albert."

Eli turned away from the bookshelves, walked back to the Lawson chair, sat down, and took a long drink from his iced tea. "Will, I gotta ask you. Why so much interest in this young woman? Why call me? It might take longer, but the state and Feds can follow up on this. Why call someone who operates with, shall I say, more flexibility?"

Will put his pen down and looked up at Eli. "A debt. I owe Tomás Delgado for the life of my daughter, Grace. When she was about ten years old, she was coming to my office downtown when a drunk redneck in a pickup lost control of his truck, which was aiming straight for her.

"Tomás Delgado was coming out of the local bank when he saw what was about to happen; so he threw down his satchel and ran in front of the truck to push Grace out of the way. He almost did it without being hurt, almost, but his hip was broken, his femur shattered, and his ankle crushed. He survived but walks with a slight limp even today. Eli, he saved my daughter's life, and is now asking me to save the life of his niece, whom he has helped raise ever since her mother, his sister, was killed.

"I have tried everything I can within the law. We both know that the state and federal bureaucracies will never find her in time, so with Lana's insistence, I called you. The girl is in trouble, Eli, maybe even dead—but I'm betting she's still alive. I'm guessing she found out something that could endanger Albert Waters's business, so they took her. We—me and Sheriff Haines in Smith County—think Maria was probably in the van that the girl who was killed Wednesday night escaped from.

"We think they were being moved to a safe house somewhere, and for some reason were, or are, being kept alive. I hope Maria is still alive and if so, I've gotta find her. I can't go to the sheriff in Jackson County since he's nothing but a paid stooge for Albert, so I need to be creative. This doesn't mean I'll intentionally break the law, I can't, but it does mean that I can take the help and advice of a man who specializes in finding information and people by means of *expert tactics*."

Eli smiled. "You know, Will, you sound like some of the bigwigs in our own government. They contract with me so they can claim clean hands if something goes down that they don't want to be a part of, but the fact is, sensitive missions like this one aren't usually solved in the sunlight, but in the dark."

Will thought about this, then said, "Eli, we haven't spoken for a long time, but I remember our time together in Viet Nam with great pride. Now, Eli, this ain't war, and I'm not a twenty-five-year-old lieutenant. My job for the last thirty years has been to uphold the law; to be an example to the people who have elected me to protect them. I'm not about to rummage around in the dark without a light to guide me."

Eli didn't say anything right away. Still silent, he rubbed his hand across *The Art of War*, then stood up.

"Will, like you say, it's been a long time. I can guess what you might think about what we do, but you don't know the whole story—you can't.

"My life since we knew each other has been very different from yours. I don't have a family, at least not now. I've been married three times, and along the way had one stepson. Traveling all over the world managing an organization of hard men working in trying circumstances doesn't lend itself to a settled life. On occasion, I regret not having what you have, but at the same time I'm proud of the work we do, and regardless of what you may think, I do have standards. I don't work for men who will lie to me or put my operation at risk, but at the same time, I don't work for the Boy Scouts, either.

"You do understand that not every country has the same dedication to the rule of law that this country espouses, but I also hope you understand that our government isn't exactly cloaked in virginal white. As I told you, I'm frequently asked by our government, as well as some foreign governments, to solve problems that don't lend themselves to the salutary glare of daylight. If you want to call it breaking the law, so be it, but sometimes the end does justify the means, whether you agree or not.

"Anyway, if you still want me to, I'll help you. It's one thirty. How long before you can get the info I'm looking for?"

Will stopped writing and focused on the wall across the room. "I'll call Tomás Delgado right now and see if his sister in Monterrey has found out the name of the man at the bus stop. I'll call Oris about hacking into the NCFC computers, but I have no idea whether or not he'll do it. Even if he agrees, no telling how long it would take him to get it done. I'm guessing tomorrow at the earliest."

Eli said, "As you've noted, if Albert and his buddies have taken Maria and she's still alive, then time is our enemy. The Latina girl's death was clearly an accident, but I agree that somebody was moving her, and probably Maria, to a secure location, meaning that they're keeping her alive for a reason.

"The accident last night that killed Jimmy Ross and the blue van driver was not an accident and obviously done to eliminate individuals with knowledge of Maria's situation. We need to know who we're fighting besides Albert Waters and the Hill fellow. I'm guessing one or more of the men on last week's bus are involved in some form of human trafficking, and that the girl has threatened their operation. All this to say that the sooner I get the information, the better."

Will shook his head, "Eli, you need a lot of information, and I'm just being realistic. We might get lucky or we might hit a roadblock."

Eli smiled, "We'll jump off that bridge when we get to it," then he paused and looked at Will. "Sheriff, you called me, so I assume you've decided that finding the girl might require some thinking and doing that fall outside the strict requirements of the law. Correct?"

Will put his pen down and leaned back. "Colonel, I can't condone actions that intentionally break the law, but being conscientious, I need to see how close to the line I can come. Believe me, I'm not trying to be difficult or naïve, but like you, I took an oath, and I get nervous when I step too far away from it. I called you to help me walk the line, but unlike our government bigwigs, I won't cut and run if the shit hits the fan; however, I'd just as soon you didn't throw a wheelbarrow full of shit *at* the fan.

"As I was stewing over my situation this morning, my wife, as she always does, helped me focus. Lana said, 'Will, sometimes Lady Justice needs to peek out from under her blindfold to find justice.'"

Eli nodded, "In that case, may I suggest that Lady Justice might benefit from having a houseguest who could help her lift her blindfold?"

Will smiled, "I was gonna suggest that, but didn't want to seem too pushy." Will got up and moved toward the door, turning to face Eli as he did. "Eli, Lana also reminded me that you're running a business; so, I will of course be glad to pay whatever the going rate is for the services of Ares Security. As the chairman of Moser Mansfield Corp., I think it's time for the company to ensure that our internal security procedures are in order and that its key officers are protected. Perhaps you could have your people send me a copy of your standard consulting contract."

Eli held up his hand, "Money is not the issue, but I will send you a contract. I never turn down an opportunity to do business; except, of course, when solicited by certain psycho autocrats or unsavory business moguls, and you don't *appear* to be either. By the way, Sheriff, as I said before, I still have standards.

"As to your kind invitation, I will need to reschedule a few things, but seeing as how your company will be a client, I'm sure we can fit you in. Fact is, Will, I'd enjoy putting the screws to the likes of Albert Waters and his merry band of human traffickers; however, discretion being the better part of valor, you'd better check with the boss before taking in boarders."

"Eli, it was the boss's idea to call you in the first place, so I guarantee that she'll love having you here."

Friday

6:00 p.m.

Jared and Dante pulled up in front of Pete's Grocery and parked beside Albert's truck. There were already two SUVs and two pickups parked to the right of the store. Albert was talking to the men who came up from Beulah, showing them where he wanted them to go. Both Jared and Dante got out of their truck, but only Jared walked over to the others.

"Ruff, here's the maps you wanted." Albert took the maps and turned back toward his men, handing one to each. "You guys know from my map where you're supposed to go, so take a few minutes and draw it out on your own map so you don't forget."

Jared motioned for Albert to follow him. As they were walking toward their two trucks, Jared said, "Ruff, I know I didn't ask you, but I called Hub Davis and asked him to see if he couldn't take an hour or two and fly over this area in his Piper Cub. He can fly the damn thing at forty or fifty miles an hour and can cover a hell of a lot of territory in a short time. I don't figure the girl will be suspecting a plane looking for her unless she thinks her family and the law in Mussel Ford paid for one, in which case she might fuck up and start waving at the plane."

Albert nodded, "Good thinking. I hope Hub's got a phone."

"Guaranteed he does."

When they got to their trucks, Jared turned to Dante and motioned him over. "Albert, this is Dante Sandoval, our partner in Monterrey. Dante, Albert Waters, president and founder of NCFC and Manpower Solutions."

Dante put out his hand. "Mr. Waters, I've heard a lot about you. It's a pleasure to finally meet you." Albert, slightly more restrained, said, "Dante, thank you for coming all this way. I'm sorry that we've had this inconvenience."

Dante gave a nod and said, "These things happen. I'm sorry that Luca Castro put you in this situation. I understand that he will no longer be a problem. My associates and I apologize for sending a man who proved to be so incompetent, but I'm sure that you and your men will quickly solve the problem that he caused."

Jared looked at Albert and said, "You should also know that Dante has an associate who arrived last weekend on the same bus the Delgado girl and the two deceased women were on. He..."

Dante held up his hand. "Jared, please, let me explain to Mr. Waters. Albert, I spoke to my associate, Ramon Castile, about the incident at the convenience store, and he says that there was absolutely no reason for Luca to have taken the Delgado girl off the bus. Neither he nor any of the other men on the bus suspected that anything was wrong in that store. They just assumed that the Delgado girl was with the other two women and was supposed to leave the bus at the gas station. Of course, Ramon knew who Valeria and the Lampe girl were, but he had no idea who the Delgado girl was. Frankly, he wasn't paying a lot of attention when they left the gas station.

"Mr. Castile is here to meet with a man who runs a very large produce operation in Jackson County. I know from Jared that you're concerned about our drug distribution plans, but I want to assure you that we never do anything that isn't well thought-out and as risk-free as possible.

"As to the background for this particular plan, it's a long story, but the quick version is that my younger brother, Germaine Sandoval, met and got to know a young American named Richard Simon. You undoubtedly know his family since I'm told that Simon Farming is a substantial business as well as an important client of NCFC.

"When Germaine met Mr. Simon, he was cutting a rather wide swath in the seaside towns on the Mexican Gulf coast. Germaine, who has had a lot of growing up to do himself, and this young man got into some serious trouble with a drug dealer in Tampico. Long story short, our father, Roberto Sandoval, who used to be a federal judge, arranged to have the two young men released from jail. Mr. Simon came running back to North Carolina to reinsert himself into his family's produce business, while Germaine, after some serious consultation, has turned himself around and is now part of our organization.

"Apparently young Simon's father is in the beginning stages of some form of dementia; so, young Simon has now taken increasing control of the family business, which, by the way, is reputedly worth millions. Germaine kept in contact with young Simon and even visited him here in North Carolina a year ago. That's when Germaine came up with the idea of distributing cocaine or heroin inside some of Simon Farm's produce… melons, pumpkins, and possibly sweet potatoes. We feel there is real potential there."

Albert, for the first time, entered the conversation. "Thank you for taking the responsibility for what that fool Luca Castro did; however, given what has just happened as a result of his actions, I can't say that anything we've done has been risk-free."

Dante nodded and said, "Well, of course I didn't mean without risk. Nothing in this life is without risk. What I meant to say is that we don't do anything where we don't make every effort to minimize risk."

Albert looked at Jared and said, "What if young Simon doesn't want to have his company used as a drug-distribution point?"

Dante smiled. "He will. We feel sure that he would hesitate

before allowing his mother and father to know about his arrest in Mexico and his involvement with drug dealers. There are, of course, photos… ugly, disgusting acts captured forever. There are arrest records to share. And there is always the fear that if he doesn't cooperate, something might happen to his parents."

Now Albert truly understood what Jared had meant when he described Dante as "a trained killer" and "ruthless." Even in his polite greeting and deferential conversation, something about Dante said, "Danger." Albert recalled the movie *Jaws*, where the shark captain, Quint, described being in the water with thousands of sharks after his ship was sunk during the war. He'd said something like, "The thing about a shark is he's got lifeless eyes, black eyes, like a doll's eyes…" Dante's eyes were like that too—so black, and worse, flat and soulless.

Albert changed the subject. "Listen, I been visiting with the black fellow who owns this store. His name is Pete Chambers and he's had this place for over twenty years. Says he's about eighty. He don't know for sure, but that's what he'd be, based on what his momma told him 'fore she died. I reckon that's about right. The old man is bent over with the arthritis, and I'm guessing only about four out of six cylinders are hittin' true in his head, but he seems friendly enough.

"I told him I was looking for my prize bird dog and was offering a two hundred dollar reward. He said he would spread the word down the road. He says his boy takes over the store at five and keeps it open 'til about eight. That's when a lot of folk around here git off work and come in for some beer or a little home brew that Pete's known to have out back. I figure all that marks this as a kind of home base in Redmond.

"Jared, why don't you and Dante wait here while the men scour the roads. I've told them to call you if they spot anybody who meets the girl's description. We don't have a picture, but according to Oris, the girl is gorgeous. She worked as a model in Monterrey and even in Mexico City."

Dante said, "Since he was on the bus with her, Ramon knows what the Delgado girl looks like, but of course that ain't gonna help the men out looking. If you give me her full name, I can have my associates in Monterrey do a little research and see if they can't come up with a picture of the girl. If she was a model, there's gotta be some published photos of her."

Albert nodded, "Okay. Jared, call the office and get the girl's full name. It ain't Delgado, that's her uncle's name. I think it's something like Puane or Punte, something like that, but no need to guess, Carla will know her name. Dante, you can have them fax her picture to the office if they find one. I'll make a bunch of copies and get 'em up here asap."

Albert took a long drink from the coffee he'd bought in Pete's store, "We'll find her. She's around here somewhere. If she got picked up by somebody, she'd have called her uncle by now, and I would have heard from Garland, since I guarantee the law in Hogg County would be hot on our trail. I told Garland to monitor any transmissions from Will Moser and his deputies. I'm guessing she's only been moving around since sunup, and that she ain't walking down the road with her thumb out in the middle of the day. She's hiding somewhere."

Dante left Albert and Jared talking while he went inside the store to talk to Pete. He knew it was always a good idea to make friends, and when he was stationed at Fort Bragg, he used to go into a lot of little country stores around Fayetteville. He thought that was why he spoke such good "Southern."

"How long you think we need to stay?" Jared asked Albert.

"'Till we find her!"

"That could be a while, and it don't look good for both of us to be away from the office for too long."

"For Christ's sake! Who's gonna notice?"

"Uhm, maybe everybody. You and I are always around the office when a bus leaves or is coming in, and remember, we got one bus coming in and two leaving tonight."

Albert nodded. "You're right. One of us needs to go back."

Jared stepped away from Albert's truck, "Listen, you go back. You're more likely to be recognized up here than me. Like you said before, we don't want to draw too much attention to ourselves. There aren't many people who know me, but lots of people know you. Shit, I bet half the farmers up here are members of NCFC."

Albert nodded. "Okay... But keep me up to date."

Dante came out of the store smiling.

"What?" said Jared.

"That ol' man is funny. He makes more money from his liquor than from his gas or groceries. I told him we was having a party in a couple of weeks and might need a few gallons of good whiskey. He said, 'No problem.'"

"You didn't tell him where you came from, did you?"

"You mean Mexico? No."

Jared smirked. "No, I mean Beulah."

Dante smiled, "Naw, I just said that I was working at a farm in the area. He asked me if I was Mexican and I said my daddy was Mexican, but I was born here and daddy's American now. I told him you and me are working for some farmers who are looking for land to rent, so we're up here calling on different folks. I told him we would be back later today. He asked me if the other fella had found his dog, and I said he got a call from a guy south of here who thought he saw the dog yesterday, so he's gonna take off."

"Okay, let's start driving around and see if we can't find that goddamn girl."

Friday

6:30 p.m.

Maria was lying on the floor half asleep when she heard voices out on the road. She rolled off of the coveralls and crawled to the corner of the room. Behind the pile of surveying equipment, she pulled herself into a tight ball. A car or truck door slammed, and a man said in an agitated voice, "Just fucking wait a minute, Bobby, 'til I check this out. You heard Mr. Waters, he said to check under every rock." She couldn't make out the reply from the truck, but the next sound she heard was of someone shaking the chain and lock on the front gate.

"The place's locked, and it don't look like nobody's been here for a while." The man in the truck said something she couldn't understand, to which the man at the gate replied, "Yeah, I know, but I don't know no place else to look." As the man at the gate walked back to the truck, she heard him say, "That bitch has either vanished or is somewhere ass-deep in pines and swamp. If she gits too far into them pines, she's gonna be making friends with either a rattler or one a' them moccasins."

She stayed in a ball for what seemed like an hour. When she was sure no one was around or had returned, she crawled out and, walking crouched down, moved over to the window to look out. Nothing. She stood up straighter, stretched her back, then moved to the door. She opened it about a quarter way and looked out… still nothing. Finally, she opened it all the way and walked into the yard. The sun was just behind the pines on her left, so she guessed it was maybe a half-hour from sunset. She didn't know what time sunset was, but she remembered Jimmy saying to Paco when they left the first house that it was almost six thirty, so it must be close to that now. She went back into the shed and sat at the table.

She closed her eyes, said a short prayer, then straightened her back, sat up, and said aloud, "Okay, Maria, here's the plan. In about an hour, leave the shed and head in the same direction as that last truck, and if you see headlights, don't be afraid to jump into the bushes. You know they're looking for you, and you can bet those last guys aren't the *only* ones around."

Friday

9:00 p.m.

Jared waited in the truck beside Pete's for the last of the patrols to call in, as Dante smoked a cigarette with his head back and his eyes closed.

"Dante, you thought any more about how to get the girl back to Mexico once we catch her?"

"No, I've been focusing on making sure we catch her, then we'll figure out how or whether to get her back to Mexico."

Jared turned to look at him. "What do you mean 'whether'?"

"Whether means whether. Why do we have to take her back? Why not just spread the pieces around up here?"

Jared paused for a minute. "Dante, if she just disappears, if nothing is ever found, that doesn't mean they'll stop looking. The law around here *won't* stop looking."

"So, let 'em look. After a while they'll quit. New cases come up every day."

"Well, some might quit, but not Will Moser, the sheriff in Hogg County. He'll stick his nose into every corner of NCFC's business. He'll have the SBI and FBI looking. He'll get court orders to access our computer files, our taxes, anything that will put pressure on us. He'll call every farmer who gets migrant labor from NCFC and ask them about how many workers they get and demand to see their pay and travel records. He won't quit until he stops up our whole operation."

Dante didn't say anything, just sat and thought. At last he said, "Sounds like you need to reason with him. When we have this problem from the law in Mexico, we sweeten the pot and make giving up a profit center."

Jared said, "I know, but this ain't Mexico, and you don't have enough money to tempt Will Moser. His family controls one of the biggest forestry and paper companies in the Southeast. I'm told he's one of the wealthiest men in the state."

"Okay, Plan B. We make him aware of the many dangers that can befall him or his family."

Jared thought about this and said, "Maybe, but you should know that he has a Silver Star, Bronze Star, and Purple Heart from Viet Nam. He don't scare easily."

"I'm sure, but his wife don't have a Silver Star. He have children?"

"A daughter."

"She got a Silver Star?"

Jared looked at Dante. "Come on, stop fucking around! What's the big deal with just taking the girl back to Mexico and getting rid of her there?"

Dante took a deep breath and exhaled, showing some pique at the current conversation. "The big deal is that any trip with a hostage is inherently riskier than one without; so, if there is an easier way to solve the problem, why not take it?"

"Because, as I've just said, having her simply disappear when her family is convinced she got on the bus will be riskier than driving her back to Mexico. Albert has told everybody that he's trying to find out what happened to the girl. When that moron Jimmy told Oris and the girl's uncle that she didn't get on the bus, we had to go along. We finally corrected the story by saying that our first information was wrong, that she did get on the bus, but got off just as it was leaving Monterrey. So, if she's found down there, Albert's story is solid, and he can express his sorrow at the terrible tragedy of losing such a beautiful young woman to all the crime south of our border. We can come out of this looking like the aggrieved party instead of the other way around."

Maria had been on the road for what seemed like hours but was probably only one or two. It was almost dark when she squeezed through the opening in the compound fence and started her trip up the road. There had been only a few cars to pass her as she walked, and each time she had hidden in bushes on the roadside. Other than the few cars that had gone by, the only sounds had been those of night birds and the barking of a dog somewhere far off.

Since she was finally well rested, her pace had been consistent but cautious. She was aware of the danger of stepping in a hole just off the road and slowing her progress, but she was determined to find help as soon as she could.

About twenty minutes after the last car passed her, she heard what sounded like a diesel truck coming up fast from behind, so she moved off the road and crouched among a patch of alder bushes. A red pickup sped past headed east. When it was well past, she moved back to the edge of the road and watched as the truck's taillights disappeared around a curve down the road.

She waited a few minutes, listening. When she got through the curve where she last saw the truck, she moved to the center of the road to get a better look at what lay ahead. There were no buildings, but when she squinted, she could make out some lights far down the road on the right. It could be a house or maybe a store of some kind. It was too far away to tell, but it didn't matter because it was at least a sign that she was near other humans—friendly ones, she hoped.

Jared was in the store talking to Pete's son, Jarman, while Dante lay on the front seat of the truck with his eyes closed. He wasn't asleep, but it had been a long day.

Having seen the lights at Pete's, Maria was moving at a trot. She could almost feel herself in the arms of her family. She slowed to a walk as she came around the back of the red pickup and toward the front door of Pete's Grocery. She glanced at the truck but didn't stop to look inside. They must be inside the store, she thought. "Hello," she called out. "Anybody here?"

Just as she reached for the doorknob, Jared opened the door and stepped out. Momentarily startled, Maria pulled her hand back, "Is this your store, sir? Do you have a phone I can use? Some men are after me. I need to call the police."

Jared looked at her and smiled, then said in Spanish, "Well, hello, Miss Puente. What a resourceful young woman! We've been looking for you. Welcome to Pete's Grocery. Sorry you won't have time to try some of Pete's moonshine and barbequed ribs. But you need to come with me and my associate back to Beulah."

She stepped back and said, "Are you with my Uncle Tomás? Are you helping him look for me?"

Jared didn't say anything, just continued smiling. "Why, no, I'm not helping your uncle." As he reached out to grab her, Maria realized he was with Jimmy! She also saw that she had but one chance to get away, so, as he stepped forward, she brought her knee up into his groin as hard as she could.

"Not today, you piece of shit!" she said as he fell to the ground with an anguished cry. She turned, hoping to find help in one of the houses nearby, only to get Dante Sandoval's fist smashing against the left side of her head.

Friday

9:30 p.m.

Lana opened the door to the library and looked at the three men. "Gentlemen, even though it's getting late, and a glass of warm milk might be more appropriate, I'm guessing that healthy beverages are not on the menu tonight. What's your pleasure?"

With his hand extended, palm up, Will looked expectantly at Hank and Eli.

Hank said, "Nothing for me, Lana. Thanks, though."

Eli smiled, "What are you having, Sheriff?"

With his hand pulling at the sides of his mouth, Will said, "Eli, I'm thinking that if the lovely Mrs. Moser can find it, I wouldn't turn down a modicum of sixteen-year-old Lagavulin."

Eli turned to Lana and said, "Madam, if you would, please double the Sheriff's order."

Lana shook her head, "All right, then, two scotches for the old geezers and nothing for the young man who could at least handle it."

When the door closed, Will looked back at Eli and Hank. "You know, the more I learn about this immigration and visa bullshit, the angrier I get. Every day you hear screams about illegal immigration and how it's taking jobs from hard-working Americans. Total bullshit. The hard-working Americans won't take those jobs.

"My daughter, Grace, works with an organization at Duke that tries to help immigrant families get settled here, and she says that every year over a hundred and sixty thousand Mexicans and Latin Americans come into North Carolina for seasonal work. I asked her if she knew how many had legal visas, and she said maybe twenty percent. Another twenty either sneaked across the border on foot or came in some cramped truck container. The rest probably had legal visas at one time, but they've long since expired.

"Grace added that when Albert Waters brings a worker in, that person pays him maybe $1,000 plus the round-trip cost of transportation on one of his buses. When the picking season is over, they're supposed to go back to Mexico, but a huge number stay past their visa date, and truthfully, Albert doesn't give a shit because they've already paid for their visa plus the round trip. He has no responsibility for insuring that they return. The real kicker is that all the money paid by the workers is in addition to what the farmer members of NCFC pay Albert for each worker. It's a goddamn racket.

"Albert Waters is nothing more than a glorified coyote. He may not smuggle workers across the border in beat-up trucks or phony, airless containers, but what he does, while safer, is just as dirty."

Eli slowly shook his head, "Will, very true, but you don't know the half of it. I'll tell you some shit that will…"

Another brief knock on the door, and Lana came in with the drinks. "Gentlemen, since you didn't specify how big a modicum is, I took the liberty of putting enough scotch in the glass to clear your brains without completely destroying them. Then I poured one for myself so you wouldn't feel so guilty."

Will said, "Well, if you're gonna have a drink with the boys, you might as well stay."

He pulled up a chair. Lana looked at the other two men and asked, "Okay with you?"

Eli said, "I was gonna suggest it even if your worthless husband didn't. Since calling me was your idea, I figure you might have other good ideas."

She handed the glasses to Will and Eli and sat down.

Will took a drink then said. "Let me fill you in on my conversation with Oris Martin, and then, Eli, you can tell us what you've found out.

"After we met early this afternoon, I called Oris. He was a bit cranky at first, but after a few minutes, he said to meet him at his office. When I got there, a fellow named Zeno Watkins or Watson was already in the room. Oris introduced him as his head of data systems. Apparently, this is the guy Maria would be working for if she was there. I don't know what Oris said to Mr. Watson before I got there, but when I told him what I needed, he just nodded and said, 'No problem, we're already working on it. We'll have the bus manifest within the hour.' Apparently, I looked a bit shocked, so Oris said, 'Will, I figured, based on our previous conversation, that this was the kind of information you'd be looking for, so I had Zeno start his search.'

"I think Oris realized how serious I was about getting this information, so screwing with me wouldn't be a good idea. I hope it was helpful."

Eli adjusted his position in the chair and took a legal pad out of his briefcase. He looked at Will and said, "It definitely was. Based on the hacked manifest, plus the name of the young man that Maria recognized from her school, we've got a lot to work on. We're lucky the aunt went to Maria's old school after leaving the bus station to find out the boy's name. Once Adrian got the list, he checked all the names against our lists of cartel members, then cross-checked them against some federal police lists."

Will interrupted, "Does this mean that a cartel member is feeding you information?"

Eli put his legal pad down on the table, "Will, I can't tell you where or how we get our information. Just believe me when I say that Adrian doesn't get bad information. We use sources we can count on. We ain't invitin' them out to dinner, but we do on occasion end up paying the bill."

Will shrugged and said, "Sorry, go on."

"One name stood out, Ramon Castile. Mr. Castile is a member of the Olmec cartel. The Olmecs are the dominant cartel in Nuevo León State and most of Tamaulipas. Their specialties are human trafficking and drugs. Ramon, like many of the cartel members, has served time in prison, so is known to the authorities. He has a reputation for being more restrained and better educated than many of the 'enforcer' cartel members, but he's still dangerous.

"The young man Maria recognized is Germaine Sandoval, and he comes from cartel royalty. His father is Roberto Sandoval, a federal judge in Monterrey until his greed got the best of him and the federal authorities dumped him. And by the way, you've got to be really greedy and corrupt for the federal government in Mexico to take action.

"The scary part is that Adrian believes the older man who was with Germaine, the one Marianna said was wearing a ball cap and had a shaved head, could be Germaine's older brother, Dante Sandoval.

"Dante Sandoval is in the top layer of the Olmecs cartel. He is smart, well educated, speaks fluent English and French, served in the Mexican Special Forces for ten years, and is a cold-blooded, soulless killer.

"What is really a strange coincidence is that I may have trained him at one point! Adrian said Dante's Army record shows that he was at Fort Bragg for three months in the late eighties. I was stationed at Bragg in the late eighties and often worked with foreign combatants. According to his record, he was a major at the time. Ain't that some wicked shit?"

Eli looked at Lana and started to say something, but she held up her hand and said, "Colonel, don't bother. Earthy language is almost like praying in this household. Keep going."

Eli smiled and continued. "Anyway, if Dante Sandoval is involved, this becomes a whole new game."

"Meaning what?" Will asked.

"Meaning we may need to call in some reinforcements on the chance that he is either here or coming. We know that Ramon Castile is here; in fact, we know what farm he was sent to: the Simon Farming Corporation in Jackson County. I asked Adrian to send me a couple of photos of Dante and Ramon. He found dozens of photos of both men, but none of Germaine. I really don't give a damn about Germaine. He's small change compared to his brother and father.

"No other names jumped out of the manifest, but there were two female names on the list, a Valeria Ovaldo and a Julietta Lampe. Adrian checked with the Monterrey police and found out that Valeria is fifty years old and is a madam at a prominent brothel in the city. It's owned by a Mr. Hector Lampe, who we imagine is the father of Julietta.

"A lot of this is guesswork since I told Adrian not to contact any of these people to confirm identities. Will, if the Olmecs are involved, and I'm sure they are, we don't want to tip them off. I'm guessing that the madam is here as part of a sex-trafficking operation. No way to know if it's connected to Albert, but that would be a good bet. You might want to check on that Simon Farm connection."

Hank cleared his throat, "I might be able to shed a little light on that one. I know or knew Richie Simon while we were both in high school. Hogg County High played Jackson in almost every sport—big rivals. Richard, called Rich or Richie back then, played ball for a while but never took it seriously. Basically, he was known as a screw-up. He spent more time at his old man's house at the beach than in school. He was famous for throwing parties that featured plenty of alcohol and drugs. Word was that you could score more than grass at Richie's parties."

Eli said, "Is this rumor, Deputy, or fact?"

Hank looked at Eli with an "are-you-shitting-me" expression on his face. "Colonel, we're talking rural North Carolina. How many black guys you think were invited to white parties?"

Eli nodded. "Sorry, just tryin' to lighten the load. Go on."

"In his junior year," Hank continued, "his parents took him out of Jackson High and sent him to one of those kick-ass military schools to see if they could straighten him out. I heard he went to East Carolina for a few years and then sort of fell off the map. One hears the occasional rumor that he spent a lot of time stuffing his nose on the beaches in Mexico."

Eli nodded. "Sounds about right. If true, then we have the possible connection between Simon Farms and the Olmecs. I'll have Adrian check with our federal police contacts and see if they have anything on Richard Simon Jr. It might be that Ramon is trying to organize something with young Simon, maybe running drugs."

Will pushed his chair back, stood up and stretched. "Goddamn arthritis." He walked over to the window behind his desk and turned around.

"I'll have to think about how to check on Simon Farms without tipping off Garland Hoots; again, maybe Oris can help. I..."

Lana held up her hand. "Excuse me, Will. I know Richard's parents, Ruby and Richard Simon, pretty well. I've taken care of Ruby's dogs for years. The Simons have two black Labs they treat like their children. As a matter of fact, they might like them more than their children. The Simons have worked all their lives to make Simon Farms a success, and I know that young Richard has frequently been a disappointment to them. Ruby and I have had lots of talks about children. A month or so ago, she told me that young Richard has been doing a lot better and is back in their good graces. I also know that Richard Sr. is suffering from a type of dementia. Nothing debilitating yet, but not good. Chances are that Richie has had to take a bigger role in the operation."

Eli nodded his head and said, "I'll bet the cartel has something on Richie and is trying to use him and his company in their plans. I'll also bet that Maria has by now found out about their sex-trafficking and drug operations. She was on the bus with the two women and may have overheard something. It's almost a sure thing that the young woman killed in Smith County on Thursday night was the Lampe girl, but if she was a prostitute, why would she jump out of the van and try to get away?"

Lana said, "Because she might have been an *unwilling* prostitute sent to this country by her father. A while ago, Grace told me about a bunch of young women who had been brought into the state as prostitutes in order to protect their families. She said that sometimes the daughters of families who owe the cartels something are made to be prostitutes in payment of the family's debts."

Eli said, "That could explain the murder of the two Mexicans and Jimmy Ross. If the short guy wearing the Redskins hoodie was the van driver, then letting the Lampe girl get away signed his death warrant as well as that of Jimmy and the other guy. If you fuck with the Olmecs, you're as good as dead."

Will walked back to his desk and sat down. Looking over at Hank and Eli, he said, "Okay, gentlemen. Let's say all this guessing and supposing is right. Let's say that Maria has unwittingly gotten herself into a situation that poses a threat to their entire operation. Is she still alive, or is she at the bottom of some swamp?"

Eli stood up, drained his scotch and started walking around the library. "Is she dead?" He stopped walking. "No, I say she's still alive. I bet she was in the blue van too and was being taken to a safe house along with the Lampe girl. I bet that Albert and his buddies want to get her out of the country. I bet they want to kill her in Mexico in order to cover their lie.

"They've already compounded the lie by telling Oris that they're working with their people in Monterrey to find out what happened to the girl. Will, they know you're trying to find out what happened to her. If she just disappears, you'll still be trying to find an answer. The last thing they want is for the SBI or the Labor Department or any state or federal agency nosing around in their business. Unless they can prove that she *wasn't* on the bus, that's what would happen. And, by the way, if we don't find her pretty soon, I'd get every one of those agencies on NCFC and Albert Waters like ugly on an ape."

Will said, "Okay, Colonel, what do you suggest?"

"Amp up the pressure. With your permission, I can have my people at Guardian monitor their phones, all of 'em. Have somebody monitor their movements in Beulah. Maybe put somebody on the ground there. Drive around town and see if you spot any of their guys. I'll have photos of Dante, Ramon, and even one of Germaine just in case. Check out Richie Simon. If your friend at the SBI is solid, you might have him drive to Beulah and nose around. Ask folks if they've seen anything suspicious. Be obvious. You carry the big stick around here—use it."

Will thought for a minute. "Might that not push them to do something rash?"

"Maybe, but if they're rash, then they've already killed her. I think what will happen is that they'll move to get her outta here as soon as they can. We just need to find out when and how. They may get sloppy and talk about things on the phone that they shouldn't."

Will said, “That brings up another point, Colonel. What if somebody finds out we’re monitoring their phones without authorization?”

“They won’t.”

Will leaned back and took a deep breath but didn’t say anything. He looked at Lana, who smiled and made a motion like she was raising a blindfold.

“Okay, Colonel. Let’s put our ears on, but don’t take that as permission.”

“What do you mean?”

“You said, ‘with your permission.’ I can’t give permission.”

“Oh, yeah. You must have misunderstood. I said ‘with our decision.’”

Will looked at Lana who just nodded.

“Okay, let’s also see if you can have your Mexican sources find out when and how Albert plans on moving Maria Puente to Mexico.”

Eli nodded. “I’ll check around, and in the meantime perhaps we can have someone cruise Beulah to see who they can see.”

Will replied, “I’ll have to think about that. I don’t want to alert Albert, and a lot of my men would be recognized in Jackson County.”

Eli said, “I might be able to help. I have a guy who sometimes works for me at Guardian. He teaches black ops and occasionally at the driving course when we have classes in offensive driving. He was Special Forces and is discreet. He could check into the motel downtown across the street from the NCFC headquarters. Nobody in Beulah would recognize him and he has the perfect cover. He works for a fertilizer and herbicide distributor in Aydlett, North Carolina, so he travels around this area all the time. We can have him check into the Motel 6 in Beulah and set up a camera. We can record everybody who goes in or out of Albert's office, night or day. What do you think?"

Will thought a minute. "Could be good, but Albert probably owns the Motel 6, so the manager is probably on Albert's payroll. If your guy has the right business card, then nobody might suspect him. You say he's reliable and knows how to melt into the background?"

"Guaranteed."

"Do it, but check with me before any major change in plans."

"Of course. I'll give him some photos of Dante and Ramon, so when he's driving around town, he'll know who to look for. I'll tell him to call us even if he just thinks he saw them. I want to know if Dante is here."

Will looked at his watch, ten thirty. "Hank, how about driving out to Simon Farm tomorrow morning and nose around? I don't know what to tell you to look for, but see if you see anything or anyone of interest. Eli, you got one of those photos of Ramon Castile and Dante with you?"

"Yeah."

"Hank, don't get out and walk around. Just see if anything strikes you as suspicious."

Lana said, "I'll can call Ruby Simon and see how her dogs are doing. I gave them some pretty strong medicine a few weeks ago, so I can just say that I'm calling to make sure it's working."

Will said, "Good idea, but don't ask too many questions."

"I won't need to. Ruby likes to talk."

Will got up. "I don't know about you guys, but I'm bushed. Lana, let's leave these guys alone and turn in."

Hank said, "I'm done. I'll see you folks tomorrow."

Eli said, "Will, I might bother you for another scotch and then call Adrian again tonight. It's an hour earlier in Mexico, and he was checking with some folks to see if they had any info on the whereabouts of Dante or Germaine. He also has a guy who might shed some light on possible human trafficking involvement by Manpower Solutions. I won't be long, but I'd like to use your landline in here. Okay?"

"Fine. I'll show you the liquor cabinet. Help yourself."

Friday

10:30 p.m.

Jared put his key in the front-door lock at the NCFC headquarters but found it already unlocked. He took a few steps back and looked up at the lighted second-floor window. Albert Waters, a slight grin on his face, was standing in the window looking down. Jared waved at him, then went into the building and up the stairs.

Albert stayed at the window for a few minutes more, gauging the peace and quiet of Main Street and downtown Beulah. The parking lot in front of NCFC was the only hospitably lighted area in town. Main Street maintained a minimum number of streetlights, and the only other lights downtown were the security lights inside the Dollar General Store and the reception area at the Motel 6 across the street. Albert looked at his watch… ten thirty.

Jared came into the office as Albert was turning around. "Like I told you, we got her. She was about to walk into Pete's when we caught her." He grimaced as he lowered himself into a chair beside Albert's desk.

Albert walked to his desk. "You get hurt?"

Jared slowly shook his head. "In a manner of speaking. The girl started to open the door into Pete's as I was coming out. I said 'Hello, Miss Puente,' and she asked if I was with her uncle. I said no, that I was with some *other* men from Beulah, and went to grab her. That's when she kneed me in the balls. Dante was laying down in the truck behind her and when he heard us, he got out of the truck and came over. While I was laying on the ground holding my balls and feeling like I was gonna puke, Dante knocked her out."

"Where is she now?"

"We cuffed her to a sink in one of the trailers out back. Dante is with her making sure she's secure and conscious."

A smile started to spread across Albert's face. When Jared saw it, he said, "Please, no smart-ass remarks."

Albert, the smile still on his face, leaned back in his chair, closed his eyes, took a deep breath, then slowly let it out as he leaned forward.

There was a knock at the door, and Jared said, "That would be Dante. I told him to come on up when he was sure the girl was secure."

Dante came into the room, and smiling at Jared, said, "How the boys hangin'?"

Albert laughed out loud. He looked at Dante and said, "Señor Sandoval, I've been told that smart-ass remarks aren't welcome tonight."

"Oh, sorry. Just being sympathetic, Jared."

Albert leaned over and took a bottle of Jack Daniels out of his desk drawer. "My friends, this calls for a drink. Dante, grab three of those glasses behind you."

The three sat quietly, savoring the warm liquid along with the comforting realization that their most dangerous liability was again securely theirs. Making the moment even sweeter was the fact that the law was still stymied as to Miss Puente's whereabouts, and had given up trying to find the driver of the dump truck that had killed Jimmy Ross.

Albert broke the silence. "Jared, what's important now is that we continue our normal routines while finalizing a plan to get the girl back to Mexico as soon as possible. I..."

Jared held up his hand, "Ruff, just lemme enjoy the booze right now. Dante and I were talking on the way back from Redmond, and we have an idea for getting the girl outta here, but right now my balls hurt so bad that I need to get drunk."

Albert looked at Dante. "You need to get drunk, too?"

"No," Dante replied.

"Then why don't you fill me in on what you and Mr. Sore Crotch are planning to make this clusterfuck go away as soon as possible."

Dante looked at Jared, now finishing his second drink. "Okay, after discarding several shitty ideas, like the baggage compartment of a bus or the trunk of a car, Jared suggested his wife's RV. I haven't seen it, but Jared says it has everything we need for an easy jaunt to the Mexican Gulf Coast."

Albert looked at Jared who nodded, adding, "You've seen it, Ruff. It's that blue and white Mountain Aire parked behind the bus maintenance shed. It gets about eight to ten miles a gallon and has a seventy-five-gallon tank. I've driven it to the Smokies and back and didn't use a half-tank. Eunice got it to carry her dogs to shows all over the place. It's registered under the name of her breeding business, 'Labrador Hill.'"

As Jared poured himself another drink, Dante said, "I figure it's about sixteen hundred miles from here to McAllen, Texas, on the Mexican border. If two people split the driving, I think we could do it in maybe thirty hours. This assumes we don't need a bunch of bathroom stops since there's one on the RV and we only need to stop for food if we want to. I calculate that with a seventy-five-gal fuel tank, we ought to be able to go about six hundred and fifty miles on a tank, which means we'll have to stop two or three times for fuel.

"Of course, there's always construction and accidents to deal with, but there's no emergency now that we've got the girl locked up. We should leave sometime in the next couple of days, maybe Sunday morning. That should also give us time to figure out what to do with the hookers who are already here.

"Meanwhile, Ramon has had a discussion with Richie Simon about our distribution plans, and while Rich ain't real happy with the idea, he understands that he ain't got much choice. Fact is, we've got a lot of work to do before we make a final decision.

"We need to solidify a plan to get the stuff into the country, but we're working on that. In fact, Gabriel had an idea that looks real promising. We've made some modifications to the Tex bus that we think are nothing short of inspirational. We'll test it when everything dies down.

"Then we need to decide on the internal distribution systems. I'm guessing that with the Simon Company's reputation and their existing wholesalers, we can hire a few new ones without making waves. Ramon has spent a few days in the packing and shipping departments at Simon and feels that, without disrupting anything, we can fill certain produce—specifically melons and pumpkins—with drugs as part of the quality-control process. QC is housed in a separate building from shipping and packing."

"Where is Ramon staying?" Albert asked.

Jared replied, "At Richie's place. Richie told his parents that Ramon is a grower from Texas who wants to distribute his produce through Simon, and since his growing season is different from that in North Carolina, Simon will have product for its customers year-round. They already buy and distribute produce from Florida and Pennsylvania, so adding Texas would be logical."

Albert added, "Can Richie be a problem for us?"

Jared, more relaxed and in less pain, replied, "I don't think so. Truth is, he's scared shitless of Dante, so he's also afraid of Ramon. This morning he asked Ramon how long he and Dante would be here because he needed to check on something at his house on the beach. Ramon said probably only for another couple of days; so, Richie said that Ramon could stay until then, but that he had to go to the beach.

"The little fucker's solution has always been to run away when faced with a problem. Anyway, Ramon doesn't need to stay but three or four more days. Just long enough to fully understand the QC and shipping operations. Now that we've got the girl, Dante doesn't need to stay. You agree, Dante?"

"Yeah, we're about done, and by the way, I don't care that Richie is scared of me. Fear focuses the mind, and Richie's needs a lot of focusing. I don't want to make him paranoid, but if I have his attention, then that's good. We tried to calm him down by explaining that we'll be using several other farming operations as well as his. We told him that if we see any unusual inspection activity at one location, we'll shut it down and move to another one.

"Ramon thinks Richie is still using drugs though, making his cooperation easier, but his work-level sloppier. Ramon has pretty well figured out how Simon's operation works, so, like you say, we don't need to be here much longer. I'd like to resolve how we reorganize the prostitution business here too, since our managers are all dead!

"I spoke to Gabriel a few hours ago and told him about the Ovaldo woman. He hadn't spoken to the Lampe girl's stepfather yet, so he said he would call him and tell him that his stepdaughter and madam are both dead. Hector Lampe is a small-time ex-pimp, so I doubt either death is gonna move him. We may have him find us another madam, or maybe we'll just get rid of him in case he has a case of regrets about sending his stepdaughter to be a whore. In any case, I want to talk to the women who are already here. We might find a new leader, a madam, among them."

Albert shouted, "Shit, shit, shit, shit… the whores! Nobody has checked on the whores today. Dante just reminded me! Their madam was killed last night, and while we were freaking out trying to find the girl, nobody has checked on the whores at the Elliot place. We need to get out there."

Jared said, "Albert, it's almost midnight. They'll all be asleep. We'll check on them in the morning. They knew the old lady was going away for a few days. That's what Jimmy told them when he picked her up. It'll be all right."

Albert got up and started to pace. "Okay, but we need to get out there first thing in the morning. I'll take Dante. You okay with that?

Dante nodded, "Good with me. How secure is the house you got them in?"

"Very. It's on a small piece of land owned by a farmer named Sam Elliot who lives on the other side of Cranston, in Smith County. Jimmy Ross rented it a few months ago and told Sam that we needed it for some pickers who were unassigned. I doubt that Sam goes out there very often. From what I understand, he mainly grows cucumbers out there, and that season is long over.

"If there is a problem, we have other places we can move them. We can use the Upchurch farm again if we need to. Anyway, Dante, meet me here early tomorrow. Say six thirty."

"Right. See you then."

Saturday
September 28th
DAY SEVEN

Saturday

8:30 a.m.

Lana poked her head into the dining room as Will and Eli walked in. "Who wants breakfast? We got eggs, bacon, toast, and lots of coffee. The Mussel Ford Food Lion was short on mangoes and papayas this week, but I do have some semi-yellow bananas and a few kinds of cereal."

Will said, "Hon, I'm not real hungry. How about an English muffin, a small OJ, and a mug of coffee?" Eli looked up and said, "That's good for me too, Lana."

"Got it," she said.

Eli put his legal pad on the table and flipped back a few pages. "Will, I had a good conversation with Adrian last night. We talked for about an hour. He's had mixed results.

"As far as the whereabouts of Dante and Germaine Sandoval, he only got confirmation on Germaine. He was seen a week or so ago in Monterrey, but Dante hasn't been seen, at least according to our source, for a while. This doesn't mean he's not in Mexico, only that our source has no information to the contrary. Adrian is still fishing, but as of last night, nothing.

"On the other hand, he found out some interesting things on young Richard Simon."

Lana came in with two plates, set them in front of the two men, and then sat down with her cup of coffee.

Eli looked up and said, "Thanks, Lana. I was just telling

Will what we found out about young Richard Simon. You'll be interested.

"It seems Junior was arrested eighteen months ago on drug charges in Tampico, Mexico, and shortly thereafter ex-federal judge Roberto Sandoval got the charges dropped. But the really interesting part is that he also got charges dropped against his youngest son, Germaine."

Will didn't say anything right away, but when Eli started to speak, Will raised his hand. "Hold it. A disgraced ex-judge pulled strings and got drug charges dropped against his own son and his son's gringo friend?"

"Correct. You heard it right."

"Holy shit! How does an ex-judge still have the muscle to have drug charges dropped?"

"Will, he may be an ex-judge but that doesn't mean he's without power. Roberto works for the cartel. It's the cartel that has the power."

Will leaned back in his chair, "I guess we now know why Ramon Castile is here, and I'll bet that his friend Dante Sandoval ain't far away."

Eli smiled, "Sharp as always, Sheriff."

Will took a sip of coffee. "Okay, so Simon Farms could be involved in the drug business, and maybe even the prostitution business, because the Sandovals and Olmecs have got young Richie by the balls."

Eli nodded, "Right again."

"Holy shit."

"That ain't all. You remember when we were talking yesterday about the drug business, and we wondered *how* they would bring drugs into the country?"

Will nodded. Eli continued, "Well, I think Adrian has an answer for that. He kept thinking that if he was Albert, how would he do it, then it hit him… AmTex. Albert brings people into America from Mexico every week. His buses are large and full of people who have legitimate visas, so they aren't inspected on any regular basis. All of the AmTex buses have been reconfigured from the mobile palaces used by rock stars and Jesus freaks back to buses that can accommodate a large number of passengers. With this in mind, Adrian looked for the company that sold AmTex its buses.

"Turns out it's a broker in El Paso, Texas. They buy used tour buses, then find companies to reconfigure the insides. Since they're just brokers, they have no facilities to modify the buses, so they sub it out, and obviously it's cheaper to do it in Mexico than in the US.

"Adrian asked the broker who sold the buses to AmTex who did their modification work, and they gave him a couple of names. The biggest and most important was a company called Xpres Engineering, owned, oddly enough, by Arco Industries. That's the same company with a factory near Raleigh. After talking to an Arco vice-president, Adrian thinks he may know how Albert and Jared Hill plan on bringing in their dope, if they haven't already.

"Arco does custom work for the government as well as private corporations. They make modifications to all kinds of vehicles: limousines, trucks, buses, almost anything that moves. In fact, they basically build from scratch the bulletproof limos used by the federal government and some of the head honchos of the big conglomerates. Fifty percent of their work is for the government and fifty percent for the private sector.

"Anyway, this Arco VP said they'd reconfigured all of AmTex's buses. When Adrian asked if they'd made any special or unusual modifications to any of the buses, the man said that on one of the buses they modified the septic tanks."

Will took a sip of his coffee. "Why is that interesting?"

"Why do you need to modify a septic tank? Piss is piss whether it comes from a country music star or a field hand."

"Okay, so what did they do to them?"

"They installed trap doors."

"And?"

Eli took a bite of his muffin and washed it down with coffee. "Will, let me give you the quick tutorial on bus septic tanks that I got from Adrian.

"To empty the holding tank, one end of a sewer hose is attached to a fitting located on the outside of the bus, and the other end is attached to a sewer. A button on the bus is pushed to open the holding tank, which allows the blue formaldehyde… along with the urine and feces… to empty from the holding tank. All of this crap goes through the sewer hose and into the sewer. After all this, they again push the button and, *voila*, the tank is empty and ready for more goodies."

Will leaned back in his chair. "Okay, got it. So?"

"So, why put in trap doors? The tank is empty, unless of course you have something else in the tank that you need to get out; like, say, a shit load of heroin! The manager said that a septic tank barrel has a displacement of about eight cubic feet. Once it's emptied, they pump more blue formaldehyde into the tank to keep down the smell from the shit. I don't know if you've ever smelled formaldehyde, but it ain't perfume. You would not only keep down the smell of shit and piss but of anything else too, like drugs.

"If dogs were brought out to sniff out drugs, all they would smell is a load of human excrement, but not drugs. I did a quick calculation. If you used half the tank or four cubic feet, you could probably put 60 to 70 kilos in a single shipment. At $150 per gram street value, that would be $150,000 per kilo or 9 to 10 million dollars per 4 cubic feet, leaving the remaining 4 cubic feet for shit, piss and formaldehyde."

Will looked at the other half of his English muffin, butter, and his favorite orange marmalade, then pushed them away. "Suddenly I'm not so hungry anymore."

Eli laughed. "Well, that's the difference between us. I spent so many years in the field that it takes a lot more than that to put me off my grub."

Lana took Will's plate and said, "I'm with you, Eli. No reason to waste a good muffin."

Eli stood up and walked toward the kitchen. "Coffee pot still work?"

Lana started to get up, but Eli held up his hand, "Never mind, I'll get it. You want any more?"

Lana smiled and handed him her mug, "Yes, please."

Eli filled his mug with fresh coffee and sat back down. "So, what do we now know? One: There is probably a connection between the cartel and Simon Farms Corporation as a result of young Simon's needs and indiscretions. Two: If we're right, then the plan is probably to use Simon as an interstate distributor for the cartel's drugs. Three: With the information from Arco Industries, we think we know how they might bring the drugs into the country. Based on all of the above, this could explain why Ramon is here and staying at Simon Farms.

"On a related matter, I talked this morning to Olan Rizzo, the guy from Aydlett that I told you about. He checked into the Motel 6 this morning and got a room on the top floor facing the NCFC building. He set up a camera and recorder aimed at the front of the building. He talked to the manager of the motel for a while and gave him one of his cards. If the manager does tell Albert, or Albert's sheriff, about Olan, and they check on him, all they'll find is a fertilizer salesman who lives and works out of Aydlett, North Carolina. I told Olan to get breakfast and call me later."

Will got up and walked into the kitchen for more coffee while speaking over his shoulder. "Since Olan has a car, what do you think about having him take a ride around Beulah to acclimate himself? He ought to know where Jared Hill lives as well as Albert. I'll give you their addresses and you get 'em to him. I also think he should learn where all of NCFC's buildings are. He can eat downtown at Mozell's. There's usually a lot of loose talk in there that could be helpful."

Eli nodded, adding, "Will, I guarantee that Olan will know what is what before the day is out. He's from this part of the state, knows the towns in eastern Carolina, and is a good listener. Plus, he has equipment that can record everything that goes on inside and outside of NCFC. If a mouse farts in that building, he'll calculate how big it is."

Will still had a worried look on his face when he came back into the room. "I talked to Ed Haines in Smith County and Thomas Pierce in Redmond, but neither one has seen or heard anything. They're still keeping their eyes open, but unless Albert and Jared are really careless, I don't think they'll see anything. I sent Hank over to the Simon Farming operation this morning to snoop around. He said he'd call me if he finds anything interesting, but as of now, it seems we're just thrashing around with nothing to show for it."

Eli wrote something down, then said, "I agree, but remember the words of Lord Tzu, 'Action undirected is pointless.' Adrian is working his sources hard, and with Olan planted in the Motel 6 we'll at least have some eyes and ears on site. I've spoken to my communications specialist at Guardian, and he's configuring a listening network with access to all of the phones at NCFC, plus Albert's and Jared's cell phones."

"Eli, like I said. No permission."

"My man was a specialist at NSA for twenty years, and since coming to me has developed a surveillance system that uses techniques that fall outside of traditional definitions of 'taps.' As I told you, we have clients in the Middle East who are 'friends' of this country, which means that we have the assistance of our government in coordinating our protection and communication efforts with theirs. Hell, you can buy systems on the internet that allow you to listen in on cell phone conversations. A traditional phone tap is like bringing a buggy whip to a car rally. Again, you said you needed to find this young woman and called me for that reason. So, let me help you."

With some frustration showing, Eli said, "Will, you can call in the Feds or the State Bureau of Investigation and wait for their mills to grind slow and fine, but be prepared to explain to yourself, as you stand by that young woman's grave, how slow-grinding was the proper way to go. You know as well as I how these organizations operate. Court orders, interviews, and by-the-book procedures."

Will said, "Look, Colonel, I appreciate your help, I really do, but please understand, I am the law here, and if I ignore it, then there's not a lot that separates me from the law-breakers, right?"

Eli took a deep breath. "I know you're the law, and you know that I spent my whole career fighting for the rule of law that this country stands for, but sometimes rules need to be broken, or in your words, Lana, blindfolds need to be raised. We don't have the luxury of any time at all, now, William.

"I don't remember where I heard it, *Elmer Gantry*, I think, but I remember a line that went something like, 'Sometimes you can be so concerned with what's right that you lose sight of what's good.' There is a young woman out there whose life is in grave danger. She's done nothing wrong, but fate has put her at the mercy of ruthless men. I'm not suggesting we break the law, only walk the line."

Eli got up and walked over to the windows overlooking the backyard with its masses of lilacs and hydrangeas. He turned around and said, "In Afghanistan we were constantly confronted by the anti-waterboarding crowd. We understood their concern, but at the end of the day we also understood that our most sacred duty was to our brothers-in-arms, and that saving their lives might mean getting information fast—in unattractive ways. You were a soldier, and a good one, so you know the code. Maria is our comrade, so we need to save her. Let's stop the bad guys who have her. Let's stop the scum who are importing the drugs that kill our fellow citizens, citizens of North Carolina and Hogg County."

Will had not taken his eyes off Eli. He wasn't sure he'd even taken a breath, but sitting there in his dining room, in the house in which he was raised, in the house where he and his wife and daughter lived, he understood that this time, good had to triumph over right. He understood what his wife had understood years before, that justice has many names.

"Okay, Eli, let's find Maria. Let's be *good* this time."

Saturday

10:15 a.m.

Hank slowed as he neared the Simon Farm compound. Since it was a little past ten on Saturday morning, the place was empty and locked. Even so, it was an impressive facility containing what appeared to be dozens of buildings. For a quarter-mile on either side of the entrance were rows of planted pine trees behind which was a ten-foot-high chain link fence. The wrought-iron entrance gates were flanked by two massive stone walls and secured by an electronic, card-controlled box mounted on a metal pole. Set in the middle of each gate was a large, hand-forged "S."

It was impossible to tell the function of the individual metal buildings from the road, but it was clear that, when in full operation, this was a substantial production facility. Collectively, these buildings comprised the grading, sorting, packaging, and shipping operations of the Simon Farms Corporation. The back-office functions of the company—customer service, accounting, data processing, and logistics—were housed in a two-story brick building about a half-mile farther down the road.

Just past the brick headquarters building was the home of Mr. and Mrs. Richard Simon Sr. Theirs was a large white, neocolonial mansion reminiscent of the houses in Natchez, Mississippi, on the bluff above the river. While no river was nearby, the house did overlook what must have been a ten- or twelve-acre lake. Young

Rich Simon lived in a smaller version of his parents' house on the other side of the lake.

Having passed the production facilities, Hank turned into the parking area of a small country store and gas station farther down the road. It sat across from and maybe fifty yards beyond the brick building that housed the Simon Farms offices. He assumed it was closed since no cars were in front of or behind the store, and he saw no sign saying that it was open. He parked in front of the pumps and got out to stretch and look at his map while checking out the headquarters building. To his surprise, an old black man came out of the store and approached him.

"Mornin', young man, can I he'p you?"

Hank, a bit startled, turned and smiled at the old gentleman.

"My goodness. You surprised me. I wasn't expecting anybody. I thought you were closed."

The old man said, "No sir, it's just slow. You can pump yo' own gas, but if you needs somethin' inside, I can git it."

Hank said, "Actually, I was just pullin' over to check my map. I'm supposed to meet a friend of mine at the Ebenezer Baptist Church near here, and I'm on my way there. I got the feelin' that I might be lost."

"No sir, you're fine. I can tell you zac'ly how to git there. Go down this road 'bout four miles, then go east on Road 815 toward Farmington. Ebenezer will be 'bout three miles down that road."

"Thank you, sir. I appreciate it. My map ain't exactly clear. So, do you own this store and gas station?"

"Naw, my boy does. I just work here some days."

"Well, it's a lovely area. I live in Hogg County and haven't been this way before. That sure is an impressive-looking building 'cross the road. Who owns it?"

"Mr. Richard Simon own it. He been here for his whole life. I worked for Mr. Simon for thirty years. I retired two years ago. Mr.

Simon ain't doin' so good these days, so his boy Richie has taked over."

Hank looked over at the building and said, "Is this part of that big operation down the road? The one with the two large stone gates and metal buildings behind?"

"Yes, Sir, they is the production part, and this building here is the office part. The Simon Farms Company is one of the biggest anywhere around."

Hank nodded while staring at the office building. "You think they might be hiring these days?"

The old man walked over to the side of Hank's car, looked at the office building, and said, "Don't know. Ever since young Rich has took over, seems they been hirin' mostly them Mexican fellas. Every week they more and more of 'em. Ain't like when his daddy was runnin' things. Young Rich damn shore ain't his daddy."

Hank looked at the old man. "Well sir, I best be goin'. By the way, my name's Henry. What's yours?"

"I'm Robert, Robert Banner."

"Well, Robert, I ain't Mexican, but I do have a degree in accounting. You think if I come by on Monday, Mr. Simon Jr. might find a job for me?"

"I reckon you could come by, but young Rich won't be there. He gone down to his place at the beach. He come by yesterday and ask me could I work on his Jeep while he's gone. I done a lot of that kinda work for his daddy over the years. I reckon I was one of his best mechanics, 'specially on them tractors.

"Anyway, young Rich says he'll be at Wrightsville and for me to call if'en I need 'im. I doubt I would 'cause I know a lot about them Jeeps. He say for me to get the key from his house, from a man stayin' there who know where it is. He say the man is doin' business with the Simon company and live in Texas, but come here to see 'bout sellin' stuff through Simon."

"Did young Mr. Simon tell you his name?"

"Yeah, he told me, but I cain't remember it right now. I 'member it's Mexican-sounding, though."

"How long is Mr. Simon gonna be away?"

"He say he be stayin' for maybe a few more days and that he might be back 'fore the man leave. Anyway, I'll get the key tomorrow."

Hank smiled at Robert, shook his hand, then walked around to the car door. "Mr. Banner, I appreciate the directions. You take care of yourself now. And God bless."

"Amen."

Saturday

12:30 p.m.

Hank strode up the brick walk and front steps of Cromwell House, a magnificent home, imposing but tasteful at once. As he started to raise the front-door knocker, he turned, as he often did, and looked out across the wide, sloping lawn with its clusters of French hydrangeas and perennial flower beds toward the Roanoke River and the forests following its banks.

Hank could never quite reconcile the mixed feelings he had while standing on this porch. On one hand, as an educated man, he appreciated the subtle beauty of such a well-preserved house and garden. On the other, the history of the house brought to mind the cruelty and ignorance of past generations who had owned and abused his ancestors. After turning this over in his mind for years, he had finally seen that, regardless of the records of past cruelties, the current occupants of Cromwell House were as close to family as he had in this world, so Hank resolved to let the past stay in the past, silent and unbidden.

Within seconds of the massive knocker hitting its base plate, Will opened the door and motioned Hank into the hall and then into the library where he and Eli had moved for sequential, but no less savory, cups of coffee.

"Join us for coffee, Deputy?"

"No, thanks, I've filled up on gas-station coffee over the last hour."

"You look mighty nice in your Sunday-go-to-meetin' clothes."

Hank smiled. "Well, Sheriff, some of us have a job other than sitting around all morning drinkin' coffee and talkin' rough."

Will sat down at his desk while Hank took the Lawson chair beside Eli.

"Afternoon, Colonel," Hank said.

"Deputy."

When Hank was seated, Will said, "You find out anything at the Simon operation?"

Hank stood up, took his suit coat off, draped it over the back of his chair, then sat back down.

"I went out there—and by the way, that is one damn-big operation—but as you can imagine, it was locked up, with no one around. It's pretty well protected by a ten-foot-high chain link fence all the way around it, security cameras all over the place, and two large, card-activated metal gates. About a half-mile farther down the road is the company admin building. It was also locked; so I pulled into a little store and gas station across the road to get a better look.

"I got out of my car and spread a map out on the hood while studying the offices. While I was pretending to look at the map, I got the shit scared out of me by an old man who came out of the store. I'd assumed it was closed, but the old man said he'd come by to get something he'd left the night before.

"Seems the place is owned by his son, who has him work there sometimes. He's a nice old man and said he'd worked for old Mr. Simon Sr. for over thirty years. When he asked if he could help me, I told him I was just stopping to look at my map in order to find the Ebenezer Baptist Church, where I was meeting a friend. He gave me directions; so I thanked him, shot the breeze for a while, and finished by asking him if the Simons might be hiring.

"He apparently doesn't think much of young Simon, who he

says is hiring 'nothin' but Mexicans' these days. I told him I had an accounting degree and might stop by on Monday to see if Mr. Simon might be interested in a hard-working young accountant. He said not to bother 'cause young Rich wouldn't be there. He said Rich went to his house at Wrightsville Beach yesterday and would probably be there for a couple of days. He said Rich asked him to work on his Jeep while he was gone, and when he asked Rich about the keys, Rich told him he could get 'em from a Mexican fella staying at his house. You think that could be the man who came on the AmTex bus last week? Ramon?"

Eli turned to look at Hank. "Could be. Did you see young Rich's house?"

"Yeah, I saw it, but I didn't see anyone around."

Eli started to say something else when his cell rang. He took it out of his pocket, looked at it, then said, "Hey, Olan, what's up? When? Who else was there? Holy shit. Okay, while you're out, go by the Simon operation and see if you see Ramon there. Hank Grier says there's a Mexican fellow staying at Rich's house and we're thinking it could be Ramon Castile. I don't know. Hold on.

"Hank, is there anywhere he can park and observe Rich's house without being spotted?"

Hank thought for a minute and said, "He could park across the road, but if anybody came by, he'd be pretty visible. I don't recall anything that would hide him or that he could blend into."

"You hear that, Olan?... Okay, call me back."

Eli closed his phone and put it on the small table beside his chair. He stared at the table for a few minutes then looked up at the other two men.

"Interesting. As you heard, that was Olan Rizzo, the guy who's now in the Motel 6 in Beulah. After he checked in and set up his equipment, he decided to take a drive around Beulah. I gave him Jared Hill's address as well as Albert's. When he drove past Jared's house this morning, he saw two men sitting on the porch drinking coffee. One of 'em was Jared Hill and the other one looked a lot like Dante Sandoval. He couldn't be sure because he didn't want to stop and the man had on a ball cap that partially hid his face, but he says he's eighty to ninety percent sure it was Dante.

"He then went by Albert's and saw him and his wife going somewhere together. So, we now know that three of the big fish are in town, and that young Rich is hiding out at his house in Wrightsville. Olan is gonna drive out to Rich's house, then come back to Beulah in order to keep a close watch for any activity at NCFC. By the way, Will, how far is Wrightsville Beach from here?"

"By car, about an hour and a half. Why?"

"Well, it occurs to me that we can listen in on phone calls all we want, but we can't listen in on porch conversations, at least not without exposing ourselves. The one person who is sure to have some knowledge of what's going on is Richard Simon Jr., a man presently at his beach house far away from the bad guys in Beulah.

"What if we were to confront young Richie with some very scary information. You gotta figure that he's not involved in this drug business through a burning desire for money; he's got plenty of money, or his old man does. It's almost a sure thing that he's being blackmailed. They have him over a barrel, and I bet he's scared to death, especially now that Dante is in town. Richie is the kind of guy that will crack wide open if confronted with the possibility of prison or even worse, the wrath of the cartel."

Will said, "I could go down. I know the area and the shortcuts. I can talk to him and point out just how slippery is the slope he's heading down."

Eli replied, "I don't know; he might figure that talking to the law would only put him in a worse position. On the other hand, if I speak to him and show him a possible way out, he might listen."

"What way out?" Will asked.

"Well, I haven't got that figured out yet, but there's always a way out." Eli saw the look on Will's face, "What, you don't agree?"

Will took a deep breath and leaned back in his chair. "Eli, you might be right about the law scaring Rich, but maybe talking to a friendly lawman, a man that's local and known to be fair, would be less scary than talking to a complete stranger, and by the way, you ain't exactly the warmest and fuzziest of fellas."

Eli looked at Will with a smirk, "Aw, now you've gone and hurt my feelings."

Hank pushed himself forward and said, "While you all figure out what our next move is, I'm gonna get a cup of coffee after all. The pot in the kitchen, Will?"

"Yeah, help yourself."

Eli looked at Hank and said, "Hold on, Deputy, I'll go with you. I gotta get rid of a cup first. Where's the downstairs head, Will?"

"It's on the way, I'll show you," Hank replied.

As Hank and Eli walked into the front hall, they heard Will's desk phone ring.

Hank and Eli walked in just as Will was hanging up, so they sat and waited for Will to stop noting the call.

When he finished, Will put down his pen and looked at the two across from him. "Interesting—another fucking twist in this never-ending soap. That was Sheriff Ed Haines in Smith County. Looks like he might have stumbled onto something. He said a couple of hours ago, one of his deputies got a call from a man who lives on a small farm outside of Cranston. The deputy knows the man pretty well and says he's a straight-up guy.

"When this fellow and his family were on their way to some kind of family gathering, they drove past an old run-down house on a farm next to his. He doesn't usually go that way, but the road he normally takes is under construction. He said nobody's lived there for over a year, but this morning he sees a bunch of women on the porch and in the yard. It wasn't any of his business, he said, but thought the deputy might want to check it out.

"The deputy asked him who owned the house and he said it was owned by a fellow named Sam Elliot, who Sheriff Haines says is one of Smith County's biggest farmers. The sheriff said the Elliots live on the other side of Cranston but farm properties all over Smith County and even in some adjoining ones.

"When the deputy went out to investigate, he found two women outside the house and four inside, only one of whom spoke any English. He said they have H-2A visas and are apparently staying there before going to work on a nearby farm.

"He asked which farm, and the one who could speak some English said she couldn't remember the name. There was a white Suburban parked out back and when the deputy checked, he found that it was registered to NCFC. He told Ed that the whole thing seemed suspicious. Most of the women were young—girls, really. The only one who looked older was the one who spoke some English. Given what Ed knows about our search, he thought I might be interested. He's going out there this afternoon with one of his Spanish-speaking deputies and wondered if I wanted to join him. I thanked him and said I'd be glad to go."

Eli leaned back in his chair and took a sip of fresh coffee. "Gentlemen, I'll guarantee you that Albert Waters' fingerprints, plus those of his buddies, are all over that house. Will, if you smell an Albert-rat, you might have Ed keep it quiet for a while. We don't want to tip off either Sheriff Hoots or Albert that we might have found one of their little human-trafficking operations, at least not until we have some idea about Maria."

Will nodded, "That won't be a problem. I have a good relationship with Ed Haines and he's a pro. Don't worry."

Eli said, "I won't, but it never hurts to keep reminding ourselves about caution. I'd like to use your office while you're out. I want to check in with Adrian to see if he's found out anything new. I might also call my commo guy at Guardian to make sure he's got everything he needs."

"No problem. Lana will be back soon, and if you need me you have my cell. If you have something of a confidential nature, call me on my secure system. I'll give you the number and I'll tell the office that you have it."

Will motioned Hank toward the door. "See if Wimbley has heard anything."

Saturday

1:30 p.m.

Jared and Dante sat in Albert's living room watching a football game, while Albert fumbled around in his kitchen. Albert's wife, Ruth, and their daughter had gone to Raleigh to shop, so the men had the place to themselves.

Albert yelled from the kitchen, "Anybody want something to eat or drink? Coke, Sprite, beer, popcorn… anything?"

Dante held up his hand. "A Saturday-afternoon cerveza works for me."

Albert came into the living room with three Buds. "Only got American cervezas, sorry."

The conversation moved from football to fishing, to hunting, to sex, finally concluding with a spirited discussion on the superiority of soccer over football.

Jared finished his beer and said, "Okay, gentlemen, down to business. The Puente girl is recovered enough to travel. She's still bruised and sore, but otherwise seems healthy; in fact, she kicked a tray of food I was bringing her out of my hands. I told her she could lick her food off the floor for all I cared, and she said I could lick the sweat off her ass. You believe that? I'll say one thing, if that girl was a man, she'd have the biggest set of cojones in the room! I'll be glad to get her to Mexico so *you* can deal with her, Dante.

"On our other matter, I assume, based on your visit to the Elliot farm this morning, that we're okay for now, but that we should probably move the women to another house once we have a manager. As an interim solution, I have a fellow who was with me at Manpower who could be an interim manager, but he isn't someone we want running a prostitution ring full-time. At least he can keep everybody calm and keep paying them so they don't get restless. I can have him check by every day until we have a more permanent solution, but for the next day or two they seem okay. Am I right?"

Albert said, "I wouldn't exactly say all right. They seemed suspicious when Dante said that Valeria had to go back to Mexico. I don't think they really gave a shit since she'd only been here for a week or less, but we're not talking about a bunch of geniuses here. I don't…"

Dante interrupted, "I think it would be better to have Ramon go over there. He was planning on staying a while longer to become more familiar with the operations at Simon Farms; so, adding a few hookers to his schedule shouldn't be a problem. He has a Simon Farms cell phone that Rich gave him, so if he has a problem and we're not here, he can call you, Albert. I told him to make sure Richie is calmed down before he leaves. One thing I've learned the hard way; if you have a shaky partner, you're better off cutting the cord right away before you get into trouble. We need to be sure Simon is the company we want to use for our distribution before we send a few million dollars worth of heroin up here."

When Dante said that, Albert looked over at Jared with an expression that said, "What the fuck have you gotten us into?"

Knowing that Albert still didn't trust Dante and his associates, Jared tried to lighten the situation. "Dante, before Ramon leaves to go home, he has to calm Richie down. You need to tell Ramon to tell Richie that he and his family are safe and under your protection—rather than your threats. Have Ramon act like Richie is his friend, that they might have some fun in Mexico someday. Confide in him. You know the game, mi amigo!"

Dante smiled, "Right."

Saturday

6:00 p.m.

Eli and Lana were sitting on the front porch when Will got back to Cromwell House.

"I gotta tell you something, Will. If I lived in this house, you'd have to call the fire department to get me off this porch. Me and the boss been sitting here for the last hour watching and listening to the wood ducks fly over the house whistling their way down to the river. It's truly a beautiful place."

"Well, thank you, Colonel. You do seem mighty calm and rested out here with your glass of single malt and smoking what I assume is a fine Cuban cigar that you have kept secret from me."

"Actually, I was about to offer you one, but since you're getting kind of snippy, I just might keep them for myself." He smiled and shook his head as he got up and went into the house. He returned with a small humidor full of Cohiba Maduro 5 Genios.

"Help yourself. I offered one to the boss, but she demurred."

Lana smiled, then to show her interest in the conversation, rolled her eyes.

Will said, "Forced generosity, the best kind. No guilt."

Hank Grier came up the walk and onto the porch. "Gentlemen."

Eli held out the box of Cohibas, "Deputy, Cuban?" Hank shook his head, "Thank you, Colonel, but those are way above my pay grade. I'm more of a rum crooks sort of guy."

Will cut his cigar and sat on the outdoor sofa facing the river.

"Eli, I would have been here sooner, but Ed wanted to go to Sam Elliot's place after we left the women."

Eli blew a smoke ring above his head and asked, "So what's their story?"

Will continued, "Well, according to the Spanish-speaking deputy, and he may have missed some of what they said, these women were brought into the country on H-2A temporary visas arranged through NCFC. Their employer was supposed to be a farm in New Hanover County, but for some reason the farmer no longer needed them. Oris explained to me the other day that Albert sometimes applies for visas for farms or businesses that don't need temporary workers, then ships them off to unqualified employers.

"Anyway, the group leader was an older woman, maybe forty, who said that their main contact wasn't Albert Waters, who she said they'd never heard of or met, but a man named Luca Castro, who they variously described as 'scum,' 'bastard,' 'son-of-a-bitch,' and a variety of other names the deputy was unclear about. They have not seen Castro for almost a week. The only other man they saw was Jimmy Ross. According to the older woman, they are being sent to a farm closer to their current house. She couldn't remember the farmer's name but said he grows sweet potatoes, which puts him in the same category as about every other farmer around here.

"Eli, there is no way these women are pickers. This is a bunch of hookers if I ever saw one. Except for the one, they're all young and clearly not field-worker types. Ed said that since they have legal visas, there is nothing he can do right now, but he's gonna call the Labor Department and Immigration tomorrow.

"He was upset that Sam Elliot might be involved in something as shitty as human trafficking, so he decided to go over there and talk to him. I said we might want to wait on that, but Ed figured Sam would probably find out sooner rather than later, and if something was amiss, he wanted to quash it now.

"We left the women there, but Ed told the leader to keep everybody at the house and not go anywhere. She said she would, but some of the younger ones looked pretty upset when we left. Ed's got the license number of the NCFC car.

"I followed Ed over to Sam Elliot's farm on the other side of Cranston. Ed was right about Sam. He lives in a really nice house with a pond out front and a three-car garage behind. He's obviously a very prosperous farmer. When we drove up, Sam met us in the driveway and quickly led me and Ed down to a little gazebo by the pond. The deputy stayed by the car. Apparently, Sam was a little nervous about his wife hearing what we might say.

"Ed tried to open with a little small talk, but Mr. Elliot quickly waved him off. 'Sheriff, cut the bullshit. Why are you here?' Ed smiled and said something like, 'Okay. Sam, what do you know about a place on your property being used to house prostitutes involved in human trafficking?' This was probably a little blunter than Sam had in mind. He swallowed hard, lost his smile and said, 'What the fuck are you talking about?'

"Ed said, 'We were just at a house on your farm off Clemmons Road north of here. One of your neighbors says it hasn't been lived in for over a year, so when he saw a bunch of people milling around outside, he called us. One of my deputies went by and found five or six women standing on the porch and in the yard. The deputy doesn't speak Spanish so he called me, and I went by with Sheriff Moser and a deputy who speaks Spanish. The women say they're field hands waiting to go to their assigned farm. I asked if they were going to Mr. Elliot's farm and they said no, but they couldn't remember the name of the farmer who has now hired them. Apparently, they were brought in by NCFC to go to a farm in New Hanover County, but that fell through. The woman who seemed in charge wasn't very forthcoming, and the others were clearly frightened. Sam, something is going on up there, and I think Sheriff Moser will agree that these ladies don't look like pickers, if you know what I mean.'

"Sam sat rigid and silent. After a long pause, he said, 'I rented the house to NCFC a few months ago. A fellow named Luca Castro was sent over by Jimmy Ross at NCFC. He said they had a few farms that had reduced their personnel requirements for the season, so, they needed some additional housing until they could reassign the workers. He said they would only need it for the season, maybe 'til mid-October. I told him that it hadn't been lived in for a while and was in pretty rough shape, but there was power, the plumbing worked, and it had a phone hookup. He said not to worry, that they would take care of fixing it up. Jimmy Ross sent me a check for the first two months, and that's the last I've heard about it. You know me, Ed, and you know I would never be into something like sex trafficking.'

"Ed paused, and said, 'Sam, I sure hoped that was the case, but there's a lot of weird stuff going down these days and I needed to check it out. Will Moser has an investigation in Hogg County on a similar matter, which is why I asked him to come with me today.' I felt like I ought to say something here, so I asked Sam, 'Sam, did Jimmy pay you with an NCFC check or personal?'

"Sam paused, then said, 'I think it was personal, but he said it was for NCFC.'

"Ed closed his notepad. 'Sam, I'm gonna call the folks at the Labor Department and Immigration tomorrow, so wanted you to know. If all these women have valid H-2A visas, it means they're legal, but I guarantee you the Immigration folks are gonna want to know what farm they're supposed to go to. I told them to stay put and said that if they tried to leave, we'd find them. I don't think you have a thing to worry about, but you should be prepared for a bunch of questions. I'd suggest you not go over to the house.'

"Sam said, 'You don't have to worry about that, Sheriff, and thank you, I appreciate it, and guarantee you that I'll be on the phone to Jimmy Ross tomorrow morning first thing.' Ed looked over at me, so I said, 'Mr. Elliot, Jimmy Ross is dead. He was killed in Jackson County in a traffic accident on Thursday night.' I thought he was gonna faint.

"'What the fuck is going on?' he asked.

"Ed replied, 'Sam, it was an accident as far as we know. Sheriff Hoots has issued a preliminary report that says it's a case of hit and run. But the driver of the truck that hit Jimmy has disappeared.'

"Sam, still dumbstruck, said, 'Then I guess I'll call Albert Waters.'

"Ed said, 'Sam, you might wait for a day or two. At least until I finish my investigation.' Sam didn't say anything, just nodded.

"There not being a lot more to say, Ed and I left."

Eli blew another smoke ring and said, "You think he'll wait to call Albert?"

Will replied, "No. I think he'll stew about it for a few hours, down a couple of stiff shots of whiskey, then call him tonight."

Eli smiled as he finished his drink, "That should flush the quail out of the bushes."

Lana got up and said, "Eli, looks like you need a fresher-upper, and the sheriff looks like he could use one as well."

Will started to say something, but before he could, Eli said, "Sheriff, hold just a minute. I need to call Olan."

Lana came back on the porch with a bottle and two more glasses. She poured Will a drink, then topped off her own and Eli's.

Eli finally put down his phone and said, "Will, while you and Sheriff Haines were out hobnobbing with the hookers, I kept thinking about informer options, and the only one I kept coming back to was Richie Simon. You gotta confront Mr. Simon, and confront him soon—like first thing tomorrow morning. When Albert finds out about the whores, and he will, all plans move up. If Rich is being blackmailed, as we think, then he's scared shitless and praying for a way out. Short of some irrational act of grabbing Albert and his buddies on sex-trafficking charges, which will never stick based on what we know now, Rich is the best chance we've got to find out what's going on.

"I'll stay here and keep an eye on things, while Olan cruises around Beulah to see if he can find out where everybody is. My communications guy at Guardian is monitoring office and home phones, plus scanning all cell transmissions, but if Albert believes he's been compromised, he might use other phones. Let's hope he ain't that smart.

"Will, you might want to call your buddy at the SBI and tell him to be available. We'll need him if we discover a drug angle or get anything concrete on human trafficking."

Will nodded. "I'll call him tonight, and given our relationship, he may be open to a little snooping around without concrete proof."

Will stood up, "If I'm gonna visit with Richie Simon tomorrow morning, I'll need to drive to the beach tonight. Lana and I have a house at Figure Eight, just north of Wrightsville, so I can spend the night there and go see Richie early in the morning. I might even go by his place tonight to make sure he's still there."

Lana stood up and, looking at her husband, said, "Will, I'll drive. You may need to use the phone, and if so, I'd rather you didn't have an accident while driving. Plus, I might be of some help with young Richard."

As Will and Lana started to go inside, Will turned, and smiling, said, "Eli, go easy on my scotch. That bottle of Lagavulin costs over $100 at our local ABC store. I'd hate to dock my first paycheck to Ares." Eli smiled, raised his glass, and said, "Dock away, Sheriff."

Will replied, "I'll call you as soon as I leave Rich's." Then Will looked at Hank and said, "You're in charge, Henry."

Saturday
11:00 p.m.

Will and Lana had only been asleep for about an hour or so when his phone rang.

"Yeah."

"Will, it's Hank. Get awake 'cause you ain't gonna believe this."

Will sat up in bed and said, "What time is it?"

"Eleven o'clock. You awake?"

"Somewhat."

"Okay, just when you think it can't get any weirder, it does. I just got off the phone with Nathan Holloway, the deputy in..."

"Yeah, yeah. I know."

"Okay, he is on duty tonight at the jail in Cranston. About an hour ago, a young woman comes into the station hysterical. She can't speak any English but is clearly in a panic. Nathan doesn't speak any Spanish, but they happen to have a Hispanic prisoner in jail for a DUI who was sober enough to translate.

"The long and short of it is this: the young woman is one of the hookers who you saw at the Elliot place this afternoon. It seems that after you left, some of the girls were in a panic and the older woman who was there started yelling at them to calm down. After a while most of them seemed okay, but this woman decided that she wasn't gonna stick around. After the others went to sleep, she sneaked out and took off. She ended up at the Sheriff's Department after hitching a ride with some long-haul truck driver.

"Anyway, the young woman says she's a prostitute who was brought to the states to work the labor camps on various farms around the area. She and the other women have been here for about a month, and the Elliot house is the second one in which they've been kept. It seems that an older woman named, get this, Valeria Ovaldo, came into the country last week to run the business."

Will interrupted, "Which means that the girl killed Thursday night is almost surely Julietta Lampe."

Hank continued, "Right. Valeria had only been here for three or four days when, on Thursday afternoon, Jimmy Ross came by the house and picked her up. He said she would only be gone a few days and for the women to stick close to the house. Nathan said the girl only knew two men, Luca Castro and Jimmy Ross, but they haven't seen or heard from Castro for four or five days, and from Jimmy Ross since he picked up the Ovaldo woman.

"Since Valeria left with Jimmy Ross, nobody has been by the house until this morning. Two men came by early to see if they were all right and told them that Valeria had to go back to Mexico for a while."

Will said, "Did she get a name?"

"Of who?"

"The men who came by this morning."

"No. Only one of the men said anything. The other man stayed in the car. They were there for maybe five or ten minutes, then left. A few hours later, the girls were out sunning themselves when Ed's first deputy came by, and by the time you and Ed got there, they were in a panic. The oldest woman, the only one who speaks any English and is maybe early forties, told them to keep their mouths shut.

"After you left to go to Sam Elliot's, the older woman got hysterical. She said for them to calm down and that they would find out what was going on tomorrow, meaning Sunday morning. That's when the young woman decided to run away. The girl says she was taken from her family in Mexico by the cartel and forced into prostitution. She was sent to the US with the other girls to start a new business, but she ran away because she doesn't want to be a prostitute. What she's really scared about is the safety of her parents in Mexico."

Will said, "We gotta get moving. When Albert finds out about all this uproar, he's likely to panic. This will undoubtedly mean a change in plans. With Jimmy Ross and the two drivers dead, and probably Luca Castro and the Ovaldo woman, Albert and Jared Hill are gonna be on the hot seat, and if the fellow sitting on Jared's porch this morning was Dante Sandoval, then their seats are gonna be red hot! The Immigration people…"

"Hold on," Hank said. "The whores may have never seen Albert or Jared. Jimmy Ross and Luca Castro were the only ones the young prostitute talked about, plus Valeria Ovaldo, and like you say, she's probably dead or gone; so, what would the Immigration people…"

Will interrupted, "Wait a minute. You just said that two men came out early this morning, Saturday morning. That one of those men spoke to the older whore, so they have seen other men?"

"Yeah, but they didn't get a name and they had never seen the man before, plus the other man never got out of the car, so like I was saying, what would the Immigration people have on Albert? He can deny everything. He can say that NCFC was misled by the women, that according to his records they were supposed to go to New Hanover County. He'll say that Jimmy Ross and Mr. Castro, plus the two dead Mexicans, must have been running a sex-trafficking ring behind his back. He'll call his buddies in Raleigh and cry foul. If Ed and the Immigration people jump on him too soon, he'll get off the hook."

Will said, "That may be, but finding the whores will accelerate everything, and the 'everything' we should be most concerned about is Maria Puente. With the runaway whore now in Ed's custody, the others are bound to get itchy feet. Ed needs to go out there early tomorrow morning and get the rest of them. Has Nathan talked to Ed?"

"I think so."

"Okay, call Eli at my house and fill him in. I'll talk to you first thing tomorrow."

Lana Moser sat looking at Will. He paced around for a minute, then turned to her and said, "Just when you think things are going in a certain direction, shit hits the fan."

She smiled and said, "Like I said, Sheriff, we've seen shit hit fans before. We just gotta step back, dodge the shit, and move forward."

Saturday

11:10 p.m.

Albert woke with a start. The ringing seemed to come from everywhere. When he had reoriented himself, he reached for the phone on his bedside table.

"Yeah."

"Albert, whash the fucking idea of parking a bunsh of whores in my howse in Shmith County?"

Albert still hadn't fully focused. "Who the fuck is this?"

"Sam Elliya, you ashhole."

"Sam Elliot. What the hell time is it?"

"Iss eleven somin'."

"Morning or..."

"Night, you dum shit."

Albert sat up and put his legs over the side of the bed. He rubbed his head and face and wiped the sleep and tears out of his eyes. "Sam, hold on. I need to trade phones."

Albert's wife was awake by this time and leaned forward as she said, "Who the hell is that? What does...?"

Albert put the phone on the bed and said, "I'm gonna take this downstairs. Hang up when I pick up."

"Who is...?"

"Nobody," he said as he stood up. "Just do what the hell I'm telling you."

Albert went downstairs and into the kitchen. "Sam, you still on?"

"Goddamn righ, I am."

"Ruth, hang up the phone." He heard the phone click upstairs. "Okay, Sam. What the hell is going on?"

"Whores is goin on, thash wha."

"Sam, you're drunk. Why don't you call me back in the morning?"

Sam rubbed his face and blinked. "Hod on. I'm gonna wash my fash." That seemed like a good idea, so Albert walked over to the sink and splashed a little water on his own face. After a couple of minutes, Sam returned to the line.

"Okay, better. This afternoon Sheriff Haines called me and said he wanad to come by the howse and talk. I said okay, come on. He showed up wif Sheriff Mozher from Hogg Couny. He said that one uf my nabors called his office to say that a bunsh of women was at my howse. The howse I rented to Jimmy Rauss for NCFC. I toll him I got no idea who wuz in my howse, that it wuz rented to NCFC. He says that the women haf visas for farmwork but they don' look like farm pickers. He says that he gonna call emagrachon tomorrow. I don' need no fuckin' guvment ashholes commin' roun' my fuckin' farm lookin' for no whores. You godda…"

Albert finally couldn't take it. "Sam, just be quiet. I know the place and know that we had some pickers living there until we could get them resituated. They were supposed to go to another farm, but the guy backed out. I'll have them out of there tomorrow. Stop worrying about it. Nobody is putting whores on your property. As you may have heard, poor Jimmy Ross was killed in a terrible automobile accident Thursday night just outside of Beulah. His funeral is this week and I'm trying to organize things around that, but rest assured that you won't have any problem with the Immigration authorities. I know everybody in the department, and it will only take a phone call tomorrow to straighten this whole thing out. Sheriff Haines is a bit over his head when it comes to immigration matters, and that arrogant asshole Will Moser is just sticking his nose where it don't belong. Go to bed and we'll talk tomorrow. Sam?"

"Yeah, okay. Les' talk tamarra."

Albert hung up and closed his eyes. He walked over to the refrigerator and took out a beer. "Goddamnit. Why don't I fucking follow my own instincts? This whole thing was a clusterfuck to begin with! Jimmy and that dumb shit Luca Castro were exactly the wrong people to trust with this shit. I knew I shouldn't have listened to them. Jared's got something to answer for as well."

With that he picked up the phone and started to call Jared, but before he got through dialing, hung up.

Albert's mind was racing. "Shit, if Ed Haines and that fucking Will Moser have already been to the Elliot farm as well as Sam's house, then they may have already called the Immigration people and maybe even the SBI or Labor Department. No phone—they may check phone records. I gotta get dressed and go over to Jared's. No phone."

Albert parked in front of Jared's house. The lights were still on upstairs but out in the living room. He knocked on the front door until he heard someone moving around.

From the top of the stairs came, "Who the hell is it?"

"It's Albert. Come to the door."

The curtain covering the front door glass panel pulled back and Jared Hill, clearly annoyed, stared out. "Your phone broken?"

Albert, equally annoyed, said, "No, it's not, but given the mounting number of fuck-ups going on, I thought it best not to leave a phone record for the various state and federal agencies that might currently be monitoring our ass."

Jared opened the door and said, "What are you talking about?"

"We got problems with the whores in the Elliot house. I..."

"Bullshit, you were out there this morning and said they were fine. Unless something has happened that I don't know about, and no one has called me, then I don't know what the fuck you're talking about."

Albert said, "No you don't, that's why I'm here, so why don't you shut the fuck up and listen?"

Jared walked out onto the porch. "Sorry. What's up."

Albert told him about Sam Elliot's call and ended by saying, "Let's meet at my office in ten minutes. You get Dante."

Jared nodded and without saying a word went back inside.

Saturday

11:25 p.m.

In his office when Jared and Dante walked in, Albert looked up at the two men without saying a word. "Dante, I assume Jared filled you in, but just in case something was lost in translation, let me reiterate. Sam Elliot just called me yelling about a visit he had this afternoon from Sheriff Ed Haines and Will Moser, the sheriff in Hogg County and the one who has been looking for the Puente girl. They asked Sam why a bunch of prostitutes were staying in a house on one of his farms. They told him that one of his neighbors called a deputy around noon today when he saw people milling about at a house that has been vacant for a year. Apparently, the man was on his way to a family lunch or something, so it was after we were there this morning.

"The deputy went out there and found five or six women in the house, and then called Sheriff Haines, who showed up with Will Moser and another deputy who spoke Spanish. The deputy talked to the women and the one who seemed to be in charge told him that they were here on H-2A visas and were waiting for transportation to their new jobs. She said they were supposed to go to a farm somewhere else, but the farmer changed his mind."

More to himself than to the men sitting in front of him, Albert said, "At least the woman had the good sense to give the party line." He shook his head, then went on. "The sheriff said that since they weren't illegal, he couldn't arrest them, but he did take their phone for now. He told Sam that he was gonna call the Immigration people, but if they were really farm workers, he had nothing to worry about. Clearly Sam didn't believe him, because he is plenty worried." Albert stopped for a minute to let this sink in, looking from Jared to Dante, then continued. "This is the kind of shit that I've been warning about. I think you'll agree that we need to pull the plug right now. I don't…"

Jared held up his hand, "Hold on, Ruff. Let's not get ahead of ourselves. Yes, we have a new problem, but I don't think it's something we can't handle. You say that Sam said the sheriff left the women there because he didn't have anything to arrest them on, right?"

"Yeah."

"Okay, so we know they're still there, thus can be moved tonight."

Albert, almost shouting, said, "Really? And just what do you think the sheriff is gonna do when he comes back and they're gone?"

Jared replied, "I think he's gonna be pissed. He'll call Sam Elliot and ask him where they went, and Sam will say he has no idea and to call you. And when he calls you, you'll say that you have no idea because as far as you knew they were on their way to another farm. You'll say that Jimmy Ross was in charge and that under normal circumstances you'd ask him, except he was killed in a hit and run accident Friday night."

"Albert slowly shook his head, pursed his lips, and said, "And you think that's gonna be it? You think that we won't be covered up with Labor Department and Immigration folks crawling all over the place?"

Jared replied, "No, I think we will, but I also think that our contacts at Labor and Immigration will call us before they come. When they get here in a day or so, they'll ask a few questions about Jimmy Ross, ask if we know anything about these claims of sex trafficking, ask where the women are now and what farm they might have gone to.

"You'll say you have no idea where they are now, but you're trying to find out what the hell is going on. You'll say that according to Sheriff Haines, the company car that was at the house is also gone. You'll say that you have alerted Sheriff Hoots about the stolen car and that he's got his department looking for the car *and* the women, who undoubtedly stole the car."

Albert, a bit more relaxed, said, "Okay, Sherlock, where will they actually be?"

"A long fucking way from here, for sure. We need to get out there tonight and pack them up. I'm thinking we need to send them to a place at the other end of the state, but right now we need to move them somewhere that's secluded and far away from nosy neighbors. We probably know…"

Albert held up his hand and said, "Shut up and let me think." After a few minutes he raised his head and said, "I've got it. The trailer on the farm in Redmond. The one where the Puente girl killed the whore. It's in the middle of a Georgia Pacific pine forest. No neighbors—and it's got a barn where we can hide the car until we can get rid of it."

Dante said, "I'll call Ramon. We can pick him up and take him to the Elliot place, get the girls, and drive them to the Redmond trailer. You say there's a barn at the trailer?"

Albert nodded.

"Okay, he can put the car in the barn, then stay there until you figure out where to send them."

"What if someone is watching the Elliot house when we go out there?"

"At eleven thirty on a Saturday night? You're overreacting."

Albert leaned back in his chair. "Okay, so they're gone. What do we say when the Immigration guys ask what farm they went to? What…"

Jared held up his hand. "Hold on, Ruff. Let me think." He got up and walked over to the window looking out over the darkened downtown, then said, "We'll say we don't have a fucking clue. Apparently, Jimmy Ross and Luca Castro had them here as part of a sex-trafficking scheme that we have only now been made aware of. We'll say that our records show that we got them visas for work on a farm that no longer needed them, and that Jimmy said he was looking for somewhere else to send them. We're just as confused as they are, and as a matter of fact, we're looking for them ourselves. Since we got the visas in the first place, we have some responsibility in helping to find them. We'll tell Immigration that we'll give them all the help we can."

He closed the window blinds, then turned to face Dante and Albert. "Albert, we can diffuse this whole mess if we stay calm and use our heads. Jimmy and Luca are both dead. The two Mexican drivers are dead. Valeria is dead. Sam Elliot knows nothing about nothing. There's nobody left who has any connection to the women and none of the women have ever seen or talked to either you or me."

Albert interjected, "Well, they probably saw me in the car this morning, but Dante did all the talking. Did you tell them who was in the car, Dante?"

"No, and they didn't ask. I just told the older woman that we would be moving them soon and not to worry. She seemed a little perturbed about Valeria going back to Mexico, but quickly got over it. She probably thinks that this could be good for her. She seemed pretty calm when we left."

Jared continued, "We won't have a hard time at all finding a compliant farmer to take them in." He turned his head toward Albert. "Shit, I just had a brainstorm. We can send them to old man Becher's place near Sparta. We send him dozens of men every year to work on his Christmas trees. He has a huge operation with tons of Mexicans, men and women. He runs at least three labor camps stuck back in the hollers of Alleghany and Ashe Counties. We can park the women there until we come up with something better. They won't talk—they're too afraid of what might happen to their families in Mexico."

Albert said, "What about Will Moser? He's obviously still looking for the Delgado girl."

"Probably, but that's not our biggest worry right now. Having the state authorities nosing around is our biggest problem, and that's why we need to get Dante out of here. Obviously, I'll need to straighten things out on the home front, but Eunice won't mind. I'll tell her that taking the RV to Mexico will give me time to discuss our recruiting needs with Dante, plus I'll have a place to sleep while I'm there. I'll say that I need to check on our operations at Manpower Solutions in Monterrey and will be home in a few weeks. If Dante and I leave tomorrow morning, we should be in McAllen by sometime late Monday." Jared looked at Dante, "That sound right?"

Dante nodded, then said, "I'll need to spend a little time with Ramon. We can talk tonight on the trip to Elliot's place. He'll need to call young Simon and tell him that he had to go somewhere and will be in touch in a day or so. He should probably call him tomorrow morning or early afternoon. I'm guessing Richie will be greatly relieved. As you said, if we leave early tomorrow, we should be in McAllen by Monday afternoon or evening. I'll alert my people in McAllen to have the border guards ready. Are you sure that that Becher fellow will let us park the whores at his place?"

Albert nodded. "I haven't told you this, but when you asked about shipping marijuana into the States, I told you that we didn't need it. That was because Robert Becher grows so much weed on his Christmas tree farms that we can supply all of North Carolina and most of South Carolina with Grade A marijuana. He grows the stuff right beside the trees, almost in the branches, and has a group of Mexicans who prune and harvest the plants. The sheriff in Ashe County is on his payroll, so Becher stores the stuff there. Believe me, he'll do whatever we ask him to do."

Jared said, "We, and by this I mean you, Dante, need to tell Richie to keep his mouth shut if anybody happens to nose around out at his place. I know that Ramon has been our contact with Richie, but it's you that he's most afraid of. If you tell him to keep quiet, I guarantee he will. Ramon has a Simon Farms phone, so you can tell Richie that if he has any questions he can call Ramon."

Albert stood up, "Gentlemen, it's eleven forty-five. You need to pick up Ramon and get the whores to the trailer. Let's meet here tomorrow morning at seven."

Jared stood up and said, "Make it six, Albert. I'm thinking that Dante and I need to get on the road by seven. You know damn well that when Sheriff Haines goes out to the Elliot place and sees that the whores are gone, he's gonna throw a shit fit. I'd just as soon get outta here before the State and maybe Federal Immigration people descend on Beulah."

Albert nodded.

Jared added, "Dante, I'll drive us to the Simon Farm. You call Ramon and tell him we're on our way. When we get the whores, Ramon can follow us in the NCFC Suburban to Redmond. You can fill Ramon in while we're driving from the Simon Farm to the Elliot place. He can stay with them until we get someone to drive them to old man Becher's farm in Alleghany county, then head back to Rich's for a day or two."

Dante looked at the other two men and said, "Boys, I do this kind of shit all the time, don't worry about it. We'll be outta here at first light tomorrow, and Jared will be sunning himself in beautiful Mexico by Tuesday afternoon." He then focused on Albert. "And you'll be having fun with the State Labor Department, the US Immigration authorities, possibly the State Bureau of Investigation, and the always-pleasant Sheriff William Moser, his own self."

Albert stood stony-faced without even the hint of a smile as Dante, a smirk on his face, brushed past him.

Sunday
September 29th

DAY EIGHT

Sunday

2:00 a.m.

Will looked at his bedside clock… two a.m., then picked up the receiver. "Yeah."

"Will, it's Eli. I just got off the phone with Olan Rizzo. The rats are getting ready to jump ship. But first, I gotta tell you about a call from Dan McReady, my commo guy at Guardian. He recorded a call made by Sam Elliot to Albert at 11:10 last night. Sam was apparently trashed and yelling at Albert about prostitutes in one of his houses and your and Ed Haines's visit yesterday afternoon. He said that Ed was calling the Immigration people and that Albert better do something about it."

"What did Albert say? Did he…?"

"Hold on. Albert said nothing incriminating. As expected, he told Sam that the women were field workers and supposed to be sent to another farm. He said he didn't know anything about any prostitutes and would straighten it out tomorrow. Dan expected that Albert would make a call right after that, but nothing. No call out or in.

"As I was speaking to Dan, I got a call from Olan Rizzo. He said that he was in his room at the motel when he saw Albert show up, closely followed by Jared Hill and Dante Sandoval. He said they were meeting in the NCFC offices as we spoke. I told him to wait until they left and then call me. About thirty minutes later he called and said that the party was breaking up.

"I told him to get in his car and see who seemed to be in the biggest hurry. He said that Albert headed toward his house, but the other two headed out of town. I told him to stay far back but follow the other two for as long as it took. He called me on my cell about twenty minutes ago and said that he was sitting on a dirt road in Redmond County looking across a field at a trailer about a half-mile away.

"Jared and Dante went by the Simon Farm and picked up someone, undoubtedly Ramon Castile, drove to the Elliot Farm in Smith County and picked up the women and the NCFC Suburban, then drove to the farm in Redmond county where Rizzo is now sitting. I told him to stay out of sight, keep his lights off, and keep me informed."

Will said, "Holy shit. We need to tell Ed Haines and Thomas Pierce, the sheriff in Redmond County, about this. Ed already knows that one of the whores is in his jail, but I guarantee he doesn't know that the others have been moved, and Thomas needs to know that they're now in his jurisdiction. I..."

Eli broke in. "Wait a minute! I understand the protocol, but if we call them now, we may fuck up our chance to find Maria. You need to find out from Rich what is going on first. I can have Olan keep an eye out at the trailer. He... Wait, he's calling me. I'll call you right back."

Will hung up and got out of bed. Lana sat up and said, "What?"

Will rubbed his eyes, "That was Eli. It looks like Albert knows we found the whores and they've already moved them. They took them to a trailer in Redmond County. I think I should call Ed Haines or Thomas..." His phone rang.

"Shoot."

"Okay, Olan said that Jared and Dante have both left and are headed back to Beulah, meaning that Ramon Castile is with the whores. I told him that we would have eyes on the trailer first thing in the morning and for him to head back to Beulah so he can keep an eye on Albert and the NCFC building. I told him to make sure to use a back stairway to get to his room in case the night clerk at the motel thinks something fishy is going on."

Will said, "I'll call both Ed and Thomas first thing in the morning and let them know about the trailer. I'll tell Thomas to put eyes on the trailer first thing in the morning and to keep it under wraps.

"Thomas is a good man. He was Special Forces, so he knows how to stay hidden. In the meantime, we need to keep an eye out for Jared, Dante, and Albert."

Eli replied, "Olan will call if anything changes, but I suspect they believe they've solved their problem for now."

"I hope so. Anyway, I'll try and get a few more hours of sleep then call you in the a.m."

"Right. I'll do the same."

Will looked at his wife and said, "Well, in the words of Colonel Kahn, the rats are getting ready to abandon ship."

Sunday

6:00 a.m.

Will's alarm went off at six a.m. He was in the bathroom, having been awake for over an hour thinking about the night's events, so he didn't hear it at first. He realized it was buzzing when Lana yelled, "Yo, Sheriff, time to get up!" He walked back into the bedroom and said, "Sorry, I've been awake for a while and forgot to turn it off."

"No kidding. I guess I gotta get up now."

"Not if you don't want to. I can go to Richie's by myself."

"Yeah, I know, but since I've met him before and know his mom pretty well, maybe I can be a calming influence. Give me a few minutes."

"No rush. I don't think we need to get there too early. I'm gonna make a phone call to make sure he's still there. If he is, then I don't think we need to get there before about eight. What say we go to Mid Island for breakfast?"

"Splendid idea."

Will walked over and picked up the phone and dialed Richie's number. After a half-dozen rings, a very groggy Rich Simon answered.

"Yeah."

Will smiled and said, "Rufus, you ready?"

Rich, halfway out of a dream, replied, "There ain't no fucking Rufus here! What fucking time…?"

Will said, "Sorry," and hung up. He and Lana had driven by Rich's house the night before, but not seeing a car parked under the house, he decided to make the early morning call. Going over after breakfast was soon enough. He wanted Rich to be in a sleepy, but not comatose state.

At seven thirty he went downstairs where Lana had already brewed a pot of coffee.

"Thanks, hon. This'll get my heart pumping before I call Eli."

He sat down at the table and dialed home. "Morning, Colonel. Hope you slept well."

"I did. How about you?"

"No such luck, but I am having a cup of black, four-month-old Dunkin Donuts house blend coffee brewed by the nice lady staying with me. After a quick shower, we'll head over to the Mid Island Café in Wrightsville Beach for a freshly brewed cup of coffee and a world-class breakfast, then head over to Rich's around eight thirty. I called Sheriff Pierce and he's organizing a stakeout at the trailer."

"Have you done a recon of young Richie's? Are you sure he's there?"

"Yeah, I went by last night and he wasn't there; so I pulled the wrong number routine this morning at six a.m. He's there, all right, and I imagine in a foul mood. We'll go by after we've had something to eat."

Will emptied a pack of Splenda into his coffee, stirred it around, and after thinking how he wanted to say it, said, "Colonel, does this McReady fellow…"

Eli anticipated what was coming, so he cut him off in mid-sentence. "Will, I told you, we're very good at this. No one can trace anything we're doing, so stop worrying. Hell, the government is the one who trained us."

"Okay, okay. Just be careful. I'll call you when I leave Richie's."

Sunday

6:10 a.m.

Maria sat on the floor of the trailer with her back against the wall. Her left eye was bloodshot and partially closed after being knocked out by Dante at the convenience store, and her face was still bruised from her beating by Jose during her trip with Julietta. Hope had drained from her soul, and the reality of her situation had begun to settle in.

She realized that she was in big trouble. These men weren't the errand boys she'd encountered before. The Luca Castros and Jimmy Rosses of the world were back on the bench and the first team had taken over. She tried to think how long it had been since she left that sunny, hope-filled day in Monterrey, but time had run together. Her new friend had been killed, and she had been forced to murder another human being. She kept telling herself that hope never dies, but she was having a hard time believing it now.

The door to her room opened, revealing the man who had tried to grab her at the convenience store. Behind him was the other man, the one who had knocked her out. Fear tightened its grip as the two men entered the room.

"We're going on a little trip, Miss Puente. We need to move you to the vehicle that's gonna take you home. Get up. Let's go." Maria didn't move.

Jared shook his head and said, "You know, you're a brave young woman, but you ain't too smart. You've already taken a few beatings, so you must know that if you don't cooperate you're just gonna get roughed up again. Why don't you be a smart girl and get up."

Maria knew he was right, but still, why not try to make his life miserable?

"Fuck you."

Jared turned to Dante. "Grab her feet. I'll take her hands."

The two bent over, picked Maria up, and carried her out of the trailer and over to the RV next to it. They opened the door and hauled her into the bedroom in the back. She was already wearing a pair of handcuffs, so they dropped her onto the floor and padlocked a chain fastened to the base of the bed to her cuffs, then tied a rope around her feet.

Jared opened a bottle of pills and shook a couple into his hand. "These will make you sleep, making the trip go a little faster."

She looked at him, her eyes huge, "What is that?" she demanded.

"It's phenobarbital. My wife uses it on one of her Labradors who has occasional epileptic fits. Basically, they're some strong-ass drugs that'll knock you right out."

"I won't take it."

Jared looked at Dante. "Dante, we gotta treat this bitch like one of my wife's dogs. You grab her head and open her mouth. I'll put a stick in her mouth crossways so she can't close, then we'll put the pills down her throat and massage 'em down."

Dante looked at Jared. "Jared, that's bullshit. Let's just knock her out and stick 'em down her throat."

Jared rolled his eyes. "Dante, if she ain't awake, then alls that will happen is they'll get lodged in her throat and she'll cough 'em out when she comes to. Just do what the fuck I tell you. I've done this with Eunice's Labs a dozen times. When they're down her throat some ways, I'll pour in some water, rub her throat, and she'll have to swallow the fucking pills 'cause of the water."

Maria closed her eyes, and when Dante opened her mouth so

Jared could put a stick across her teeth at the back, she bit down as hard as she could just before Jared got the stick into her mouth.

"Motherfucker!" yelled Dante as he pulled his hand back. "The bitch about bit my fucking finger off."

With that, Dante hit Maria with his fist against the side of her head. Jared, seeing that she was momentarily dazed, put the stick across her mouth and pushed the pills down her throat. Almost at the same time, Dante poured a half bottle of water down her throat causing her to gag, but also to swallow the water—and the pills.

The two men stood up, Dante shaking his hand and cursing while Jared checked the handcuffs and chain.

Dante sucked the blood off of his finger and said, "I tell you one thing, Mr. Hill. Killing this bitch is gonna be a pleasure."

Sunday

6:30 a.m.

When Albert came into the office with his cup of coffee, Jared and Dante were already there.

Without any greeting, Albert sat down, took a sip, and started to say something when Jared held up his hand. "Ruff, before you say anything, you ought to know that we may have another problem. When we picked up the whores at the Elliot place last night, we learned that one of the young women had run away.

"The older woman said that sometime after eleven, she was told by one of the girls that Trissa, the youngest of the girls, had taken off. She said none of the other girls knew anything about it beforehand. As they were going to bed, this girl said she wasn't sleepy and was gonna stay up for a while longer. She said she was gonna get some air outside. The other girls said they didn't pay any attention until a half hour later when she didn't come back into the house.

"We asked if any of the girls knew where she might have gone, but they all said no. We're guessing that she panicked after the sheriff showed up and just took off. I don't think it will be a serious problem since she doesn't speak any English and doesn't know anyone around here. She's probably just wandering around trying to figure out how to get home."

Dante added, "We have her name and our people in Mexico

will straighten it out. It won't affect our plans for getting the Puente girl outta here."

Albert snarled, "Well, why not? Everything else has been fucked up. Where's the RV?"

"Behind the maintenance shed," Jared replied. "We tied the girl up in the bedroom and gave her a heavy dose of phenobarbital. I gotta tell you; I'll be glad when we're shed of that girl. She ain't nothin but trouble. Anyway, we'll be ready to go just as soon as we make sure we're all on the same track."

"Okay, so what's our track?"

Dante said, "I've talked to my people in McAllen, and they're set for us to arrive sometime Monday afternoon or night. Staying on the interstates will be safe since no Immigration folks are likely to come nosing around here until sometime late tomorrow or Tuesday. Taking 95 South, then I-20 to Atlanta, 85 to Montgomery, 65 to Mobile, and then I-10 to Houston will be the quickest route.

"From Houston we can head to Corpus, and then straight south about 165 miles into McAllen. We shouldn't have to stop but two or maybe three times for fuel. I figure somewhere around Montgomery, Alabama, for our first fill-up, and then again around Houston. That ought to take us to McAllen. We'll stop to switch driving duties whenever we need to and probably a few times for a decent meal. I've got a 9mm and an AR15 in case of any unforeseen problems."

Jared said, "I'll have my cell, Ruff, but don't figure to use it unless it's something important. Have you talked to Robert Becher yet?"

Albert took a long swig of coffee and said, "Talked to him this morning. I'd say he wasn't real pleased with the idea, but after a bit of convincing, came 'round to our way of thinking.

"This afternoon I'll have Rico Mendez drive the Everlasting Kingdom activities bus to the trailer and load up the whores, then drive them to Becher's place in Ashe County. Ramon and I will follow him to the trailer in my truck, and after he leaves, I'll have Ramon follow me in the NCFC Suburban back to Rich's place where he can stay until the Monterrey bus goes on Wednesday.

"I'll make sure he calls Rich at the beach and tells him that he'll be leaving on Wednesday, so Rich should stay in Wrightsville until then." Albert paused and opened the bottom drawer of his desk, taking out a bottle of Jack Daniels. After pouring some into his coffee, he looked at Jared with a dour expression and said, "Since I'm sure Sheriff Haines, and probably that asshole Will Moser, will call the Immigration people, I'll prepare myself for a lot of bullshit questions while you're sunning your lazy ass in Mexico."

Jared didn't bother to reply, only stood up and turned toward the door. "Ruff, as the big dog, you gotta be the one doin' the barking."

Albert didn't bother to get up as Dante and Jared left the room.

Sunday

8:05 a.m.

Will parked across the street from the house in the space Rich maintained for his boat dock and gazebo. The house was a typical North Carolina beach retreat: three stories high with a porch on the second level above an open carport. The porch and living quarters were ten feet above ground level as protection from the devastating surge of water that often accompanied the increasingly frequent hurricanes that blew up the South Atlantic coast.

Will and Lana climbed the stairs to the porch above the garage and knocked on the front door. Nothing. Will knocked again, but louder and longer. Within a minute or so he heard from inside, "Who the fuck is banging on my door at this goddamn hour?"

"Mr. Simon, I need to speak with you."

Rich came to the door and looked at Will through the glass panel. "Who the hell…?"

"It's William Moser, and I'm…"

"I know who the fuck you are! What do you want?"

"I'm here about a young woman who is missing. Please open the door. I won't take much time."

Rich opened the door halfway, but blocked Will's entry. Lana stood behind Will and to his right.

"How the hell am I supposed to know where some girl is? I'm

a fucking farmer and nobody who works for me is missing. Sorry, but I can't help you."

"Mr. Simon, can we discuss this inside? I just need ten or fifteen minutes."

"Like I said, Sheriff, I don't know nothing about no missing girl. Now please leave." Rich tried to close the door, but Will put his hand out to keep it open.

"That's fine, then perhaps your friends Dante Sandoval or Ramon Castile can help me."

With that, Rich's expression went from anger to horror.

"Wha', uhm, what the hell are you talking about?"

"Your friends, Dante Sandoval and Ramon Castile, of the Mexican drug and human-trafficking cartel the Olmecs. You know, the gentlemen who are presently at your place of business discussing a possible distribution system for their products."

Rich swayed backward as if he was about to faint. He closed his eyes and put his hand over his forehead while emitting low guttural sounds, almost groans.

Will put his hand on Rich's shoulder, "Why don't we go inside? I think we're going to be more comfortable talking there."

Rich stepped backward, a look of panic and disbelief on his face. As Will opened the door, Lana stepped forward, "Good morning, Richard. I hope you don't mind. I drove Will here."

Richie didn't say anything, only backpedaled into the living room.

"Very nice, Rich," Will said as he entered the room. "Is this yours or your folks'?" Richie didn't say anything as he walked over to a large upholstered chair beside the fireplace and sat down. Will continued to walk around the room, taking in the books and bric-a-brac that filled the shelves. Lana sat down in the chair farthest from Richie.

"Somebody really loves conch shells," Will said as he passed the last shelf.

When he got to the large sliding-glass doors that opened onto the ocean side porch, he said, "You know, Lana and I have a place north of here at Figure Eight Island. Do you know…?" Without finishing, Will turned to see if Rich was still there. He hadn't said a word, but was sitting in his chair gripping the arms so hard that his knuckles had turned white. And the look on his face was abject terror as he stared out to sea.

Will sat down in the armchair across from Rich and to the right of Lana. "Rich, like I said, we're here to find a young woman who was supposed to be on one of AmTex's buses early last week but never showed up. The truth is, I don't think you know anything about her disappearance, at least I hope you don't; however, I think you do know something about what Misters Waters, Hill, and Sandoval are meeting about, and we believe they are the ones who may be holding Miss Puente, the missing girl."

Rich started to say something, but Will held up his hand. "Let me finish. On Friday, I was visited by an old friend who has offered his assistance in finding the missing girl. My friend has access to an unlimited amount of information and resources. I can't disclose who he is, but take my word for it, his capacity to assist is formidable.

"He is the reason I know so much about Dante Sandoval and Ramon Castile. He is the reason I know about your past problems in Mexico. He is the reason that we have a very good chance of finding the young lady; however, we currently lack the information that ties Albert Waters, Hill, and Sandoval to our missing person. We believe they've taken her because she knows something which can be harmful to their plans, thus perhaps to yours… Rich. We know that they're involved in sex trafficking, but don't believe you are. We assume they're using information about your problems in Mexico in order to force you to cooperate with their future plans."

Will paused when he saw Rich lean forward in his chair, lower his head, and begin to cry. When Rich sat back up, Will said, "Take a minute. I'm sorry. That's a lot on you all at once."

Rich wiped his eyes and again looked at Will then at Lana.

"Dr. Moser, do my parents know what the sheriff is talking about?"

Lana shook her head. "No, Richard. That's why the sheriff is here. We want to find the young girl but don't want to involve you or Ruby and Mr. Simon in this mess."

Richie cleared his throat and said, "Everything you've said is true. I know nothing about a young girl being kidnapped. I know nothing about sex trafficking, but I do know that Dante and Ramon have talked to Albert Waters and Jared Hill about the possibility of distributing drugs.

"Sheriff Moser, I never planned on any of this. Yes, I got into trouble in Mexico along with Germaine Sandoval. Yes, he and his brother have incriminating evidence, pictures and court records, but you gotta understand that if that was all, I would refuse; however, they not only have threatened to show these things to my parents, but have threatened harm to them if I don't cooperate. You gotta understand who these people are! You gotta understand that when they say something about harming my mother and father, they aren't kidding. That's how they conduct business. You don't know…"

Will held up his hand and stood. It was clear that Rich had surrendered any attempt at noncooperation. He was in shock.

"Rich, I believe you, and I promise that as much as I can, I will help you, but right now I need to find that girl before they do something to her. You obviously know what they're capable of, so I don't need to explain what 'do something' means. What are

Dante's plans? Why is he here and how long did Ramon say he was staying?"

Rich took a deep breath and leaned back, relaxing for the first time. After a minute he said, "I saw Dante a few days ago. When I asked Ramon why he was here, he said that he had business with Albert Waters and Jared Hill. Ramon knows that Dante makes me really nervous, so he said something like, 'If Dante being here makes you so nervous, why don't you leave town for a while?' I didn't really like the idea of him staying at the farm while I would be away, but he said that he was just gonna spend a little more time with my foreman trying to understand our operation.

"When I said that I might have some things that needed looking after at the beach, he said it would be a good idea for me to go. He seemed as anxious for me to leave just as I was. When I said that my parents might need something, he said that if anything came up, he would call me, and I could come back. He, and maybe Dante, obviously wanted me out of town for a few days. When I asked how long they were gonna be here, he said, 'I don't know, probably early or middle of next week.'"

"How did Dante get here?"

"I don't know—I figure he flew into Raleigh from Mexico. He's staying at Mr. Hill's, so I guess he picked him up."

"Rich, have you heard anything about how he plans on going back to Mexico?"

"No, but Ramon came on one of NCFC's buses, so I'd guess that's how he'll leave. When I talked to Ramon yesterday, he said he…"

Will held up his hand. "How do you communicate with Ramon?"

"He's got a Simon Farms cell phone that I gave him when he came last week. I told him…"

Again, Will held up his hand. "I need that number, Rich."

Rich looked a bit startled, then said, "Sure, it's 910-444-6000."

Will picked up his phone and called Eli. "Eli, give Mr. McReady another number; 910-444-6000, I'll explain later."

With that, he picked up his hat and motioned to Lana. They started toward the door. Will said, "Rich, stay here and wait to hear from me. We may want you to call your foreman at the farm and find out where Ramon is and if he's doing anything strange. But you have to sound calm, like you're just curious… no panic or worry in your voice. Can you do that?"

"Absolutely, but I won't call until I hear from you."

"Good. Have you got a pencil and paper, Rich?"

Rich went to the shelves and got a pad of paper and pen. Will said, "Write down my cell as well as Henry Grier's, my chief deputy. Then write down your cell plus the house number here." Rich wrote down all the numbers, gave his to Will, and kept the rest. As he was finishing, Rich looked up and said, "Sheriff, I'm sorry about the girl. Who is she?"

"I can't say, but you would know her family."

Rich got up and walked to the door with Will and Lana. "Sheriff, if you can please check on my parents? I know we're not in your district, but I can't ask Sheriff Hoots to do it. He's paid off by Albert Waters."

"You're right about that, Rich. I'll see what I can do." Lana put her hand on Rich's arm as she paused at the door. "Richard, I'll call on Ruby today. It's about time for Purdy to get his distemper shots, so it won't seem strange to your mom or dad." She looked at Will then back at Richie. "I, of course, can't say anything about what we've just been talking about, but I can make sure everything is okay with your folks. I'll keep an eye out for any trouble. I always have a reason to be at your folks' house."

Richie smiled for the first time. "Thank you, Dr. Moser. That makes me feel a lot better."

Will opened the door and turned as he walked out. "Don't panic, Rich. We'll get to the bottom of this, but no matter what, don't say anything to Ramon if he calls. Just act like nothing is happening."

"I will, Sheriff, and thank you."

As Will walked down the steps and headed for his car his phone rang. "Moser."

"Will, it's Eli. Where are you?'

He turned and smiled at Rich, who was standing on his porch. "We're just leaving Rich Simon's house at the beach. What's up?"

"Can you talk?"

"Yeah, just a second." He put the phone to his side and walked across the street to his car. He got in and closed the door, turning slightly to his right as if he was speaking to Lana. Rich was still standing on his porch looking down at them.

Will put the phone back to his ear. "Okay, I'm private. What's up?"

"I went over to the motel talk to Olan a few hours ago, and don't worry, I went up the back stairs so no one saw me. I wanted to listen to the tape he tried to make of the conversations at last night's meeting at NCFC to see if I could make out anything. No luck there; so, I fast-forwarded to about six this morning, but again, nothing. Anyway, what did you find out?"

Will said, "Well, everything we thought about Rich and the Sandoval-Albert Waters connection is true. They're looking to use his farm as a distribution point. He said he doesn't know anything about sex trafficking or whorehouses or a kidnapped young woman, and I believe him. After about ten minutes of pretty tough talk, I told him that we're looking for a young woman who we think has been kidnapped. I said we're desperately trying to find her. When I asked if he had any idea of where they might have taken her or how they might plan on moving her, he drew a blank. The number I gave you is for a Simon Farms cell phone that Rich gave to Ramon last week. Your commo guy needs to put that into your system. I have a feeling that if Ramon is in Redmond County with the whores, then he will be in contact with Dante and maybe Richie pretty soon."

Eli replied, "Already done. Have you spoken to Sheriffs Haines or Pierce yet?"

"Yeah, I talked to Thomas Pierce early this morning and he's got some undercover guys checking out the trailer. They're dressed in Georgia Pacific uniforms and headquartered in a small metal building near the road to the trailer. As a matter of fact, they said that the guy from Georgia Pacific who opened the building for them said that it looked like someone had recently been in there. I told Thomas to keep me informed, but not to move in unless they tried to leave the trailer.

"I also talked to Ed Haines and asked him to hold off talking to the Immigration people until we have more info. He said he had talked to the runaway female in his jail but got nothing new. He was really pissed when I told him about Jared and Albert moving the women last night. He started yelling about calling Immigration right then, but I calmed him down. I told him to go out to the Elliot place like nothing had happened, and then to call Sam and yell at him. He said it would be a pleasure and easy to do since he was really pissed. I imagine when he does, Sam will call Albert and hopefully your commo guy will find out something."

Eli said, "I'll keep checking with McReady, but he knows to call me with anything interesting." After a brief pause, he added, "Will, there's something else you ought to be aware of. Early this morning your housekeeper came into the kitchen where I was having a mug of coffee and said there was a snake on the back porch. I asked her if it was alive. She said no, that it looked dead. I asked where, and she said it was in front of the back door. She said there've been snakes around before but this one was different. When I asked what she meant, she said, "You gotta see for yourself, Colonel." I told her to stay in the kitchen, that I would check it out.

"Will, it's pretty clear that you're getting under the skin of Albert and his Mexican buddies. When I opened the back door, I saw what I assume is a dead water moccasin laying on the floor, but this one had a couple of feathers in its mouth and five or six tied around its neck."

Will said, "What the fuck does that mean, Eli?"

"It's a message from the Olmecs. The feathered serpent appeared in ancient Olmec art and later in the Aztec culture. The Aztecs called it Quetzalcoatl, and it was one of their most powerful deities. The cartel uses it as a warning; kinda like in the *Godfather* when one of the men comes into the kitchen with a fish wrapped in a newspaper."

Will imagined the snake on his back porch with a band of feathers around its body. His temperature started to rise. "Like I said, what does it mean? Is somebody dead?"

"No, but it does mean that Dante or Ramon wants you to back off. Like I said, it's a warning."

Will opened the car door and got out. He walked to the gazebo in front of Rich's house and looked out over the harbor behind Wrightsville Beach. His breathing had become more rapid. He was still holding the phone but hadn't said anything for a minute or so. Lana got out and walked over to his side. She said, "What?"

Will just looked at her, shaking his head.

Eli said, "Will, you still there?"

Will looked at Lana then cleared his throat and said, "Yeah, I'm here. I'm just considering what to do about their warning. I've been threatened lots of times. My family has received threats. But

I've never considered those as much more than some pissed-off citizen, probably drunk—or more likely a damn coward trying to make themselves feel tough. This is different. This is serious. This, I take personally."

Eli cut him off. "Hold on, Will. It's just a cheap trick. I imagine Dante had one of the men who came to town on the bus slip over to your house last night and throw the snake onto the porch. They don't have the muscle up here to do anything; plus, I've got some men from Guardian coming over this morning. Remember, you're a client now and I've never lost a client."

Will took a deep breath and said, "I'll tell Hank to check my in-house security cameras and see if they recorded anything. Anyway, I'm coming home right now. Keep me informed and I'll talk to Hank on the way back. I'll have him call Wimbley Johnson and see if he's heard anything; plus I'll check in with Sheriffs Haines and Pierce again.

"But Eli, if they want to play *Godfather*, fine. Let's find their prize horse."

Sunday

12:00 p.m.

Will got back to Mussel Ford by midday and called Eli to meet him at his office for lunch. Lana took the car home and said she'd call Ruby Simon that afternoon, then would call Will if Ruby mentioned anything amiss.

Janice brought in sandwiches and a couple of local beers. As they were eating, Eli recounted his earlier conversation with Olan Rizzo. Olan had little new information, but he'd seen Albert go into his office early that morning. Olan added that if Jared or Dante was with Albert, he hadn't seen them. Other than a few very early trucks and cars on their way to work, there hadn't been any downtown activity until later.

Will was recounting his conversation with Rich Simon when his phone rang.

He put it on speaker.

"Go, Thomas."

Sheriff Pierce said, "Will, we got some activity out here. As you know, I sent two deputies dressed as Georgia Pacific timber workers out to a little metal shed on the road just down from the trailer entrance road. About ten minutes ago my chief deputy, Fred Fowler, called and said that a church activity bus just drove past his location and turned onto the trailer road. A minute behind that, a pickup, driven by your friend Albert Waters, followed the bus to the trailer.

I sent my other deputy through the pines to a spot in the woods just opposite the trailer. He said he was twenty feet inside the pines on the other side of a bean field, so was invisible to the people at the trailer but close enough to see what was going on. Fred… Hold on. Will, I'll call you right back."

Will clicked off the phone and looked at Eli.

"So, what do you make of that?"

Eli shook his head and said, "I'd say that Albert is getting ready to ship the fair damsels to some distant location. It might not be a bad idea to have Sheriff Pierce interdict the bus and bring the women to his offices for a few questions. I'll bet a few of them would like to join their already-escaped friend. Like her, I bet most of these girls aren't here by choice." He stopped when the phone rang.

Will hit the speaker button. "Yeah, Thomas."

"Will, Fred says the bus is loaded with that bunch of women and is starting to head out. Albert and another man are still there but look like they're also getting ready to leave. What do you want to do?"

"Thomas, where are you?"

"I'm sitting a few miles down the road at a small gas station and store."

"Are you in a patrol car?"

"Yeah."

"How about your chief deputy."

"He has his own pickup."

"Okay, have your deputy follow Albert and the other man when they leave. Tell him to stay way back but see where they go. I think the fellow with Albert is here legally but is part of that Mexican cartel I told you about. I don't know who's driving the bus, but I imagine it's somebody who works for Albert."

Thomas said, "Will, I've got another deputy riding with me,

so we'll stop the bus and haul the whole bunch to our lovely jail here in Redmond. I can't remember the last time I had a jail full of hookers."

Will continued, "Can your deputy who was in the trees across from the trailer get back to the metal shed to go with your chief? I'd prefer to have two men following Albert."

"No problem, I already told him to come back to the shed. He's probably already there. I'll stay in touch and let you know where Albert and the other fellow go."

"Thanks, Thomas. Good job. Maybe we can start to clean up this damn human-trafficking mess."

"Will do."

Will leaned back in his chair and just as he started to say something, Eli's phone rang.

"Go."

"Colonel, it's McReady. You got a minute?" Eli put his phone on the desk and turned on the speaker.

"I'm here. You're on speaker with me and Sheriff Moser."

"Okay. I just recorded a call from Ramon Castile to Rich Simon. Ramon told Richie that he was going back to Mexico on the Wednesday bus, so Rich should stay in Wrightsville until then. He said he would get in touch with him within a few weeks.

"Rich then asked about Dante, and Ramon said he'd already left, adding that Dante and Jared Hill should be in Mexico by Monday night or Tuesday. Rich asked where he was, and Ramon said he was following Albert Waters and was on his way back to Rich's farm. He said he wanted to spend tomorrow working at the shipping operation, so Rich should have his foreman spend the day with him answering his questions. Rich didn't say anything after that."

"Ramon didn't say how Dante and Jared were traveling, did he?"

"No."

Will said, "Mr. McReady, can you tell where Ramon was?"

"Yes sir, within a certain area."

"Where did he call from?"

"Somewhere in Redmond County. I'd say on the southern border with Smith County."

"Anything else?"

"A call this morning, about ten thirty from Sam Elliot to Albert's office, was like the one last night. Sam was yelling about a call from Sheriff Haines, who told him that the women weren't at the house any longer and asked did he know where they were. Sam raged on about what the fuck was going on, and Albert finally told him to shut up. He said that the women had been sent to their new workplace, so there wouldn't be any immigration nonsense. That seemed to pacify Sam."

"Thanks, Dan. Keep listening."

Eli turned off the phone and looked at Will. "On the way, huh. Jared and Dante are driving to Mexico. That's the only safe way to get Maria out of the country and I'll guarantee they're not in one of AmTex's buses, but they may be in one of the in-state vans. Any way to get an inventory of NCFC's vehicles? And while we're at it, let's find out how many cars Albert Waters and Jared Hill own personally, and if possible where they are."

Will started to say something when Hank knocked on the door. "Sheriff, you wanted to see me?"

Will looked up, "Hank, you heard anything from Wimbley?"

"Nothing. I talked to him last night and said for him to see if his wife could find out anything from her friend at NCFC, but I haven't heard anything today."

Will said, "We just got off the phone with Eli's man at Guardian. He just recorded a phone conversation between Richie and

Ramon. Ramon said that Jared Hill and Dante have left for Mexico and should arrive by Monday night. This means they're driving. Call DMV and get an inventory of all vehicles registered to NCFC as well as to Albert Waters and Jared Hill personally. Also get the make of and license number for all the vehicles, plus a description of each."

"Right. Be right back."

Eli said, "Will, my guess is that they left either last night or early this morning, meaning they've got a long lead on us. I'm gonna call Adrian in Houston and tell him to stay close to a phone because we may need some manpower on the road looking for that car or truck or whatever."

Will nodded. "Let's hope Jared uses his phone so McReady can track 'im."

Within five minutes Hank came back in. "Gentlemen, they're working on the list of vehicles at NCFC. Albert Waters has a pickup and a Suburban. The Suburban is in his and his wife's name. Jared Hill has two vehicles registered to him—a BMW sedan and a GMC pickup. You need to have Olan check by NCFC, Albert's house, and the Hill's to see what's there and what's not."

Eli said, "I just spoke to Adrian in Houston, and told him to round up a half- dozen men."

Will replied, "Good, and he also needs to get hold of four or five vehicles. They should be different makes, models, and colors. We need to set up a picket line on the highways along their probable route. Eli, I'm guessing the route you described, I-95 or I-20 to Atlanta, 85 to Montgomery, 65 to Mobile, and I-10 to Houston, is the one they'll take, and if they've already gone then we probably should try and intercept them somewhere in Alabama or maybe Texas. There's no reason for them to speed since they probably believe they have plenty of time."

Eli said, "If we're right, then their crossing point into Mexico will be through Brownsville or McAllen."

Will got up and went to the door. "Janice, if you don't mind, I could use a cup of high-test coffee." He looked at Eli and Hank, "You guys want any?"

Eli said, "Silly question. Of course, I want some. I was in the Army for twenty years, remember?" Hank just shook his head.

Will started to say something when his phone rang.

"Moser."

"Will, it's Lana. I just talked to Ruby Simon. She said they're okay, but she's taking Richard to the doctor this afternoon. He's getting worse. You find out anything about the girl?"

"No, but we did find out from a call between Ramon Castile and Richie that Jared Hill and Dante have left Beulah and are headed to Mexico. It's a sure bet that they've got the girl with them. We're trying to find out how they're traveling, so we're getting a list of all the cars registered to NCFC, Albert Waters, and Jared Hill. So far, not much. Albert has a pickup and a Suburban, and Jared Hill a BMW and a pickup. I don't think any of those seem like a smart way to transport a hostage. Hank is checking on what vehicles are registered to NCFC. He says that, according to our deputy friend in Jackson, no AmTex buses have left town in the last day, but it's highly unlikely that they'd take the girl on a bus anyway. We better find out something soon."

Lana nodded and said, "I just hope…" She stopped and said, "You said that the Hills have a BMW and a pickup?"

"Yeah."

"What about Mrs. Hill's RV?"

"What do you mean?" Will asked.

"Eunice Hill raises pedigreed Labs. She has an RV that she uses to cart them off to shows all over the country. I took care of her dogs for a while, but she's so lousy about paying her bills that I told her to find another vet."

Will said, "Well, if the Hills have an RV, it ain't registered under their name. What's the name of her kennel or dog business?"

"I think it's 'Labrador Hill.'"

Will looked at Hank, "Check with DMV and see if there's an RV registered to a company named 'Labrador Hill' or Eunice Hill." Hank nodded and left the room.

Will said, "Thanks, Lana. I'll fill you in when I learn anything."

He turned to Eli. "Eli, you know, I don't really want to wait to see if Jared uses his phone. Maybe we can force the issue. I have a good friend in Raleigh with the Commerce Department. I've known him for a long time—we can trust him. I could have him call NCFC and ask for Jared. He can say something about hearing rumors of human trafficking and wanting to see how they might have started. He can say that he knows Jared is responsible for the visa program, so would like to talk to him about the rumors. I'm guessing the NCFC folks will say Jared is unavailable, so maybe Albert could help. Whether Albert agrees to talk to him or not, I guarantee that Albert will call Jared, and when he does we should be able to track the call and confirm or negate your estimation of their route."

Eli nodded, and started to say something when Hank returned. He looked at the two men and said, "Bingo. There is a Newmar Mountain Aire RV registered to the 'Labrador Hill Kennels, LLC.' President and CEO, Eunice Hill. I've got the license plate number and vehicle description."

Will said, "Good. See if you can find out the specs on that model. Mileage, speed, fuel, anything helpful."

Eli said, "William, if it turns out that they're in the RV, we've got to have a plan on how to interdict. Remember Sun Tzu: 'Bad planning creates waste.' I need to call Adrian. I just wish I could be on-site. I have more tactical experience in this kind of operation than he does. I'd get one of Guardian's planes, but we got nothing but a single Pilatus in North Carolina, and I think it's being used for a DC trip. Shit."

Will leaned back in his chair and took a deep breath, "Civilian jurisdictions are my specialty, Colonel. We should both be there." He started to say something else when he stopped and, looking at Eli with a sly smile on his face and holding up his index finger, said, "Give me a minute."

He picked up the phone and dialed.

"Good afternoon, Doris, is Dooley in? It's Will."

After a brief pause, he said, "Dooley, Will. I need your help. I've got an emergency on my hands and need to use the plane. Right now. To Texas. I don't know, probably two days, maybe less. I can't tell you right now, but for the purpose of the flight log, let's say it's to visit Lone Star Resources about a lease on their land in New Hanover." Laughing he added, "I didn't say that was the emergency, only that that's what the logbook will say. I'm at the office… Okay, call me right back. And thanks."

He turned to Eli who had a curious look on his face and said, "That was my first cousin, Dooley Marshall. He's the CEO of Moser Mansfield Corp. I'm the Executive Chairman. One of the benefits of being the chairman of a company with a plane is that you often get to use the plane." Five minutes later the phone rang. "Moser… Yeah, great! Thanks Dooley… Houston. Hold on." Will turned to Eli, "Which airport?"

"Tell him, Ellington Airport, southeast of Houston."

"You hear that?" Will asked. "Okay, thanks… Yes, I promise. I'll call you back, probably within the hour… There'll be two passengers, me and Colonel Elijah Kahn. Yes, that Elijah Kahn… Yeah, I know. I wouldn't ask if it wasn't important… Thanks, Dooley. Tell Jimmy to call me when he's twenty minutes out… Okay, I will. Right, later."

Hank came into the office. "Like I said, the RV is a Newmar

Mountain Aire. It's a diesel and has a seventy-five-gallon fuel tank. The dealer in Raleigh says it gets about eight to ten miles per gallon, depending on how fast you drive. The Hill's RV is royal blue and white. You've got the license plate."

Will said, "Thanks, Hank. Stay close. Eli and I are going to Texas in about an hour, so you'll be in charge while we're gone. Keep your cell handy." Hank nodded and returned to his office.

Eli looked at Will. "Sheriff, not to be a bore, but you do realize that this might not be something done strictly by the book."

Cold, stone cold, was Will's expression. He looked at Eli as a mongoose studies a cobra before delivering the fatal blow. "Colonel, like I told you this morning. This is personal. You don't threaten my family. I haven't asked a lot of questions, nor have I ordered anyone to break the law, but the fact is, I'm sick and tired of these scumbags coming into my county and my state, bringing in drugs and prostitutes.

"I want Albert Waters and his ilk put away for good. They're sucking the blood out of this place, leaving it with dead migrant workers, enslaved prostitutes, and people vitiated by drugs. I already told you, I'm looking out from under the blindfold, Eli, and I hate what I see. So let's go to Texas and lance the boil infecting this country. And by the way, I wouldn't be at all surprised to hear on the news that a Mexican drug lord and his American partner were killed by rival gangs while in the US."

Sunday

4:30 p.m.

The Citation CJ3 touched down in Houston at 4:30 Central Daylight Time and taxied to the fixed-base facility at the south end of the airport. After the engines shut down and the stairs were lowered, Eli stepped out and was met by Adrian Gavalas.

"Señor Gavalas, I believe," Eli said as he descended the stairs.

Adrian smiled and stepped forward, "Eli, didn't think I'd see you so soon, but glad you made it!" As they shook hands he added, "We've got a good group. They're waiting for us in the situation room I've set up over at some NASA facilities."

"Good to know. So, who's on our team?" Eli asked.

"Well, first and foremost, Wesley Dunlap is the mission leader. He has six men, including himself. All have combat experience. Four as members of Special Ops and two combat medics. I think you've only met one of them, Sergeant Rob Wilde, whom you met in Iraq."

Eli turned as Will descended the stairs, "Adrian, meet Sheriff William Moser, known many years ago in the Mekong Delta as First Lieutenant Moser of the 18th Military Police Brigade. He is also the Chairman of the Board of Moser Mansfield Corporation, the owner of this fine aircraft. Sheriff Moser and I have had two hours of uninterrupted pontification on the way down here, so I'm anxious to hear what the real experts think about our mission."

Adrian smiled and said, "Right this way, gentlemen."

Two Impalas and a black Suburban were parked beside the entrance to the building adjoining the fixed-base operation. Ellington Airport had originally been called Ellington Field and was a training facility for pilots during WW1. The City of Houston annexed the field in the 1960s as a public field but one without commercial traffic. The airport was now primarily used by private aircraft, but still had a large military presence as well as a large contingent from NASA. In fact, the building where Adrian had reserved a room still belonged to NASA.

Adrian led the way through the fixed-base offices to the two-story, attached building at the back. Two men in Air Force uniforms came out of the conference room and said to Adrian, "Sir, I think we have everything you wanted. If you need anything else, just call."

Adrian replied, "Thank you, Sergeant, I think we'll be fine." Then he added, "Coffee and a supply of soft drinks and beer are located in the kitchen at the back of the room."

As Will, Eli, and Adrian came into the conference room, the six men Adrian had assembled turned and nodded but continued with their work. The team leader, Wesley Dunlap, an ex-SEAL who worked with Eli while in the service and for five years since his retirement, got up and walked over. Extending his hand, he said, "Colonel, we're a bit rushed, but I think we got everything we'll need."

Eli smiled as they shook hands. "Wesley, I appreciate your getting a team together so quickly. You know I wouldn't call you on such short notice unless it was urgent." He turned to Will, "Will, this gentleman is the finest tactical officer I know.

"Wesley, this is William Moser, sheriff of Hogg County, North Carolina, and the best combat MP I had the honor of working with in Viet Nam."

Wesley smiled and said, "Sheriff, a pleasure, and let me say that having been forced to endure countless hours of bull manure from the colonel, we clearly have a something in common."

Will shook hands and replied, "Undoubtedly, Mr. Dunlap. And may I add that it appears we still have countless hours of bull manure ahead." Eli held up his hands, "Where's the respect?"

After all the appropriate introductions had been made, everyone took a seat at the front of the room. When all were seated, Eli stood and said, "Gentlemen, first, let me say that I appreciate your quick response to our call. Sheriff Moser and I are in pursuit of two individuals who have kidnapped of a young Mexican woman.

"These kidnappers are part of a human-trafficking operation in North Carolina that includes Mexican partners, specifically, members of the Olmec cartel in Nuevo León and Tamaulipas states. It is our belief that the young woman found something that made her a threat to their illegal operations.

"Specifically, we are looking for two men, Mr. Jared Hill from North Carolina and Mr. Dante Sandoval, a senior member of the Olmec cartel. Henceforth, they shall be known as Thug 1 and Thug 2. Since Mr. Sandoval is clearly the biggest thug, he is Thug 1, Mr. Hill, Thug 2."

Wesley interjected, "Colonel, did you consider Scum 1 and 2, or was Thug the winner all around?"

Eli smiled. "As I recall, Sheriff Moser and I decided on Thug because of how closely it echoed 'drug,' which is also on their agenda."

After a brief pause to let the laughter fade, Eli continued. "Gentlemen, back to business. You are being given photographs of both Thug 1 and Thug 2. Keep them close.

"We believe Mr. Hill and Señor Sandoval are transporting the young woman, Maria Puente, in a Newmar Mountain Aire RV owned by Thug 2. We believe they left North Carolina sometime early today and are heading for McAllen, Texas, and then into Tamaulipas state where they plan to eliminate Ms. Puente. After confirming the location of all their other potential escape vehicles, we have concluded that this RV is their most likely transport. We could be wrong, but after looking for the subject RV at all of its recent known locations in North Carolina, it's nowhere to be found."

Wesley raised his hand. "Colonel, why bother taking her to Mexico? Why not get rid of her in the US?"

"Good question. Will, you want to fill in?"

Will stood. "Ms. Puente was coming to work in North Carolina on an H-1B three-year visa. She was traveling on a bus owned and operated by a labor company called NCFC, or North Carolina Farmers Collective. This collective is responsible for recruiting thousands of temporary workers from Mexico to work as agricultural laborers in the fields of North and South Carolina. Ms. Puente was supposed to arrive in North Carolina a week ago, but when she didn't show up, her uncle, a close friend of mine, called me and told me that something had happened to her.

"When we contacted NCFC, they lied. Their story was that Ms. Puente had never gotten on their bus in Monterrey. However, her aunt, my friend's sister, called her brother on the day she put their niece on the bus and told him exactly when and from where the bus left. As the Colonel just said, we believe Ms. Puente saw or heard something on that journey that endangers the operation of NCFC and their partners, the Olmecs.

"Their problem is that they said she never got on the bus in Mexico, so if she turned up dead in North Carolina, their lie would be exposed; however, if her body was never found, they understand that our investigations would continue, and the resulting interrogations might seriously endanger their operations.

"We believe they want to offset both possible outcomes by taking her back to Mexico and killing her there. There is no doubt in my mind that they intend to kill her, since they have recently killed four other connected people that we know of and probably two others that we also believe are dead. Yesterday, the sheriff in Smith County discovered one of the prostitution facilities being used, thus accelerating the exodus south of Thugs 1 and 2 with Ms. Puente. Colonel Kahn and I have a plan that we believe will yield the best and most reliable result, namely the capture of the RV and the successful recovery of Ms. Puente." Will turned to Eli, "Your turn, Eli?"

Eli got up and, moving to the large display board Adrian and Wesley had set up, said, "As you have seen from the map on the board, we believe that Thugs 1 and 2 are presently traveling South on Interstate 65 from Montgomery, Alabama, to Mobile. As we were landing, I got a call from Dan McReady, our commo guy at Guardian, who is monitoring a number of phones belonging to NCFC and the private individuals involved. Following a phone call Sheriff Moser made to an associate of his in the North Carolina Commerce Department, a call was made to NCFC headquarters, and within the hour, another call was made from NCFC headquarters to Thug 2's cell phone. Dan traced the most recent call to a spot just east of Montgomery, Alabama. Based on the performance data for the model RV they are driving, we estimate that they will need to refuel in the Montgomery area.

"We don't believe they feel any pressure to get to Mexico on a specific schedule, only that they want to arrive sometime tomorrow afternoon or evening. This says to us that they are probably traveling at a normal rate of speed, say 60 to 65 MPH, and only need to stop to refuel, change drivers, and perhaps eat. While they can carry food with them and use their own bathroom, we believe they will stop for both anyway.

"As Sheriff Moser just said, the sheriff in an adjoining county discovered one of NCFC's prostitution operations, and while potentially dangerous to NCFC and Thug 2, we don't believe any action will be taken against them by the state or federal authorities until later this week; thus, the lack of panic the kidnappers currently feel.

"Given our most recent location estimate, we assume the RV is headed toward Houston, so whether they take Interstate 20 to Meridian and then South to Interstate 10 or take 65 to Mobile and then 10 toward Houston, they're coming this way. We estimate that barring any unforeseen circumstances, they should arrive in the Houston area by four or four thirty a.m. Sheriff Moser and I believe the best place to intercept them is Beaumont, Texas.

"Whether they go through Mississippi or Alabama and Louisiana, they've gotta come through Beaumont. The good news is, there's plenty of light in Beaumont. If they get there at, say two thirty a.m., while it's still dark, we'll be able to identify the RV using the numerous streetlights in Beaumont. We will have one car on the east side of town and one south of town. Since they'll have had to fill up somewhere around Montgomery, they won't need to fill up again until near Houston, so we follow them until they pull off to refuel and grab the RV and the girl without incident. I'm guessing that since the monster they're driving is a diesel, they'll stop at one of the big truck plazas just off an I-10 exit.

"We'll divide into three teams: Red Team, White Team, and Blue Team. Major Dunlap will be Red 1 and Sergeant Wilde, Red 2. The same designations will be applied to both the White and Blue Teams. Red and White Teams will be driving the Impalas, while the Blue Team will have the Suburban. Since the Blue Team is EMT trained, they will need the Suburban to transport the medical equipment necessary for the evaluation and treatment of the young woman. Sheriff Moser, Adrian, and I will monitor from here as Citation 1.

"We hope to get additional information on the location of the RV from Dan McReady at our communications center in North Carolina, but that will depend on their cell phone usage, and at that time in the morning, it doesn't seem likely. Let's pray they get sloppy and leave their phone on.

"It's about an hour and a half from here to Beaumont, so you'll need to leave by eleven o'clock. Questions?"

"Colonel, what if they don't stop for fuel within our range? I mean, what if they fill up in a rural area instead of waiting until they're almost empty? I'm thinking maybe Lake Charles, Louisiana, thus being able to bypass Houston."

"Then we'll have to improvise. Truthfully, I think it's unlikely since they're not trying to avoid anything, but I'll think about it and we'll be in touch. I assume you're all fitted with the SCS systems we used in Afghanistan, so we'll have the ability to rework our plans on the fly." He looked at Wesley, "Everybody equipped with 9mms and silencers?"

"Roger that, plus, we've all got M16s and gas, and both Red and White have tasers and stun guns."

"Okay, get some rest, and we'll regroup before you head out."

Sunday

6:30 p.m.

The RV slowed as it pulled into a travel plaza and fueling station outside Montgomery, Alabama. Dante was heading for the only vacant pump at the plaza when Maria started yelling.

"Hello! Bad men, can you hear me? I gotta go to the bathroom."

Dante looked over his shoulder at Jared who was sitting at the kitchen table looking at some maps.

"Jared, tell that bitch to shut the fuck up! We gotta get some gas and don't need nobody outside hearing some loser yelling about taking a piss."

Jared got up and walked to the back bedroom. When he opened the door he looked at Maria. She was sitting on the floor beside the bed. The drugs had kept her more or less passed out since leaving North Carolina, but now they had about worn off.

"Okay, you can take a piss, but if you open your mouth one more time, I'm gonna tape it shut. We ain't got anymore pills, but duct tape will do just as good."

Maria was handcuffed and secured to the base of the bed with a padlocked chain similar to the one used by Jimmy Ross at the trailer. Her feet were bound as well. Jared kept standing in the doorway without moving.

"See, when I said I had to go to the bathroom, that meant I

wanted to pee in a toilet not on the carpet. By the way, how're your nuts feeling?"

Jared walked over and released the chain that was around the base of the bed, then the rope around Maria's feet.

"You're a real class act, lady." He pulled her up and briefly held her arm since she was still groggy from the phenobarbital. She held out her hands hoping he would unlock the cuffs.

"You can pull your pants down with your hands cuffed together. And I don't wipe asses."

"No? You look like you do."

"Shut up and do your business."

Maria went into the bathroom and pulled her pants down. She was still groggy and unbalanced from the effects of the drugs, but stable enough to navigate the bathroom. She looked for something that might be of help in picking the handcuffs, but the room had been sterilized and cleaned.

"You finished?"

"Patience!"

"Look, hurry up. I don't want to have to come in there."

Maria got up, pulled up her pants and opened the door.

"Listen, Jared, or whatever your name is. I don't know who you're working for and I don't care, but my uncle is a wealthy man and he will pay you whatever you want. You can't be getting rich working with that Castro creep or Jimmy Ross, and with their madam dead, they have to be close to being out of business. I promise I won't say anything. I don't care what you guys are up to; I just want to live with my uncle and go to my new job. Please, we'll pay."

Jared led her back to the bed and re-locked the chain around its base.

"First off, the Castro creep and the whore are by now little more than bits of flesh in some alligator's stomach, and Jimmy Ross was in a car crash so bad that his coffin could be a shoe box. So, don't worry about me; you're the one with the worries. And by the way, your uncle, Tomás Delgado, ain't that rich; plus him and his buddy, Sheriff Will Moser, have already given up looking for you."

With that Jared re-tied the rope around Maria's feet and then tied it to the handcuffs so she couldn't move her hands to her face. Tears were starting to form in her eyes, but she fought them. She stared at Jared, her face hard and resolute.

"No matter what happens to me, I'll guarantee you one thing. You don't know my uncle. In his whole life, he never gave up on anything, and one way or the other, he'll find me or at least find out what happened to me, and when he does, you're a dead man."

Jared stood up and went into the kitchen, returning with a roll of duct tape. As he wrapped it around Maria's head and across her mouth, he said, "Dream on sister."

Sunday

10:30 p.m.

Eli and Adrian returned to the conference room and roused the teams. "Gentlemen, we don't have any new intel on the exact position of the RV, so we're still assuming it's coming south toward Houston. Major Dunlap will go over your action plans again, and then you can head to your designated initial observation assignments." Eli looked around the room. "If we do this right, we'll save the life of this young woman while taking out some cartel scum. I, like you, would love to see a win chalked up for the good guys."

Wesley stood by the display board and the area map. "Okay, once more. You will drive north to your designated positions," He turned to face the map, "Red Team here, and White Team here. We assume that Red Team will be the first to spot the RV, but if not, then it will be White. Once spotted, Red and White will take up a position behind the vehicle at a secure distance. Red Team will take the front position with White Team a quarter-mile back.

"Every three or four miles, Red and White will change places in case the driver of the RV senses he's being followed. While we don't believe either Thug 1 or 2 will think they're being followed, it makes sense to assume they might. Blue Team will be a half-mile back and only come forward when the RV exits for refueling or, should events call for it, is disabled.

"Since we have calculated that they will need to refuel somewhere in the Houston area, our primary plan is to secure the vehicle when it has stopped for refueling. Once it has stopped and Thug 1 or 2 has exited to refuel or stretch, we will secure the vehicle, subdue both men, and free the young woman. Blue Team will enter the RV once secured and determine the condition of the young woman. Questions?"

"Have you decided what to do if they stop before they reach us?"

"As Colonel Kahn said, we improvise. They're not in a panic, but they are in a hurry to get to Mexico, so, stopping early doesn't help them; however, if they do, then we move to Plan B."

"Do we have a Plan B, Sir?"

Wesley looked at Eli and said, "Colonel?"

Eli said, "After considering all options, and assuming they've refueled early, Sheriff Moser and I think our only option is to slow the RV down by having the Red Team move to its front and decelerate, thus slowing the RV down, while White Team comes up from the back left side. If Red can slow the RV to a manageable speed, White can take the driver and shotgun passenger out. This assumes that both men are seated in the front.

"If this is not the case, then our only option is to shoot out one of the back tires. We will use a silenced Glock 9mm and hope the driver won't see us do it. If we are successful, the driver will simply think he's had a routine blowout and will pull off the road. At that point, Red Team will take the driver out and White Team will breech the RV door and take out the other occupant. Any more questions?"

"Colonel, what if, when we try to subdue the bad guys, we encounter deadly force? What is our permission?"

"Use your silenced Glock to blow their fucking heads off, but if this occurs while at the refueling station, make sure the gas pump is off. We don't want you to blow yourselves up."

Laughter released the tension from the room and restored the swagger that characterized the men.

Since they had no more questions, Wesley said, "Good hunting, Gentlemen, and before we go, let's have one more commo check."

Monday
September 30th

DAY NINE

Monday

12:30 a.m.

Will's phone rang. He put it on speaker.

"Moser."

"Will, it's Hank. I just got a call from Wimbley Johnson. He says a half-hour ago a fire alarm went off at Jared Hill's house. Said the fire department was there and has it under control."

"Anybody hurt?"

"Don't think so, but I didn't ask. Seems like it started in the garage behind the house. It's too early to tell how it started, but apparently it doesn't look serious. You just never know about these old buildings."

Will looked toward Eli who was by now looking at him. He smiled slightly, then said, "Keep me advised, Hank. Thank goodness no one was hurt."

"Yeah, right, thank goodness."

He put the phone down and said, "I'm betting that you're gonna get a call from your man McReady in a few."

Just as Eli was about to speak his phone rang.

"Colonel, McReady here, I just monitored two calls to Jared Hill's phone. The first was from ADT, the security company. The next was from Mr. Hill's wife notifying him that…"

Eli said, "He had a fire at his house?"

Dan laughed, "Damn, Colonel, you must be psychic or something."

"No," he said, looking at Will, "Just surprised. But cut to the chase. Where is he?"

"I'd say he was about twenty miles past Lafayette, Louisiana. I couldn't get a definitive fix, but that should be close."

"Thanks, Dan. Keep it up."

Eli looked at Will. "Sheriff, you wouldn't know anything about some pyromaniac running around Jackson County, would you?"

Will took a long sip of coffee and said, "I'm not familiar with the criminal element in Jackson County, Colonel. But more importantly, where are the thugs?"

"Looks like they're just past Lafayette. Maybe an hour and a half from Beaumont. Think I'll call our men and tell them that they have a few hours yet."

Will took another sip of coffee, and after checking the big board in front of the room, said, "You never know what fate will bring, do you?"

Eli said, "Nope, not unless fate had a helping hand. Of course, being a conscientious guardian of the law, you have no idea how such a tragedy could have occurred, do you?"

"Not a clue."

Monday

2:00 a.m.

Jared sat down next to Dante, who'd been driving a while, and held up a map. "Per our last estimate, we should refuel sometime in the next sixty to ninety minutes." The streetlights of Beaumont illuminated the inside of the RV so that he didn't need the overhead lights.

"Based on these calculations, I think the best place to stop is the Love's Travel Plaza in Baytown. It's outside of Houston, so there'll probably be less congestion, plus it has a Denny's Restaurant. I could use something to eat other than week-old tamales and beer."

Without taking his eyes off the road, Dante replied, "I don't really give a shit where we stop, but I need some fresh air and a break from your damn whining."

Jared shook his head as he folded the map. "Such a pleasure traveling with you, Dante. I guess being pissed that my garage almost burned down falls under your definition of whining?"

Dante snorted, "Yeah, it does."

Jared slowly folded the map while staring at the lighted streets of Beaumont. He was beginning to hate Dante Sandoval. After more hours than he cared to remember, he had come to understand the indifference that Dante had toward killing people, forcing young women into prostitution, and addicting a whole generation of his own people.

Dante pursued personal power the way most people pursue oxygen—without a thought. Even with his own culpability in prostitution and the rapacious wrangling of poor immigrant farm workers, Jared Hill still clung to an aspiration of civility. He did this by demonizing the people whom he abused, while giving himself credit for the few instances of generosity that he and his wife offered to the poor in Jackson County. Whenever he took clothes to the Goodwill Store or food to the local food bank, he made sure his name would appear on the list of contributors in their next publication.

But even with these few acts of generosity, people in Beulah didn't think of Jared as a generous, kind-hearted man. They thought of him as a man who was trying to buy respectability. Neither Albert nor Jared fooled anybody. Albert rarely went to the Everlasting Kingdom Pentecostal Church even after paying for its new sanctuary, and Jared's gifts to the local charities were seen as meager for a man who lived the way he did. A big house, new BMW, and a $200,000 RV should equal more than a bundle of hand-me-down clothes and a few boxes of canned goods, the townspeople thought.

"Citation 1, this is Red 1."

Eli sat up. "Roger, Red 1, go ahead."

"We have identified subject vehicle as well as Thugs 1 and 2. We are following at a safe distance. White Team has also joined. Blue Team will join in two minutes."

"What is your position, Red 1?"

"We're about two klicks west of Beaumont. Traveling at 65 miles per. Will alternate position with White as directed."

"Roger, Red 1. Advise change in status."

Will got up from a cot at the back of the room.

"What's up?" Will asked.

"That was Wesley. They're following the RV after identifying Dante and Jared. They're continuing south and were about two kilometers west of Beaumont. Now they just follow and hope the RV pulls off to refuel in the next hour or two."

Will said, "I've told Jimmy to refuel the plane and be ready to leave within the next four or five hours. I'm guessing that whatever is gonna happen will happen in that time frame, and I want to be ready to head home as soon as the guys from Blue Team say it's okay."

Eli said, "If she's in really bad shape, we ought to take her to Methodist Hospital here in Houston. I know the president, and he's already talked to the head of emergency about a room. As you can imagine, we have lots of contacts around Houston; in fact, Ares owns five condos within two miles of the airfield. Adrian lives in one, and the other four are for visiting personnel."

Will replied, "If Maria's in serious shape, we'll definitely keep her here, but if she can travel, I've arranged for a room at Duke Hospital. I'm on the board of the Nicholas School of the Environment and am good friends with the Chairman of the hospital board. I know Tomás will want to be near her, so if she can travel, I'll take her back. Let's just hope she's well enough to fly."

Monday

3:30 a.m.

Adrian came into the conference room through a side door, walked over to the galley, and poured himself a cup of coffee. "You guys need any coffee?

Eli shook his head as did Will. "We've had all we need, thanks."

"I couldn't sleep anymore, so I figured I'd come back to the airport and bother you two."

Will replied, "That seems fair; you go home to sleep, and we get the army cots. Good plan!" Will grinned and started to say something else when Eli's commo link clicked on.

"Citation 1, this is White 1."

"Go ahead, White 1."

"Subject vehicle is leaving the highway at Exit 789, Baytown. Am following."

"Roger, White 1. Red 1, did you copy?"

"Roger, Citation 1. Am in sight of White 1 and following. Blue Team is two klicks back and will follow."

"Citation 1, subject vehicle has turned onto Thompson Road and then left into a Love's Travel Plaza. We are twenty yards behind and are parking in the automobile lot to the left of the restaurant and shops. Subject vehicle has pulled into Bay 3 of the refueling line. We are in the far space closest to the fueling bays."

"White 1, this is Red 1. Am moving to the air pumps and car vacuum area at your twelve o'clock. Do you copy?"

"Roger, Red 1. I have eyes on."

Red 1 continued. "White 1, have White 2 walk to rear entrance of restaurant to monitor movements around subject vehicle. Keep a low profile. When Thug 1 or Thug 2 exits to begin fueling, you approach and engage in conversation."

White 1 replied, "Roger that. White 2 has exited and is moving to location. Am awaiting RV exit to move."

Since it was almost 3:40 in the morning, there were only five or six trucks in the entire refueling plaza. A break for Red and White Teams. Blue Team arrived and parked in front of and far away from the restaurant. An Old Dominion truck was refueling in Bay 6 with nothing between it and the RV.

Dante turned off the engine and walked back through the RV to the outside door. He opened the door, but rather than immediately stepping out, he stood twisting his neck and breathing in the warm Texas air. After a brief pause, he stepped down and walked to the nearest diesel pump.

Jared stepped out right behind him and headed toward the plaza restaurant. "I gotta take a piss and can't wait to do it in something that ain't moving."

Dante mumbled something like, "Who gives a damn?" then said, "Come back as soon as you piss. I need to take a shit. You can get breakfast after that."

Dante shoved the pump handle into the RV's tank. He put the handle on automatic and stood back, making sure the diesel was flowing.

Jared walked toward the restaurant, shaking his arms and hands and twisting his head from side to side to rid himself of the tension that had been building over the past few days. Especially over the last few hours. Their whole money-making project had become more and more tenuous, what with the whores being discovered and all the damn killings. He couldn't get far enough away from the killings.

Albert had never been enthusiastic about the prostitution business, and even less excited about the drug-distribution plan, but Jared knew now that they had no choice. Working with the Olmecs was the only way they were going to be able to recruit enough pickers to fill the growing demand for cheap seasonal help, so his job now was to convince Albert that they simply had to swallow the garbage and make the best of it. He also needed to get Dante and his buddies to back off for a while, but how to persuade that cold, soulless bastard was another matter. They needed to let things settle down, and especially to make sure Richie Simon was stable before risking any money on him.

If they started the prostitution business again, they needed to put somebody in charge that wasn't a total fuck-up. He also wanted to make sure that he and Albert stayed in control but were shielded from the day-to-day operations.

He was still shaking his hands out and mumbling to himself when he passed a man standing outside the restaurant smoking a cigarette and talking on his cell.

"Red 1, this is White 2. Thug 2 just walked past my location and went inside. Do I follow?"

"Negative, White 2. See where he goes and stay put."

After making sure the diesel pump was running, Dante walked back to the open vehicle door. White 1 got out of his car and slowly walked around the RV, looking it over. He went to the back and then moved around to the front. As he walked pass the door, he smiled at Dante while still staring at the RV. When he was ten or twelve feet away, he said, "Man, this is a beauty. You own it?"

Dante tried to ignore him, but when White 1 repeated his

question, Dante finally said, "No. The fellow who went into the restaurant owns it."

"You think he'd mind if I took a look inside? I've always wanted to own one of these babies."

Dante, who was now leaning against the RV's door, pushed away and moved to block the entrance.

"There's somebody asleep inside."

White 1 walked closer, "I'll be real quiet, I promise."

"Like I said, someone's sleeping."

"But…"

Dante turned to face the man and, wearing his most threatening look, said, "Fuck off, buddy."

White 1 shrugged his shoulders walked away. When about fifteen feet away he said, "When the owner comes back, maybe I'll ask him."

Dante said, "He'll say the same thing, but you do what you want, asshole."

White 1 was still walking around the RV when White 2 said, "Thug 2 is coming back."

Dante waited until Jared was back at the trailer then said, "That asshole standing at Bay 4 wanted to look in the RV. I told him to fuck off, that someone was sleeping inside. He might come back and want to look inside, which I'm sure you agree would be a stupid move."

Jared nodded, "Yes, it would. I'll take care of him. Go shit so I can go back and get a decent breakfast. We still got a long way to go."

Dante walked toward the restaurant. As soon as he was through the doors, White 1 came back to the side of the RV.

"Hey, friend, your buddy didn't seem too keen on me looking inside of your RV. He said someone is sleeping, but all I want to do is just put my head in the door. I'm thinking of buying one of these and would to love to see the layout and how you've fixed it up."

Jared smiled at the guy and said, "I understand, but our friend inside is a very light sleeper. Sorry, but no dice."

Just as he said that, there was a loud banging from inside the RV. Maria, realizing that the RV had stopped and then hearing a stranger talk to Dante and now Jared, began banging her feet against the bedroom wall. The smile left Jared's face. "Now you've woken him up, you jerk!" Without another word, he turned and stepped into the trailer. The instant his back was turned, White 1 took out his stun gun, pressed it against Jared's back, and shot 400,000 volts and 4.5 milliamps into his body. The force of the electric shock knocked Jared forward onto the floor of the RV. He lay quivering, his body jerking in small convulsions. White 1 leapt into the RV and pulled the door closed, turning the lock as he did.

"Red 1, this is White 1, I have Thug 2 under control. Vehicle now secure. I will locate victim. Send Blue Team to RV."

Wesley said, "Citation 1, did you copy last transmission?"

Eli immediately responded, "Roger, Red 1. Did copy. Have Blue Team move."

White 1 looked around the RV. Spotting the door to the bedroom, he entered and saw Maria lying on the floor, still gagged and tied up, but conscious and apparently alert. She had pushed herself against the wall and raised her feet as protection.

White 1 held up his hand and said, "Ms. Puente, relax, I'm here to free you. I'm with Colonel Kahn and Sheriff Moser from Mussel Ford."

Maria put her feet down and began to cry as her rescuer untied her feet and removed the duct tape from around her mouth and head.

"Are you okay?"

She took a deep breath and, after regaining some composure, said, "Yes, I am now. Where is Mr. Hill and the other man?"

White 1 replied, "Mr. Hill is unconscious on the floor out

there and Mr. Sandoval is in the restaurant where our team is probably taking him into custody about now. A medical team is on their way to check you out."

"I'm fine, but I'd really like to get these cuffs off since I've been wearing them for two days."

White 1 said, "Does Mr. Hill have the keys?"

"Yeah. Pretty sure."

White 1 went out into the living room and looked through Jared's pockets until he found the keys. Jared didn't resist; in fact, he no longer moved. White 1 came back into the bedroom just as the Blue Team arrived.

"Where's the girl?" called the chief medic.

"Back here!" White 1 replied.

After unlocking Maria's cuffs and the chain that held her against the bed, White 1 went back into the RV's living area while the head medic began to check Maria's vital signs. The second medic was kneeling beside Jared as White 1 came into the room. He was pressing a stethoscope against Jared's back but after a brief pause, removed the stethoscope and looked up.

"He's dead. Probably died of a heart attack from the stun gun." White 1 started to key his mike when Maria came into the room followed by the medic.

She looked at Jared lying on the floor, then up at the two medics and White 1. "I told him that Uncle Tomás and his friends wouldn't give up looking for me. I told him that one way or another, he'd be a dead man." She paused, looked at the three men, and said, "I gather from your faces that I was right."

The men nodded, then the medics guided Maria to the waiting Suburban.

"Red 1, this is White 2. Thug 1 in restroom. Do we secure?"

"Roger, White 2. Red 2 will join now."

Wesley drove his Impala to the back entrance of the restaurant. Rob leapt out and, along with White 2, entered the restaurant.

Dante had entered the bathroom a few minutes before, but had stopped in front of one of the mirrors to comb his hair with water and check out a small laceration on his cheek. He'd have to see a dermatologist when he got home, then get a good facial, maybe with some special massaging, too. "Home is looking real good," he thought, winking at himself, "You handsome devil!"

Dante pampered his body with every cosmetic enhancement he could find. His complexion had always been a problem, so correcting any perceived flaw was of great importance. As he was standing before the mirror, White 2 entered the restroom, closely followed by Red 2. Since neither expected to encounter Dante so soon, neither could suppress his immediate look of surprise. In that second, Dante saw their reaction and turned to face them.

As they reached into their pockets, Dante struck White 2 in the throat and kicked Red 2 in the kneecap, effectively putting both out of action long enough for him to flee the restroom. White 2 was on the floor and couldn't speak, so Red 2 keyed his mike.

"Red 1, White 2 is down and I can't pursue. Thug 1 just ran out of the restroom. Don't know direction, but assume he is armed."

Wesley turned his head to the back door but didn't see any movement, so he quickly accelerated to the front of the restaurant. Just as he came around the corner of the building, he saw Dante throw a woman to the ground and leap into her car. The woman lay on the ground screaming, but no one was outside to help.

Dante backed her Jeep Cherokee out of its parking place with smoke billowing from the tires, then slammed the car into drive and raced out of the parking lot toward I-10.

"Citation 1, this is Red 1. Did you copy last transmission?"

"Roger, Red 1."

"Am in pursuit of Thug 1. If Blue Team is at RV, have White 1 follow."

"Red 1, this is White 1. Blue Team will remain at RV, secure Thug 2 and assist victim, who is alive. Am moving. Advise location."

"White 1, am heading west on I-10 toward Houston. High rate of speed."

"Red 1, this is Citation 1. Take out Thug 1 if possible. What is location?"

"Twenty yards behind Thug 1. Can't talk. Will advise."

By now, Dante, looking in his rearview mirror, saw that Wesley was on his tail. Their speed fluctuated between 60 and 90 MPH depending on the traffic ahead. Within a matter of minutes, they approached a bridge over what looked like a river or perhaps a finger of Galveston Bay. Traffic was starting to increase as they got closer to Houston, so Dante attempted to shake tail by moving from right to left and back.

After it crossed the waterway, the expressway made a sharp turn to the left, so Wesley kept to Dante's left side, hoping to force him to the outside of the curve. As he came up beside Dante's car, Wesley saw him take a pistol out of his jacket, so Wesley lowered his head and rammed into the Jeep, hoping to make Dante drop the pistol. No such luck. Dante looked over at Wesley once, raised his gun, and started to fire, but was about to run into the back of a large truck. Since Wesley was blocking his left, Dante swung right to get around the truck. However, Dante was already in the outside lane, and had nowhere to go. An exit ramp loomed ahead.

While Dante was looking for somewhere to go, Wesley fired two shots out his passenger side window. One hit Dante somewhere in the left shoulder or arm, the other perhaps in his left chest, but either way he was forced off the highway at a high rate of speed and down the looming exit ramp. Wesley turned hard to the right and braked as hard as he could. His car, smoke pouring from the tires, ran over a slight drop-off just past the exit ramp.

At the bottom of the exit, Dante's car hit the guard railing on the right, bounced back to the left, then hit a concrete island divider. Given its speed and the fact that Dante had been shot twice, the car, now turned sideways, flipped over two or three times, ending up in a small patch of woods on the far side of the intersection.

White 1, who had been following, saw Wesley's car, pulled over at the top of the ramp, got out, and raced over to the driver's side window. "You okay, Major?"

"Fine, but Thug 1 may not be. Go down and see if he's still alive. If so, then take him out. I already put two bullets in him."

"Roger that."

Wesley keyed his mike. "Citation 1, this is Red 1. Do you copy?"

Eli immediately replied. "Roger, Red 1. What is status?"

"Thug 1 shot and forced from highway at high rate of speed. Stolen car flipped twice or more at the bottom of exit ramp and at present is upside down in a small wooded area. I don't know exit number but is first exit after crossing river."

"Roger, Red 1. See what I believe is your 20. What is status of Thug 1?"

"Don't know, but White 1 is on scene and checking status. Will advise."

After stopping at the bottom of the exit ramp and getting out, White 1 got back in his car and backed up the exit ramp, pulling his car in behind Wesley's. By this time, Wesley had gotten out of his car and was standing on the shoulder looking down at the wrecked Cherokee. "Well?"

"As you can see, there are several cars already pulled over down there. One of the civilians is on his phone calling the cops.

I imagine Thug 1 is dead, but I couldn't verify. The car is crushed, and he's deep inside."

Wesley said, "Plus he's probably got two 9mm slugs somewhere in his upper body."

He keyed his throat mike, "Citation 1, White 1 thinks Thug 1 is dead but cannot verify. Civilian presence at scene and expect police and EMT on scene momentarily. Do you want me to stay at scene and monitor? Advise next."

Eli responded, "Negative, Red 1. You and White 1 return to RV and meet Blue Team. No need to expose ourselves to questions from local authorities. Am advised by Blue that Individual 1 is secure and able to travel. Will await your arrival at Ellington."

"Roger, Citation 1."

Eli looked at Will and Adrian. "Gentlemen, almost home." The three men smiled and shook hands all around. Adrian said, "In the finest military tradition, may I suggest a brief celebration?"

Will and Eli nodded. "Such as?"

Adrian went to the galley and returned with a bottle of twenty-five-year-old Macallan single-malt scotch. "I brought this from home in hopes that we would have use for it. May I assume you both will join me?"

Eli said, "You may assume, sir."

As the three men savored the smooth liquid, Eli said, "I talked to the lead on Blue Team and he said that Ms. Puente's vitals are sound, but she has clearly been drugged for some time. Probably not on a narcotic, more like a strong sedative. He guesses something like Valium or a similar drug. With that in mind, I think taking her back to Duke would be fine."

Will raised his glass, "Gentlemen, thank you. As a new client of Ares, Moser Mansfield Corporation deeply thanks you. And on a personal note, I thank you. This repays a debt that I never expected I could repay. Once we're on the way home, I'll call Tomás and have him meet us in Durham."

Eli returned the gesture and said, "On behalf of Ares, you are welcome. My invoice will be forthcoming."

Will laughed, "That's the one item I wasn't worried about."

Turning more serious, Eli looked at Adrian. "How strong are your connections in the Houston Police Department?"

"Very."

"We need to find out whether Dante has been taken to the morgue or the hospital. That's a potential loose end we need to tie up."

Adrian said, "I'll call my friend, the assistant chief, and find out in a matter of an hour. I assume that if he's been taken to the morgue, case closed, but what if he's at a hospital?"

Eli leaned back and thought. "Then I think the chief needs to know who he's got so he can consider some security. We don't know if Dante had a phone and was in contact with his people in Mexico, but we should assume that he did and was. The police don't need to know about Sheriff Moser, only that Ares was pursuing a drug kingpin and kidnapper on behalf of a client when they witnessed a gun battle between two drug factions. You can say that you were contacted by me and conducted an operation on behalf of one of our clients."

"No problem. I'll talk to my guy as soon as the office opens. Where are you going now?"

"I'll return to North Carolina with Will, get my car, and return to Guardian, but first, I want to debrief the teams. Okay with you, Will?"

"Fine, no problem, but I want to get Maria to the hospital as soon as we can."

Eli said, "We shouldn't need more than forty-five minutes to debrief the teams."

Eli's commo link rang. "Citation 1, Red 1."

"Go, Red 1."

"As reported, Individual 1 is okay; however, Blue Team leader advises that Thug 2 is deceased."

Eli looked at Will and shook his head. "Say again, Red 1."

"Blue Team leader advises that Thug 2 has died of a heart attack. One of the dangers with a stun gun. What do you advise?"

"Wait, Red 1."

Eli got up and walked to the front of the room, turned and walked back. "Shit. Gotta be something."

Will got up and walked to the front of the room. "Okay, listen. Albert and Mrs. Hill both know that Jared and Dante were driving to Mexico, so when they're told by the Texas authorities that Jared has been found dead of a heart attack, they won't be shocked. Perhaps saddened, in the case of Mrs. Hill, but not shocked." He paused, looked at Eli, then started walking.

When he got to the map on the board, he stopped, placed his finger on a spot east of Baytown, then turned and looked at Eli and Adrian. "Okay, here's what we'll do. We'll have Red Team drive the RV to a location several miles away, a gas station or truck plaza east of Baytown, put Jared on the floor next to the driver's seat, and leave the RV running. Since a stun gun was used instead of a laser, there won't be any holes in his back. It will look like he had a heart attack as he was starting to refuel his RV. Neither Albert nor Mrs. Hill will ask about Dante, and if anybody does ask about him, they'll say they never heard of him. White and Blue Teams can return here as soon as they feel Ms. Puente is able."

Eli said, "What about the security cameras at the Love's Travel Plaza? They're bound to have surveillance on the refueling bays."

"Good point. Tell Red 1 to secure the tapes from the system. They can either bribe the night attendant with a large amount of cash or distract him long enough for one of them to steal the disk or tape. I imagine you've had them do something like that before."

Eli keyed his mike. "Red 1, are White 2 and Red 2 operational?"

"Roger that, Citation 1."

Eli then instructed Wesley to drive the RV to another location and stage the heart attack after securing the surveillance data from the Love's Plaza. Blue and White Teams would return to Ellington Airport.

By eight o'clock Tuesday morning, the Citation CJ3 was on its way back to the Raleigh Durham Airport with a groggy but generally healthy Maria Puente safely on board. Will called a jubilant Tomás Delgado, who said he would leave immediately for Durham.

Eli decided to stay in Texas to debrief the teams and make sure he and Adrian could manage any controversy that arose from the night's events.

Thursday
October 3rd

DAY TWELVE

Thursday

2:00 p.m.

Maria lay in her bed on the fourth floor of Duke hospital in Durham, North Carolina, with her eyes closed and a slight smile on her lips. Fall colors were starting to clothe the trees surrounding the Duke campus, and sleep was again her friend. It had been three days since her deliverance from Jared and Dante, and she was feeling stronger every day. The effects of the phenobarbital had dissipated, and her bruises were beginning to fade.

While her beauty would, in her own eyes, forever be tarnished, to those who had never met her, Maria was still a beautiful woman. Her Uncle Tomás and Aunt Sofia were staying in Durham near the hospital and had been by to see her every day since her return. Life was starting to look as though it might hold promise for her once more.

One thing she couldn't shake, however, was thinking about the murder she had been forced to commit. It kept returning to her in dreams, like the night terrors soldiers often experience after being in battle for prolonged periods of time. She now understood both the concept and working reality of PTSD.

But this wasn't on her mind today. Today she was thinking about her Aunt Marianna and her Uncle Luis, and the joy that her Uncle Tomás and Aunt Sofia had elicited in her. She started to get up when she heard a knock at the door. Assuming that it was either Tomás or Sofia, she said, "Come in."

Instead of her aunt or uncle, though, Lana Moser opened the door and put her head into the room.

"Maria, I'm Dr. Lana Moser, Sheriff William Moser's wife. I hope I'm not disturbing you."

Maria said, "Not at all, Dr. Moser. Please come in. I've heard so much about you." Lana took off her coat, walked across to the bed, and put out her hand.

"And I've certainly heard a lot about you. I can't tell you how pleased I am to finally meet you and tell you what a remarkable young woman you are! I feel I've known you forever. Your uncle and aunt are so proud of you and, needless to say, much relieved that you're safe and finally part of their home."

Maria started to get out of bed, but Lana said, "Please, don't try to get up. I just came by to say hello and see if I can do anything for you. Will and I are in Durham to see our daughter, Grace, a student at Duke. I spoke to Tomás and asked if it would be all right for me to come by." Maria pushed back the covers, smiled and said, "Actually, I've been in this bed far too long. I need to get up and walk around."

Lana said, "In that case, if you would like a walking partner, we can take a short stroll around the hospital." Maria nodded and put on her bathrobe.

"I would love a stroll mate."

The two women walked out into the hall and headed toward the elevators.

"So, how have you been doing since your terrible ordeal?"

"Quite well, really. Though at times it all comes back to me. My dreams seem to always be about some of the things that I have tried to forget, but the doctors say that that will get better." Lana didn't say anything, only nodded and walked on.

"I have been so fortunate in my life, and for the first time I realize how…" She groped for a word.

"Lucky?" Lana said.

"Yes, lucky. Lucky and protected. I know that Mexico is full of dangerous people, people like the Sandovals and Albert Waters, but I never came across them until a few weeks ago. I never saw a person killed, like poor Julietta. She was so young. And I never thought that I…" She stopped walking and put her hands to her face. She was starting to cry, so Lana guided her into a small coffee shop and atrium. There were only two other people in the shop, so they went to the far end and sat at a table at one of the large windows looking out onto a garden. Lana helped her sit down and then went to the counter and ordered two cups of coffee. When she came back, Maria had regained control of herself and had wiped her eyes.

"I'm sorry. I…"

Lana put her hand on Maria's arm and said, "You're doing fine, Maria. Memories become less vivid as they retreat further back into your brain. We all have them."

Maria, her eyes taking on a hard, resigned expression, looked at Lana and said, "Yes, but not memories of killing someone. Not memories of the sounds and smells and struggles of someone strangling to death by your own hand. I don't think those memories have anywhere to hide in my brain."

Lana didn't respond at first, but after taking a sip of coffee, she said, "Well, perhaps not; still, time has a way of eventually anesthetizing the brain. I know it has with me."

"Yes, but I'm guessing you never had to hide memories like those."

"No, but almost as painful. You know, sometimes we can feel guilt for a death without actually having it be a hands-on responsibility. I, too, have some memories I would rather not keep. But you know, the human brain has no erase button."

Maria didn't say anything, just looked out of the window at the garden; then, more to herself said, "Yes, but just feeling responsible can't be the same thing. Feeling responsible is real but too general, like feeling responsible for a disloyalty to one's school or town. This feeling I have attacks all my senses and doesn't let me breathe freely. It's like a bad song that I can't get out of my mind."

Lana kept her eyes on Maria and after a minute or two said, "Maybe not, but don't discount another's pain or expression of pain when you don't know their story." Lana moved her chair so she was facing Maria. "Maria, let me tell you my story."

Lana recounted the death of her first husband, Paul Reavis, and the quickly following death of her son, Paul Jr. This clearly made an impression on Maria, but what followed made more of one.

"After Paul died and then Paulie, I decided I couldn't rest until justice was done. I couldn't rest until the men responsible for the death of my husband and then my son, my beautiful baby boy, paid for their sins.

"I knew because of his power and ability to delegate his dirty work to lesser men, that making Oris Martin Sr. pay for his crimes in a court of law would be almost impossible, so I swore to try and destroy everything that was important to him... his power and wealth. Looking back, I confess that this wasn't a rational decision, but rational decisions weren't high on my list then.

"Killing the woman who stood in your way, Maria, who was part of the group of men who killed your new friend, Julietta, and would probably have killed you without a care, wasn't something that a rational person would want to do, but it was something that a brave woman who wanted to survive had to do. And 'had' is the key word here."

She paused and also turned her gaze to the garden outside. "Maria, I've never told anyone this part of my story, not even Will, but I was the one who infected thousands of Oris Martin's hogs with the deadly cholera virus, a disease that, if it spread, could have wiped out many of the farmers and much of the economy in Eastern North Carolina. I was the one who, by this planned act of revenge, undoubtedly caused the eventual death of Oris Martin Sr. and his murderous henchman, Eugene Winslow."

Maria was staring at Lana but didn't say a word. Lana moved her gaze from the garden back to Maria's face. She smiled and said, "And here's the really strange part, the man whose life I ruined and probably killed was the father of the man who has hired you to work in his company."

Maria still didn't say anything, only watched in thought. Lana leaned back in her chair. "Of course, Maria, that confession needs to go no farther than this room—you do understand that, right?"

Maria replied, "Absolutely, Doctor. And may I say that if what happened to you had happened to me, I'd probably have done the same thing. I guess what has been the hardest for me is having to admit to myself that afterwards I didn't feel sorry for the woman. I remember saying to Jesus that I was sorry, but I also knew that he knew I was lying. It's only been now, a week or so later, that blame has started to creep into my mind. I hope, as you said, these memories will eventually retreat to the back of my mind, but I know they'll always be there."

Lana smiled and said, "Yes, they will, but I also believe God knows we're both sorry and will forgive us. I hope you can come to believe the same thing."

Maria smiled. "Thanks, Doctor. I'll try."

EPILOGUE

Friday

October 25th

6:00 p.m.

Almost sunset. Will Moser, his eyes closed, relaxed as the smell of fallen leaves wafted up from the borders of the Roanoke River and across the porches of Cromwell House. He listened with contentment to the primal call of wood ducks as they whistled an approach once again to the quiet waters flowing beneath the cypress trees and water oaks along the river. Satisfied, Will opened his eyes only when he heard Lana come out onto the porch.

"What's up, Hon?"

"Nothing. I thought you might like a little late-afternoon toddy."

Will sat up. "Thank you. You are indeed a mind reader." She handed him a glass and sat down beside him.

"What you thinkin' about?" she asked.

"Not much. You know, the last month. How incredible it all was, and how lucky we are."

Lana smiled, "Yep, but I've known how lucky I am ever since I married you." Will smiled and leaned over to give his wife a kiss.

Lana took a sip and said, "I saw Ruby Simon today. She says Richard is doing a little better, but what she's really grateful for is how much better young Richie is. He told her all about Mexico, and she told him she suspected something like that. I think he's going to a program in Charlotte to work on his problems."

As they were speaking, a car approached the house. When it came to a stop, Eli Kahn got out, waved, and headed toward the porch. It had been almost four weeks since Will had left Eli in Texas, and two weeks since they had last spoken. Eli had said nothing about coming by Mussel Ford, so his unannounced arrival was a surprise—a surprise mixed with a dose of foreboding.

Will stood and the two shook hands. "Colonel, an unexpected pleasure—I hope."

"Always a pleasure, Sheriff, yet, an ambiguous pleasure at present. I'm on my way over to Guardian but wanted to stop by and fill you in on some events of the last week in Texas. Good to see you as well, Lana."

"Thank you, Colonel."

"Do you want to go inside?" Will asked. "We might be more comfortable in the library."

"Actually, I love this porch and view. I think we can talk here unless you feel otherwise."

"As you wish. Have a seat." He paused for a few beats then said, "Lana and I were just having an afternoon cocktail. Care to join us?"

"A scotch might be in order," Eli replied.

Will went inside and came back out with a bottle and another glass. He poured Eli a drink and topped off his and Lana's.

Eli took a long, slow swallow from his glass, then looked up with a worried expression. "Will, there's been a serious incident in Texas. Two days ago, Dante Sandoval was being taken from Houston to the federal medical facility in Fort Worth that I told you about, when the ambulance in which he was being transported and its accompanying security vehicles were attacked. They had stopped at a Pilot Travel Center just outside a flyspeck town called Buffalo, Texas, when two large vehicles carrying a number of Mexican cartel members trapped them by the gas pumps and opened fire. The long and short of it is that four of the six security personnel were killed, one was wounded, and one survived unharmed. Six of the attackers were killed, and given the amount of shooting, it's likely that several others were wounded. The two medical personnel in the ambulance who were monitoring Dante were seriously wounded… and Dante was taken.

"The single survivor recounted a somewhat muddled description of the events. He was part of a security detail comprised entirely of Texas Rangers, and since Adrian is friends with the head of the Texas Rangers, he got a full rundown on what the surviving Ranger said.

"When the detail pulled into the travel center, one of the Rangers got out of his car to refuel the ambulance when a black Suburban drove up behind them and a masked man got out of the Suburban and shot the Ranger. When the rest of the security detail saw this, they moved their cars into defensive positions and engaged the shooters. As they did this, another Suburban drove up to a position opposite the first car, thus boxing the Rangers in.

"As I said, the surviving Ranger was a bit vague about what happened next, but the end result was that dead bodies lay everywhere, and Dante Sandoval was gone. Whether he suffered additional injuries in the exchange is unknown. He could have. Where he is now is unknown, but it's not hard to imagine that he's either dead or in Mexico."

Will kept his eyes on Eli but said nothing right away. Finally, he asked, "Okay, but what does all that mean?"

"I don't know. For sure it means that the cartel lost a bunch of highly-trained men, but it also means that they have Dante Sandoval back. Whether he is alive or dead is unknown, but frankly I don't think the cartel gives a damn. The Patron of the Olmecs is a man named Romero, nicknamed 'The Executioner,' and if he has decided that Dante is a danger to the cartel, he'll either let him die from his wounds or kill him. Killing him wouldn't be out of character since Romero is reported to have killed one of his own brothers for a perceived disloyalty.

"We're not dealing with humans here, Will, but with animals presenting themselves as humans. Many of them, like Dante, are intelligent as well as wily, sociopathic, and craven to the extreme. If Dante is alive and Romero is now protecting him, we need to consider what that may mean. They're not gonna pursue something that looks like a lost cause, so if Albert is in as much trouble as you've said, they'll just cut off their relationship with him. If Richie Simon is perceived as a risk, they might kill him or just leave him for later use. They have plenty of time and can find someone else to work with when they want, but I guarantee they won't quit supplying forced labor, prostitutes, or debilitating drugs to the US."

"What does that me for me and Lana?" Will asked.

"I don't know, but it certainly means that you need to be even more cautious, and, not to be too self-serving, it also means that you need Ares to continue doing what we do to ensure that your security is inviolable and cannot be breeched. I still have men here and have already spoken to them.

"What we primarily need to do is have Adrian and our team in Mexico go deep and find out what the situation is with Dante. I also want to know the status and whereabouts of Germaine Sandoval, Dante's brother, as well their father, Roberto. If Dante is dead and they put the blame on us, then there's always the possibility of revenge raising its head.

"Romero is hunted by not only the Mexican authorities but by the leaders of the rival cartels as well. He is loath to show his face anywhere; however, we have our people on the lookout. If, as you have said, the authorities decide to deport Ramon Castile rather than incarcerate him here, that will add another wrinkle, but we have some ideas about that.

"One of my clients is a wealthy industrialist in Mexico City, and has had a beef with the Olmecs for years. I know he would love to be involved with any plan to take Romero out, and given his money and influence, we couldn't have a better partner. But right now, caution is the best advice."

Will got up and walked to the porch railing, then turned. "You know, what really concerns me is Grace. She has been very active with the SFFW on the issue of migrant rights. I think it might be wise for her to lower her visibility, and we might think about having a member of the Ares team check in on her at Duke from time to time.

"Just last week Grace and her group of labor advocates confronted the North Carolina Secretary of Labor at a public meeting about the Secretary's turning a blind eye to the enforcement of regulations governing the living standards of migrant workers.

"The Secretary replied, 'You bleeding-heart liberals in your ivory towers want to put the hard-working farmers of this state out of business just because some of the migrants who come here to work don't have all the comforts of a four-star hotel. I'm in office to serve my constituents—the farmers, hourly workers, and God-fearing North Carolinians who have made this state what it is, not the noncitizen laborers who are just here temporarily.'"

Eli took another long drink and closed his eyes. "Like I said, Will, the country is for sale. Maybe always has been. I dealt with that bitch at the Labor Department while we were trying to get licenses for Guardian, and believe me, if you want something out of her department, get ready to fork over some campaign cash."

He shook his head as he took a cigar out of his pocket, lit

it, and finished his scotch. He looked at Will and started to say something, then smiled and said, "Sorry, how about a Cohiba?"

Will stepped forward with his hand out. "Thought you'd never ask."

Eli lit Will's cigar, then added, "You know, the ideal of civil service envisioned by Madison and Hamilton and the other founders has been buried and forgotten. We now have career jingoists who will sell what is left of their souls to stay in the spotlight of Washington or whatever state capital they inhabit."

Will didn't comment right away, but took a few puffs on his cigar, another sip of scotch, and closed his eyes.

"Sheriff, are you thinking or are you praying?"

Will replied, "I don't know, which should it be?"

"If Dante's alive, you might do both."

"And how about you, Colonel? How many death lists are you on?"

Eli smiled. "If you were to count all the hate lists that I'm on, you'd need a computer with more terabytes than a snake has scales. For you, I'm guessing the list is shorter and mainly comprised of local felons rather than international terrorists; however, enemies is still enemies—and we got plenty!"

"So, Eli, do you think that if Dante is alive, he'll come here, or if he's dead, that his family will?"

"You never know what motivates a sociopath."

"Well, no point sitting around and guessing. We'll see what we'll see, but in the meantime, keep the clock ticking on the Moser Mansfield contract."

Eli said, "Don't worry about that. Like I said, I have clients who will be very interested in information about Dante and the Olmecs. We'll let everybody share the costs of this one. It's time to change the game."

Will walked over to the table, took the bottle of scotch, and refilled his and Lana's glasses. He handed Eli the bottle then turned to look out over the darkening river. More to himself than to Eli, Will said, "*Nemo me impune lacessit.*"

Eli took a sip of scotch, "And that means?"

Will, his eyes still on the river, said, "That was the motto of the Stuart dynasty in Scotland. The founder of Hogg County was a Scotsman named Josiah Moir Hogg. He came to America in 1756, and twenty years later, when hostilities broke out between The Colonies and Great Britain, he enlisted in Washington's Army. Josiah rose to the rank of General, and after fighting non-stop for six years, was killed at the Battle of Guilford Courthouse, in 1781.

"After living under the crushing authority of the British crown, the possibility of freedom and dignity meant more to him than his own life. On his coat of arms, he adopted the Stuart dynastic motto, the one appearing on the Hogg County coat of arms to this day: *Nemo me impune lacessit...* No one attacks me with impunity."

Will, turned and looked at Lana, who raised her glass and said, "To Josiah Moir Hogg and Lady Justice."

"Hear! Hear!" Will and Eli pledged, raising high their own.

Acknowledgments

I am again grateful to Linda Whitney Hobson for her editorial assistance and encouragement. Her keen eye and insightful suggestions are always appreciated. I am also indebted to Mr. David Sontag for his cogent and sharp observations on plot development, timing, and character development. I appreciate the time and expert advice and information supplied by the Research Triangle Institute; Ms. Melinda Wiggins, the CEO of Student Action with Farmworkers; and various individuals with the North Carolina Commerce Department, Attorney General's office, and local law enforcement personnel. Researching the complexities of immigration, human trafficking, and political influence within the state system presented challenges that I have never encountered before. Given the topical and emotional public sentiment surrounding these subjects, it proved difficult and more than delicate to gather meaningful information, especially attributable information. So, I thank those unnamed individuals who shared their knowledge and insights into these subjects.

About the Author

Photo Credit: Lloyd Aaron

Eldridge C. Hanes—Redge to his friends—was born in Winston-Salem, North Carolina, and graduated from Woodberry Forest School in Orange, Virginia, and then from Duke University in 1967 with a BA in Economics. He graduated from the Army Combat Engineering Officer Candidate School at Fort Belvoir in June of 1968 and served three years of active duty, the last of which was in the Republic of Vietnam and earned him the Bronze Star. After the army, Redge worked seven years for Hanes Corporation and then left to start Xpres Corporation, which eventually became The Russ Companies, for whom Redge served as chairman for three years before retiring in 2011. In addition to his business interests, he has served on a number of boards in the education, environmental and arts fields. Redge has published two novels, *Billy Bowater* and *Justice by Another Name*, in addition to contributing essays and articles to various publications. His essay *"Helen of Marion"* appeared in the recent UNC Press anthology, *Mothers and Strangers: Essays on Motherhood from the New South.* Redge has been married for fifty years to Jane Grenley Hanes. They have a son, Philip, and a daughter, Lara, and are grandparents of five lively and beautiful grandchildren.

SELECTED TITLES FROM SPARKPRESS

SparkPress is an independent boutique publisher delivering high-quality, entertaining, and engaging content that enhances readers' lives, with a special focus on female-driven work. www.gosparkpress.com

Final Table: A Novel, Dan Schorr, $16.95, 9781684631070. Written by a former New York City sex crimes prosecutor and current sexual misconduct investigator, this suspenseful political thriller brings readers along for a deep dive into a sexual assault survivor's fight to come out on top—as well as the worlds of high-stakes poker and international politics.

Indelible: A Sean McPherson Novel, Book 1, Laurie Buchanan, $16.95, 9781684630714. Murder at a writing retreat in the Pacific Northwest, but this one isn't imaginary. Authors only kill with words. Or do they?

Enemy Queen: A Novel, Robert Steven Goldstein, $16.95, 978-1-68463-026-4. A woman initiates passionate sexual encounters with two articulate but bumbling and crass middle-aged men, but what she demands in return soon becomes untenable. A short time later she goes missing, prompting the county sheriff to open a murder investigation.

Tracing the Bones: A Novel, Elise A. Miller. $17, 978-1-940716-48-0. When 41-year-old Eve Myer—a woman trapped in an unhappy marriage and plagued by chronic back pain—begins healing sessions with her new neighbor Billy, she's increasingly drawn to him, despite the mysterious circumstances surrounding his wife and child's recent deaths.

So Close: A Novel, Emma McLaughlin and Nicola Kraus. $17, 978-1-940716-76-3. A story about a girl from the trailer parks of Florida and the two powerful men who shape her life—one of whom will raise her up to places she never imagined, the other who will threaten to destroy her. Can a girl like her make it to the White House? When her loyalty is tested will she save the only family member she's ever known—even if it means keeping a terrible secret from the American people?

Cold Snap: A Novel, Codi Schneider, $16.95, 9781684631018. When a murder shocks her peaceful mountain town, Bijou, a plucky house cat with a Viking spirit, must dive paws-first into solving the mystery before another life is taken—maybe even her own.